# When I Met You

## A Hearts of Broadway Novel

ISBN 978-1-7373942-5-9
Second Edition

*When I Met You*
Copyright © 2022 by Carolyn Johnson

Cover art and design
Copyright © 2022 by Dorothy Ewald

Also available in eBook by Uncial Press, an imprint of GCT, Inc. Visit us at uncialpress.com

To Lena, who taught me to work hard
and love harder.

If you would like to enjoy the playlist that accompanies
this novel, please search for
*When I Met You* on your favorite music streaming site.

You can also visit Avery on her Instagram or Tiktok
@averyeastonwrites where you will find the links.


Spotify
Amazon
YouTube
Apple Music

# MATEO WILLIAMS FINALLY STEPS OUT

An *OMGCeleb* Exclusive
by Roger Smallwell

Fifteen years ago, Mateo Williams was plastered over every cover of every grocery store pop culture magazine. He was in your locker, on your bedroom wall, and in our tender little hearts. Who didn't bop around to his hit single, "Your Heart is Mine", at your high school dance? It topped the charts for the entire summer.

At fifteen years old, Mateo was a prodigy, right? There he was, selling millions of records, selling out stadiums, being interviewed by everyone in the world, and he was still a humble kid from Inwood through it all. His mom was ever-present at his side, and we loved that relationship, didn't we? A sunny boy with a smile that could light up the world, and he loved his mama to boot.

Were we not obsessed, kittens?

Mateo was everywhere and we lapped it up. He was an Usher sun with John Legend rising, playful and soulful, and we couldn't keep our eyes off of him. His stage presence even at that young age was dynamic. After a Grammy nomination for Best New Artist, he began selling out stadiums around the world. Pure, sweet, gorgeous Mateo. We all wanted the world for him.

Until his third album flopped and the bad choices began. And he seemingly kicked his Mama Manager to the curb. And then he took up with Ariel Star, and we all know how that ended. Clubbing, obvious overspending, an engagement ring the size of Montana, and a very public breakup. Let's be real, we lapped that up too, didn't we, babies? We did. You know we love the drama.

After being messy for a while in front of the cameras, something changed. The breakup seemed to destroy him, no one in the industry would touch him, and Mateo Williams disappeared. He went into hiding and since then, we haven't seen that sunny smile. Barely a photograph has emerged in the last ten years as he's lived in Manhattan, somewhere on the Upper West Side. The paparazzi quickly bored of trying to get a glimpse and we all moved on to the Real Housewives.

We haven't seen him for over a decade. So why are we talking about him now? Because . . . the mysterious Mr. Williams was spotted, babies! He was on 46th Street, coming out of the Equity office. For those not in the know, that's the theater actors' union. Is Mateo making a comeback on the stage? Stay tuned, honey, we have a delicious feeling . . .

# One ♪

The notice was a sunshine yellow. It blared at Jazzy Summers, the cheerful color belying the words on the page. In inky black letters, it read:

SOMETHING BLUE
will be closing this coming Sunday.
Please plan accordingly.

Jazzy let the words wash over her slowly. They sank into her consciousness as her breath stuttered in her chest. She laid her palm against the notice, wanting to rip it down, but not surprised that *Something Blue* was coming to an end. She had been warned. Still, the reality of it shocked her. Propping herself up against the cinderblock wall behind her, staring at the notice across the stairwell's landing, she swallowed hard.

She was out of a job. Her stomach pinched.

The meeting she'd had the day before with Shawn, the young director, seemed surreal. He had sat her down in a hard chair across his desk in his tiny, cluttered office. He told her that it was likely that *Something Blue* would be closing soon and he wanted her to know so she could line something else up.

Jazzy had focused on the piles of scripts and empty coffee mugs, swallowing the tears rising in her chest. She would not cry. "When?" she asked him, all that she could choke out.

Shawn had taken a deep breath and shrugged. He toyed with the pen in his hand. "I'm not sure yet. A month? Maybe two, but that might be pushing it. The numbers just aren't there."

Jazzy had let her shoulders relax. A month would give her time to get another gig, to prepare for those in-between moments an actor has in their career, though hopefully not too often. A month would give her heart enough time to say goodbye to her show family and clean out her dressing room. A month would give her time to say goodbye to her character, Abigail, whom she loved deeply.

She could handle a month.

But Shawn had been wrong. It wasn't a month. It was three days.

That wasn't enough time at all.

The stairwell leading to all of the dressing rooms of the Booth Theater was cold and a shiver went down her spine involuntarily. She let her head fall back against the wall, the memories of the journey that was getting this show to the Broadway stage washing over her.

For years, it had been in workshop, going through dozens of rewrites and table reads, and she was at them all. She was tethered to *Something Blue* in a way that she wasn't with most of her other work. She had helped create Abigail. Some of the songs were written specifically for her voice and she'd even given input to the creators when asked.

Finally, *Something Blue* had gotten the backing to do an out-of-town tryout in Boston. It was grueling, and the first week of previews brought in mixed reviews. For the next two weeks, Jazzy and the rest of her cast had rehearsed the revisions during the day and performed at night. When the show was finally frozen, they'd officially opened, exhausted but hopeful, on a chilly Boston evening.

After opening, the reviews were better, but still middling. It felt like a miracle when they were picked up for a Broadway run.

Jazzy had wanted a year. One year with this show in the historic Booth Theater. She knew it wasn't a perfect musical. The book was a little stilted, and maybe it was a little long, but the songs were good. And Abigail. She loved playing the headstrong journalist with a heart of gold, who got an incredible eleven-o'clock number, one of the most favorable parts of the show.

But what she really loved was the audience's reaction every night. Connecting with hundreds of people in a room together, all of them giving her energy which she absorbed and gave right back to them. She loved the stage door, where she could connect with her fans and admirers. The little girls who told her they wanted a career just like hers. The folks who had watched her grow up and had come to every show she'd ever done. What drove her was the unique way that live theater transformed people. She took people out of their lives for just a few hours, gave them reprieve, made them laugh and smile.

That was her purpose. But now, for the time being and much too soon, that was being taken away from her.

She blew out the breath she'd been holding. Jazzy Summers was a professional. And she could take this blow.

Probably.

"Jazzy." Neil, her co-star, stood to her left, his heavy black bag over a sculpted shoulder. His blue eyes met hers and he dropped his bag to the ground looking like a scorned puppy. He wrapped her in a warm hug, and she could feel his breath hitch in his chest underneath his soft blue t-shirt. Neil wore a cologne she loved, something clean and lemony, and she breathed in his familiar scent. A small comfort.

"I can't believe this," she whispered.

His arms tightened around her. "I can't either. Shawn said we'd probably have a month."

She nodded and pulled back. "That's what he told me, too."

"Guess not."

A beat or two passed as Jazzy gazed into his eyes, wondering if they would stay this close after closing. Based on her experience, the answer was no, and that thought made her even sadder.

More goodbyes.

Against the odds, Neil smiled almost cheerfully, his perpetual optimism shining out of him. That was why he was one of her favorite show friends of all time, why she loved playing opposite him. He'd also been with the show from the beginning and he gave her his all every night. And even though his constant cheerfulness could be a bit much, especially after a long, frustrating day of rehearsal, in this moment, she was grateful. It was why they worked. He balanced her consummate professionalism with his desire to make the work fun.

"At least we have three more shows. Could have just shut us down today," he said. He pulled her close again and kissed the top of her head.

Jazzy just nodded as anxious chatter reached them up the stairwell. The rest of the large cast had arrived and greeted them with sad but unsurprised eyes. Jazzy led them into the sizable green room where the people she'd spent much of the past few years of her life with surrounded her on the musty couches and arm chairs. The air was thick with melancholy.

No one on the production team had come to talk to them. No company meeting had been called. They were just . . . closed.

"Well, it's not as if we didn't see it coming," Neil finally spoke up, his voice on the verge of jovial. That broke the tension and a smattering of giggles flowed through the room. He picked up Jazzy's hand and squeezed.

She squeezed back. She had worked for fifteen years on Broadway and had absorbed everything she'd learned from the legends she had worked with. With that in mind, she addressed her cast. She was the leader, and if they were going out, they were going to put on the best damn show they possibly could on the way. "I think the best thing we can do is give these last three audiences the performance of a lifetime. They wanted to see our show, and dammit, we're going to give it to them."

"Hell yeah." Neil spread his arms wide and the cast came together in a gigantic group hug, all forty of them piling in, patting backs and wiping away tears. He grinned a little sadly at Jazzy from over the top of some of their heads.

Shakily, she smiled back.

The hug broke up when Shawn stepped in the room. He was followed by their stage and company managers, as well as their fight and dance choreographers. The cast quieted and turned to give Shawn their full attention.

"I'm sorry, y'all." Shawn's slight Georgian accent was even more pronounced when he was bummed. He ran his hand through his shaggy brown hair. "This isn't how I wanted it to happen, it's not *when* I wanted it to happen, and you deserved better. I have been on the phone all day, and by the time I could have called a company meeting, it was too late." He shoved his hands in his pockets, but kept his head high.

"It was an honor working with all of you. It was an honor watching you mold this show into something truly great. I'm proud of each and every one of you, and I'm excited to see where you go next. Now, you still have three performances left, and those people bought tickets. So go get 'em."

Murmurs of *thank you, Shawn* and *it's been such a good run* echoed around the room as Shawn shook hands and exchanged hugs. The cast dispersed for fight calls and stretching, or for a moment alone in their dressing rooms. Footsteps and chatter on the stairwell echoed as Jazzy caught Shawn's eye. Next to her, she could feel Neil stiffen a little.

Shawn let the loaded moment pass between them. He walked over and wrapped them both in a three-way hug. "Thank you, kids. You made me so proud."

"It's been an honor, Shawn. I hope we work together again soon." Neil squeezed his shoulder and left for his dressing room, his optimism finally waning.

Jazzy crossed her arms over her chest and looked down, chewing the inside of her cheek. She heard Shawn take a deep breath.

"I'm sorry, Jazzy."

Her eyes widened and she looked up to him. "Don't be sorry. This isn't your fault. The reviews, the ticket sales . . . We all saw it coming."

"I know, but you've been with us—with Abigail— since the beginning. I understand how hard it is to say goodbye." He reached out and placed his hand gently on her arm.

Alarmingly, Jazzy felt actual tears spring to her eyes. She sniffled and tried to blink them away. "I'll be okay. I just wish I had something I could focus on next."

"Hey, maybe consider taking one or two days off. No one will blame you." Shawn was going for playful, and it almost worked.

Jazzy supposed she did have a reputation as a workaholic. She chuckled a bit. "Maybe one."

Shawn slung his arm around her shoulders as she began to head for the stairwell and her dressing room. "If there's one thing I know, it's that Jazzy Summers is going to come out on top." He chucked her on the chin, a half-smile on his lips.

She gave him half of a grin back and then turned and walked down the stairs, her footsteps heavy.

§

The red curls of her wig fell around her ears as Jazzy adjusted the pins that held her mic. She sighed at her reflection and picked up her powder brush.

Closing night.

The last two performances had been more fun than any had been in a while. As the lukewarm reviews had come in over the last six months, the audiences had dwindled. The online buzz had faded into nothing. Closing rumors swirled around them, which had caused the cast's energy to take a significant dip. But now, knowing they were going out, they were doing it with a bang. Their energy during the last two performances had given the show a new breath of life.

Jazzy loved her character and the story. She believed in this show. Perhaps a regional theater company could take it and make it something truly special. She gave one last swipe of the brush across the apples of her cheeks and went upstairs.

Neil met her backstage before their entrance. "You ready for this, babe?"

Jazzy sighed. "You know what? Yes. Let's go on to the next chapter, right?"

"Absolutely." Neil beamed at her and she looped her arm through his. Together, they stepped into their spotlight.

§

"Let's go, kids, we're doing *shots* tonight!" Neil's voice rang through the stairwell and into every dressing room, all of which were full of energy as the cast packed up what they could carry out that night. Everything else would be picked up by movers and delivered to them later.

Jazzy placed a last framed photograph into the box she'd brought and closed it, glancing around the room she'd made her second home for the last six months. The pale pink walls were bare. The counter was cleared of her makeup and wigs. Her little gold coffee table was bubble-wrapped and ready to go.

Out of her door, up and down the stairwell that led to the other dressing rooms, music played. Someone had put on a pop playlist and she heard her castmates singing along with a young man's voice. "Your heart is mine, mine, mine" rang out through the hallways. It was kind of familiar and definitely a bop, Jazzy had to admit. She tried not to feel the emptiness that was nearly consuming, not knowing how long it would be until she heard the sounds of a familiar show family again.

"Yo," Neil appeared in her doorway, a bottle of Jack Daniels swaying dangerously from his dangling hand. "Paige Parker and everyone from *On Her Own* are meeting us at Bar 54. You're coming tonight, right? Come on, we don't have to work tomorrow. Hey, or possibly, ever!" He grinned a little maniacally and took a generous swig.

Jazzy understood the feeling. She looked at her name taped to the door of her dressing room. Half-giddy and half-sad, she pulled it down before grabbing the bottle. "You bet I am."

What could a little fun once in a while hurt?

A lot, it turned out.

The next afternoon, Jazzy rolled over in her bed, casting aside fluffy pillows and the giant down comforter, feeling around for her phone. She moaned to herself when she turned to the side of the bed facing the window.

It had been a long, long time since she'd been hung over.

She remembered the bar last night, the exuberance with which she and her castmates had downed shots of tequila and toasted to their production team, to their characters, to each other. The *On Her Own* cast were super supportive, and she certainly hadn't paid for a thing. Arms were thrown around her and she was cuddled close on banquettes. They all danced to a new single by a pop star Jazzy had never heard of and screeched with delight when Neil tried to get her to dance on a table. Security nearly tossed him out. Then there were promises of brunch in the morning, of texts when they got home safe, and staying in touch.

The night had ended with the deeply held belief that they would always be this way. They would always be together and love each other like this.

As the night of debauched memories came back in waves, she found her phone and woke it up. Perhaps someone wanted to do brunch, or now, late lunch. Or maybe Neil had checked in to make sure she got home safely.

The screen was blank.

"Of course. You know better than that." She flopped back against her pillows and pulled another one over her face.

Though she knew shows could bring new, lifelong friends, it had never happened to her. The *Something Blue* cast was no exception. They were show friends. Oh sure, there would be grand plans to meet up for coffee. Those would get cancelled at the last minute. And there would be hugging and shrieking and reminiscing at industry parties when they saw each other again. More plans would get made, but they wouldn't follow through. There would be inside jokes texted to the group thread once in a while, but eventually, even that would dry up. Even with Neil. Just like every friendship she'd ever had.

She supposed it could be her fault. She always kept a slight distance, always kept things professional. A reputation as being difficult or unprepared or dramatic was much worse than one as a workaholic. So it was easier to play everything close to the vest. To reveal nothing and keep a metaphorical distance between her private life, which was really non-existent, and her work. She gave as much of herself as she needed to and no more.

Soon she would begin another show.

And the cycle would start again. She would leave that next show, too, eventually, the same way she started it.

Alone.

# *Two* ♫

Jazzy peeked out from under her hair. After discovering that no one had contacted her all day—no one but her agent confirming a call with the rest of her team to talk next steps, anyway—she'd fallen back to sleep. The light coming in from the window suggested dusk already.

"Oops," she whispered. "Ugh." Her mouth felt like sandpaper. Staggering up, she crossed her oversized studio and took her gold water bottle from the refrigerator. Resting against the counter, she glanced around her home. Her haven. She made decent money as an actor, but on the Upper West Side, even a one-bedroom was out of the question. But her studio suited her needs perfectly: a nook for her bed against a dark gray wall next to the walk-in closet that led to the bathroom. The large living area was painted a dove gray and opened into the most perfect little kitchen where she liked to cook the meals she ordered from a meal kit program. Cooking she could do, but shopping for food? No thanks.

In one go, she downed the entire water bottle. She flicked the switch on the kitchen lights and was surprised at the clutter that greeted her throughout the rest of the apartment. Her show bag was about to tumble off the teal club chair near the front door. The box of things from her dressing room was tipped over on its side. Her boots were scattered, one under the couch and one caught somehow between the bed and the wall, the rest of her outfit discarded on the floor near her bed.

She never drank while a show was running, and it made her a lightweight. Drunk Jazzy had made a bit of a mess.

She chuckled at herself and moved across the room to straighten things up when she caught sight of herself in the vintage gold mirror hanging next to the television. A pile of blonde hair and a tank top she didn't remember putting on greeted her in the reflection. The dark blue eyes generally fawned over in the press were, at present, red-rimmed and marred by last night's smeared mascara.

"Oof. Get it together," she told herself. She marched to the bathroom and let the steam of the shower settle around her. "Alexa, play 'Jimmy' from *Thoroughly Modern Millie*," she said as she shampooed. Her device heard her, and the speakers wired in her perfect little square of New York filled with Sutton Foster's incredible voice.

Wrapped in a fluffy bathrobe, she dried her hair and then pulled it back into a low bun. She padded out of the bathroom directly into her walk-in closet, where she chose a plain white tee and a pair of NYU sweatpants, gifted to her when she did a talk to the theater students there some years ago.

Her studio was quiet and dark. She picked her show bag up from where it had finally fallen on the floor and placed it carefully on the club chair. Sighing, she momentarily rested her hand on the character shoes right on top. She scooched the box of her dressing room things under the chair in the hopes that she would use them again soon. Her scattered boots went onto her neatly lined shoe rack in the walk-in closet.

Another look in the mirror showed her eyes now clear and bright, her skin pink from the heat of the shower. She wandered to her bed and sat down, at a total loss. The days and weeks of nothing to do stretched ahead of her, and she began to feel an itchiness already, a desire to move.

There was an emptiness in her gut, but not from hunger, though she should take care of that soon. The loss of the show crept around her body, the loss of Neil, of playing Abigail, of the family they'd all built together. Jazzy snaked an arm around her middle and slumped over for a moment. Just *one*. There would be no giving in to feeling sorry for herself. She was lucky in almost every way. But this one moment of un-Jazzy Summers behavior, she allowed. Then she stood abruptly.

She would be just fine. Feeling a bit shaky, she turned on the bedside lamp. Dusk had turned to night. The lights of the city winked at her through the sheer curtain of the large window on the kitchen wall. She opened it a crack and a chilly March breeze flowed in. As she turned in a circle in the middle of the apartment, the sounds of life reached her ears. A baby cried. Someone shouted at a cabbie. A siren screamed by and faded. Laughter rang out, from a group of friends, no doubt.

Jazzy closed her eyes and grimaced. Some feet away from the bed nook, a rose-colored couch was draped with a white furry blanket. She considered climbing under it and sleeping for a week, as if she could do such a thing.

"Yes, Jazzy, some people have friends and don't just focus on their work." She straightened a pile of books on the gold and glass coffee table. "They go shopping and get drunk and—" She moved to the gold side table and lit the cinnamon scented candle on it. "—tell each other all of their secrets." On the other side of the couch, she turned on the ceramic cat-shaped lamp. She'd bought it when she'd considered getting a real one but had never had the time. "They probably haven't overworked

21

themselves to the point where they got to age thirty without any friends. They haven't cancelled every plan out of concern for their voice or body or . . . auuugggghhh . . . "

With more force than necessary, she brushed some crumbs off of the kitchen island, surprised she'd missed them the morning before.

Hands flat on the island, she said, "What . . . do I . . . do?" She drummed her fingers on the smooth marble.

"Talk to the walls, apparently," she answered herself, before chuckling and burying her face in her hands. "Talking to yourself this much can't be the sign of anything good. Right?"

Her phone pinged and she hurried to it, hoping for a text from Neil, or anyone in the cast, really. But it was just a supportive I love you from her mom. She answered back quickly, then flopped onto the bed, phone in her hands. On a whim, she texted Neil to see if he would like to get coffee in the morning.

"I have friends," she told the ceiling. "See?" She gestured to the wall above the couch. A few moments later, she got up to look at it, which she didn't often do. All of the memorabilia from a life spent performing hung on this wall in a neat collage, pristinely framed in shabby chic frames.

There was the tiny girl with blonde curls in a tiny tutu, hands above her head. At seven, in her first production at a community theater in Indiana, where she'd grown up. The inevitable *Annie* wig at eleven. Spreading her arms wide in Times Square at thirteen, when her parents decided the move was inevitable as she burned up every stage Indianapolis had to offer.

Clippings from her hometown newspaper when she got her very first lead on Broadway at fifteen years old. Playbills from each subsequent show, snapshots of her with Stephen Sondheim and Lin-Manuel Miranda, a photo with the cast of "Law and Order: SVU" when she filmed her seemingly-required-for-a-Broadway-actor episode. Backstage in various Broadway houses with Ethan Carter, with Patti Lupone, with Liza Minelli, Audra McDonald, Hugh Jackman, and even the Obamas.

Her whole career, all of her accomplishments, hung on this wall. She kept them up as motivation, to make herself keep going even when she felt like collapsing. Fifteen years of long-running shows, all of which she'd left voluntarily for something new or a short, planned break. *Something Blue* was the first she'd left without knowing what exactly came next.

Jazzy Summers didn't take days off, other than one vacation a year with her parents. And that was planned well in advance so that ticket holders would be prepared that they weren't going to see her. Though she didn't like to think about it, she was a commodity to producers, and she hated calling out of shows and disappointing her fans.

She didn't care that she was famous, or that she had nearly five hundred thousand Instagram followers. She didn't mind getting stopped in a coffee shop if it meant connecting with someone who was affected by her work. She didn't care that stage doors could take up to an hour, because that was the point to her. The fame part didn't mean anything to her.

It didn't matter that she was Jazzy Summers, Broadway star. It mattered that she got to interact with her fanbase, who were loud and silly and so much fun. That's what the work meant to her: connecting with people from all over the world, bringing a little light and entertainment and brevity into their lives. When Jazzy felt the energy of nearly two thousand people coming at her when she stepped on a

stage . . .

. . . that is where she truly lived.

She didn't care about the late nights or the impossibility of a social life. And forget about real relationships. She refused to have a "showmance" and that limited her choices significantly. It was beyond her how any of her peers dated, let alone got married. Then there was the anxiety over whether or not a show would be received well. But that was all worth it for the privilege of connecting the way that she did with so many people, eight shows a week.

She hadn't been out of work, with nothing coming up next, for fifteen years.

WHEN I MET YOU

"Hm." Jazzy stepped closer to the wall and inspected a more recent photo she rarely paused on. Paige Parker had one arm slung around Jazzy's shoulders as they smiled brilliantly into the camera. Behind them, a glittering party was taking place. They looked for all the world like best friends.

But the photo was an illusion. She had only met Paige in passing a few times. The longest conversation they'd ever had was the night before, when she'd expressed how sad she was that Jazzy's show had closed. Jazzy had put the photo on the wall as a reminder to reach out to Paige, who was in her first principle role in *On Her Own*.

She considered texting Paige for a moment.

But she knew she probably wouldn't, even though now, here she was: thirty years old and yearning for friendships she should have started building years ago.

Her stomach grumbled.

"Well now, *that* we can take care of. See, Jazz? One step at a time." She pulled up an app and began to order from her favorite vegan place out of habit, then paused.

A wicked smile spread across her face. "No show? No obligation to sing or dance any time soon? Pizza it is."

An hour and a half later, Jazzy shoved the pizza box away from her and leaned back against the couch cushions, sated. The credits for *Funny Face* rolled across her television screen, and she let them play as she washed her face and brushed her teeth.

She plucked one of the books from the coffee table, a popular romance she'd been meaning to read for ages. As she flipped through the pages, she said, "Reading! Remember reading? You have time to read now." Satisfied, she turned off all the lights but the one by her bedside, fluffed her pillows, and settled into her comfortable bed.

Some time later, proud, she closed the book with a bookmark. "See? I can relax. That was at least half an hour."

Her phone told her it had been seven minutes. And Neil had never responded. Nor had she gotten any other texts from any other person to whom she wasn't related.

"Augh!" She hastily flipped off the lamp, pulled the covers over her head, flopped over onto her side, and eventually drifted off.

§

The next morning, Jazzy inhaled the smell of beans being ground at H&H Bagels, which was blessedly not too busy. Just a block from her building, the small shop was famous for its bagels, but what she loved was the coffee. She stood in front of the display case full of waters and juices, staring at the dark wood floor, waiting for the barista to finish pouring her coffee. The tables for two, surrounded by the red vinyl chairs, were all taken at the moment, but she could wait for one to open up. She was just glad to be out of the house.

"Mateo?" the barista called. Jazzy watched a tall, striking man weave his way through the other patrons and past her to scoop up his coffee.

Oh, wow. A scent of citrus and cinnamon wafted over her. He smelled amazing on top of all that handsome.

"And . . . Jessica?"

Jazzy tore her gaze from the gorgeous stranger and smiled at the barista, glad she'd decided to meet herself for coffee since no one else wanted to. She'd brought her book and intended to read to her heart's content before a call with her management team that afternoon.

"Uh, whoops." Those two simple words melted into the air. The good-smelling stranger had a voice like the first sip of hot chocolate on a winter's day.

She looked up to meet twinkling brown eyes.

"I think you stole my coffee." The guy smiled down at her, a ten-watt, full-force, not-suitable-for-work kind of smile that stopped her brain from working properly. He kept smiling as she stared at him, then hitched up an eyebrow.

"I . . . Oh!" She noted the side of the cup she was holding where 'Mateo' was written. "I'm so sorry. Here you go."

Mateo, as he was apparently called, graciously accepted his cup and handed hers over. His fingers lingered for just a moment on hers, and she felt a burst of starlight somewhere around her heart. "Thank you."

"Of course. Sorry . . . um . . . again." Her brain couldn't seem to send signals to her mouth.

"No biggie." He gave her that disarming smile again and walked over to the counter where he took the lid off his coffee and added an almost laughable amount of sugar. She inadvertently followed him over, needing some almond milk herself, and definitely not to stay close to him. Not at all.

He had placed himself directly in front of the jug.

"Sorry, again. Excuse me." She gestured to the jug and noted the laughter in his eyes.

"Guess we're just destined to be in each other's way today." A beat passed as he held her gaze, then he handed her the almond milk jug.

"I guess so." She took the jug, slippery with condensation, and met his eyes again. For a moment, she was lost in the depth of them until the jug slipped out of her hand, not falling over but making a bit of a messy splash on the counter.

"Oh shoot! Did I get you? I'm so sorry." She felt a blush sweep across her cheeks.

He bit his lip and reached for some napkins to toss onto the spill, clearly trying not to laugh. "It's okay, you didn't get me."

She also grabbed some napkins and began to help. "I'm not this clumsy usually, really. I'm not."

"I know." He said it so off-handedly that it almost didn't register, then she stopped mopping.

With trepidation, she met his eyes once again.

At the look on her face, his smile disappeared and his mouth opened slightly in alarm. "Shit, not like that, I'm sorry! I mean, I just . . . know who you are. You're Jazzy Summers. I love your work. I'm not a stalker, I swear." He raised his hands as if in surrender.

Her shoulders relaxed. Just a fan. She grinned at him again and finished cleaning up her spill. "That's a relief."

His lips curved upwards as he put the lid back on his cup, with nearly the whole of the shop's sugar supply inside of it. "Why'd you say your name was Jessica for the cup?"

She tossed the wet napkins into the trash. "Just easier that way. Jazzy usually requires explanation."

"I think it's a solid name." He turned and relaxed against the counter as she finally added her almond milk to her coffee.

Jazzy stirred and watched the liquid turn a light brown. "It was my agent's idea. And it grew on me. I'm definitely not a Jessica anymore." She snapped the lid on her cup. "What's your name?"

He turned his cup to her, his full lips curved in a mischievous grin.

Jazzy closed her eyes, feeling totally thrown. Silly. It felt like he was flirting. Oh god. Was he flirting? "Right. Mateo. I knew that. Seriously, I'm usually not like . . . whatever it is I'm being right now."

He gestured for her to move away from the counter so the other caffeine-deprived patrons could dress their coffees. "Hey, it's okay. Not to sound like even more of a stalker, but I'm sorry about *Something Blue* closing. I thought it was great."

Taken aback, Jazzy gazed into his face again. Beyond the deep brown eyes and the full lips, he had dimples as deep as the Grand Canyon, golden-brown skin, and a natural afro about an inch long.

This was a disarmingly handsome guy. Charming as hell, too. As evidenced by what a weirdo she was being. She cast about her brain for normal words. "Thank you. It wasn't a huge surprise but closing came fast."

A couple got up from a nearby table and Mateo gestured to it, a question on his face. She glanced around the shop, not quite believing that a handsome stranger wanted to sit and have coffee with her.

Little sparkles of starlight zoomed around her chest as she walked to the empty table. Smiling again—going for coy but probably ending up somewhere around awkward weirdo—she took a delicious sip and scooted into the chair with its back to the wall.

He took the one opposite, settling into the chair and spreading out his long legs, far more at ease than she felt. "So what did you do on your first day of freedom?"

Jazzy snorted and thought about the hangover and the relaxing she had tried to do. "Mostly just talked to myself."

"Oh yeah? I'm a big fan of talking to yourself. I think it shows you're good at being introspective. That you're willing to examine your own thoughts and feelings out loud." He grinned as he took a sip. "You know, I've heard that pets help mask it, so your neighbors don't think you've lost it. You can always say you were talking to the cat. Do you do that a lot?" It seemed like he was perpetually on the verge of a laugh.

Jazzy had never thought of her neurotic need to talk to herself like that before. She felt a blush creep into her cheeks again. "I do. Maybe too much. I've lived alone for a long—"

"Mateo! *¿Que pasa?*" A redheaded woman poked her head in the door of the shop and Mateo turned and looked at her. "You said five minutes!"

"*¡Lo siento, Judith!*" Admonished, Mateo turned to Jazzy and hit her with that smile again. "Duty calls." He stood and tapped the table with his knuckles. "See you around, Jazzy Summers."

"Yeah . . . that . . . great, sure. Yes . . . " By the time she was done stammering, Mateo had made it to the door.

He turned, as if he'd forgotten something, that grin lighting up the whole shop. "What are you going to do today?"

She grinned back at him, finally finding her words. "You know, I think I'm going to adopt a cat."

# Three

Mateo's laughter faded as the door slowly closed. Jazzy placed a hand over her heart. She felt as if she were seeing stars, but not in a cartoon-dog-hit-on-the-head kind of way. In a who-the-hell-was-that-and-when-do-I-see-him-again kind of way. "What . . . was that?"

"Oh my god, girl, what's he like?"

Jazzy turned to the counter. The shop had emptied a bit and the goth-looking barista, whose name badge said Kara, was obviously trying to hold in a squeal. Her black hair was in pigtails and her blunt bangs sat above bright hazel eyes that were gleaming in anticipation.

"What? Who? That guy?" She pointed to the door, still flustered.

"That *guy*? That was Mateo Williams, girl!" Kara seemed shocked that Jazzy didn't know who she was talking about.

Jazzy frowned. "Mateo Williams . . . It rings a bell."

Kara's mouth dropped open. She slapped her towel down on the counter and leaned forward as though they were best friends. "Mateo. Williams. *Mateo Williams*. Pop star. 'Your Heart is Mine.' Didn't you go to your school dances?"

Jazzy, who'd been gazing at the door a bit wistfully, turned back to Kara and shook her head. "No, actually."

"Oh. Well. That kind of explains it. But he was huge, back in the early aughts. On "TRL" all the time. Played stadiums. I was only eight, but I was out of my *mind* in love with him."

Jazzy turned back to the door again, her brow furrowed. This information was very new and very weird. "Oh."

Kara jumped up and down a bit. "Oh? *Oh!* Mateo Williams just sat and had coffee with her and all she says is 'Oh!'" She was laughing now, clearly giddy about her run-in with the pop star.

Jazzy laughed too, enjoying the chat immensely. "I'm sorry, my life is weird! I don't really listen to pop music and I didn't go to conventional school—"

Kara held up a hand. "Trust me, he's worth a Google. Oh my *god*, you just had a *coffee* date with Mateo *Williams*!" Kara squealed again.

Jazzy laughed, thinking of Mateo's kind eyes and stunning smile.

§

"Here you are, Patti. You and I are going to be great friends. I hope you like your new home. And please don't pee on everything." Gingerly, Jazzy opened the soft gray cat carrier, left it on the floor near the door, and walked over to her bed where she sat down. She didn't want to make any sudden movements.

A small, white face peeked out and took in her surroundings.

"Hi, Patti," Jazzy said in a low voice like the woman at the shelter had instructed. Calm, loving. "Come on in. Welcome home."

Patti placed one delicate paw on the hardwood floor and sniffed the air. As she walked all the way out into the room, her tail was held high. Jazzy's heart skipped a beat when the little furball walked straight over to the brand-new cat tree under the window, hopped up, and looked outside. Slowly, Jazzy rose and walked over to the kitchen. Patti turned to look at her and blinked slowly.

"Oh you sweet girl, I just knew you'd love it here."

An hour after her chance meeting with the handsome stranger, Jazzy had brought half of the pet supply store up to her apartment, then walked to the Tenth Life Rescue a couple of blocks from her building. The woman who had helped Jazzy had told her that Patti, at five years old, was a little harder to adopt out than a kitten. When Jazzy had sat on the floor, the snow-white ball of fluff with bright blue eyes had immediately curled up in her lap and started purring. She'd dubbed the cat Patti, after Patti Lupone, Broadway legend, and she knew a lifelong friendship had begun.

"Here you go, love." She placed a dish of wet food on the ground and Patti immediately hopped off the tree to gobble it up. Jazzy clasped her hands, feeling like Snow White.

For a few minutes, Jazzy watched as the curious cat walked around her apartment, sniffing. When she discovered her litterbox in the closet and used it, Jazzy blew out a breath, glad she wouldn't have to worry about that.

The perfect little being sniffed around the bathroom and closet next, making curious chirping noises.

She wished she had Mateo's number so she could text him a photo of Patti. She let herself imagine the text turning into a stream of witty banter, then Mateo would ask to meet her for a drink. She would show up in a perfect outfit, and they would talk all night, wandering the streets of New York just like Carrie Bradshaw. She would wear something fancy instead of her regular wardrobe, which could be generously described as "chic" but was really just "mostly black". Mateo would be so taken with her because she would say complete sentences that he would pull her close and kiss her, his lips soft and persistent . . .

Her phone rang, interrupting her daydream. *Mateo? No, basket case. That's impossible.* "Hello?"

"Jazzy, this is Sandra over at the Booth."

"Oh, hi Sandra. Great to hear from you." Mateo and his dimples faded from her mind.

"We're gonna miss your sunshine around here, honey."

"That's very nice to hear, thank you. I miss you already, too." Jazzy sat down on the couch as Patti now inspected underneath the coffee table.

"Listen, we just had all the dressing rooms cleaned out and the delivery guys will be making their way around tomorrow with your things. But I just did a walk through and found a photo in yours. It looks like you and your parents? I found it under the counter."

Jazzy knew the one. A white and gold frame surrounding a photo of her mom and dad and her at the Grand Canyon from a few years ago. "The one in Arizona?"

"That's the one. I can call the delivery drivers back if you'd like."

She furrowed her brow and checked the time. Still a while before her Team Jazzy call. "No, that's not necessary at all. Can I come by and get it?"

"Sure, that would be great. Just let me know when."

"How's now?" She was itching to be back in the theater.

Sandra sounded surprised. "That's just fine, if you'd like."

Jazzy began putting on her boots one-handed, hopping about gracelessly. "I would, thank you. I'll be there in twenty minutes."

Patti had completed her assessments and was now bathing on the pale teal rug near the coffee table. Boots successfully tied, Jazzy knelt down to her. The cat stopped licking one paw and nuzzled into her hand. "I'll be back in a bit, sweet girl. You explore as much as you like. Enjoy your new home."

§

Entering through the front doors of the theater felt very odd. This entrance was grand while the stage door was industrial. The lobby was plush and elegant as opposed to the cinderblocks and mismatched furniture of backstage. Still, she took a deep breath, thrilled to be back in this historic place. After thanking Sandra for the call, she wound her way through the building and took the familiar stairwell to her—what *used* to be her—dressing room.

The photo was on the dressing table. Jazzy picked it up and gazed at it for a moment, before putting it in her bag. She turned slowly. The pale pink walls looked somehow sad, bereft as they were of her photos and personal touches. Soon, another show would move in and all traces of her would be gone. *Something Blue* would just be another ghost of the Booth.

On her way out, Jazzy saw Neville, one of her favorite people. He was sitting on a cushy chair near the stage door, with a radio on his shoulder, scrolling on his phone. She smiled and waved at him.

"Well, isn't this my lucky day? How's it going, Summers?"

Jazzy laughed. "Pretty good, Peterson." They performed the complicated handshake they'd made up when he was the doorman for one of her very first shows.

"You okay, kid?" Neville's voice held a note of concern. "That wasn't the way any of us wanted to go out."

Jazzy sighed. "I'll be fine. I'm just a little sad. And a little—" She made a sweeping gesture. "—what do I do with myself?"

He chuckled. "I've never seen anyone work harder than you. You deserve a little break. Give yourself one."

"Thanks, Neville. What about you? Got another gig around the corner?"

"The revival of *Carousel* is moving in next month. They'd been trying to get a theater for a while and—" He shrugged, not unsympathetically.

"And ours became suddenly available."

"It did." He looked into her eyes, as if assessing her. "You have someone to talk to while you look for the next amazing thing you'll do?"

Jazzy thought of Patti and felt herself smile. "You know what? I do." She glanced behind her to the hallway that led backstage. "Hey, do you mind if I . . . " She gestured.

"Not at all. The crews are gone for the night."

"Thank you."

"Have a nice goodbye," he said softly as he picked up his phone again.

She walked down the darkened hallway to the even darker backstage. None of the prop tables or smaller set pieces she'd grown so accustomed to maneuvering around in the past six months were there. After dropping her bag by the wall, she walked through the legs—the long black curtains—and stepped onto the empty stage.

A solitary bulb glowed brightly on a stand in the middle of the stage, illuminating the rest of the theater dimly. Yes, it was for safety purposes, but Jazzy preferred the superstitious reason. Every theater was haunted in some way, and she liked to think the light was for the ghosts left behind.

Her footsteps echoed across the scuffed floor. The vastness of the stage without the elaborate set, the height of the fly system, the emptiness of the space, felt as if it were engulfing her.

She stopped at center, as she had hundreds of times before, right next to the ghost light. Around her, her show seemed to come to life. The opening number in beautiful nineteenth century ball gowns, the duets with Neil, her big ballad toward the end. The charming ensemble danced gracefully, performing the beautiful choreography. She kissed Neil, time and time again, as the music gained momentum and rushed to the finale. Raised arms, deep bows, tears in her eyes, grateful for the job she'd been given, the one she was so lucky to get to do. She could feel the energy of the crowd, hear the cheers, the lights bright on her face.

She remembered the sweet moments backstage, the little rituals she'd shared with each cast member. Tea with Neil an hour before curtain. Warming up with the girls who played her sisters. The fight call. The high five she and the stage manager performed every night, without fail, after her biggest number. The post-show ritual of the actor who played her father poking his head in and telling her to get home safe. Every inside joke, every silly routine, every precious memory of the *Something Blue* months passed through her mind in a rush. She felt a palpable loneliness at the thought of losing yet another family.

None of whom, she couldn't help thinking, had contacted her in the past two days.

She opened her eyes and the theater held only ghosts. Only silence. The actors had faded into the shadows. She was alone on an empty stage.

"Goodbye," she whispered into the darkness.

She turned and walked into the wings, scooping up her bag on her way out, leaving the ghost of Abigail behind.

§

When she got home from the Booth, she found Patti on her pillow. For the next twenty minutes, they got acquainted with each other as, deep in thought, she ran her hand through the cat's soft fur.

Her phone stayed silent, and she couldn't help but feel more alone than she ever had. Not lonely, not exactly, but alone. She had always had something else to focus on immediately after a job. But in this instance, she had nothing but time. And she couldn't think of a single person, not one, who she could text for coffee or meet for a bit of shopping.

What she wanted was someone who knew her, someone she wouldn't have to explain herself to, someone who understood her. She'd spent too much of her life working on the career that so fulfilled her, she'd forgotten about the human connection part *outside* of that.

Now, with nothing to focus on in front of her, she felt the need to connect with another person, a longing she'd never really experienced before.

Of course, there was the coffee stranger. She smiled at the thought of him as she dialed into her call.

"All right, I think we're all here, yeah?" Joshua, Jazzy's agent, had a commanding voice, and everyone else on the conference call murmured assent. "Great. Jazz, we're so sorry that *Something Blue* closed so suddenly. But we all have ideas for where to go next."

Jazzy wanted to do something, but she didn't know what, or how, and these were the people who could help her decide. But she only half listened as her team prattled on about next steps. Unable to truly focus, she made noises of agreement now and then, feeling very unlike herself.

Next to her, Patti began to knead the blanket, purring up a storm. Jazzy smiled and scratched her little head. "At least I've got you," she whispered.

"What do you think, Jazzy?" Joshua's voice boomed at her from the speakerphone.

She jumped a bit and wondered what had just been discussed.

"I'm so sorry, team, I missed that last part. I'm a little scattered today." She bit her lip, feeling badly. She always paid attention in meetings.

"No problem, kid. That's understandable. But I was saying that a couple of weekends have opened up at Lowenstein's. Do you want to do a solo cabaret show?"

Jazzy smiled widely, sat up, and hugged Patti to her chest.

"That is *exactly* what I want to do."

# Four ♫

The plans for the Lowenstein's show lit a new fire under Jazzy. In the week since they'd talked about it, she allowed herself to relax. It had been years since she'd performed at the little cabaret dinner theater, and before planning for it in earnest, she gave herself the break everyone was always telling her to take.

She binge watched TV shows she'd been meaning to forever. She finished her book and began another, went on long runs in Central Park, and played with Patti. They settled into a routine—mostly of waking up at seven every morning to Patti sitting on her chest and begging for breakfast. And if she happened to go to H&H every morning for coffee it was only because she wanted caffeine and it didn't have anything at all to do with a charming guy she kept daydreaming about.

On a whim, when she'd realized she hadn't really talked to anyone in days, she'd texted Neil again. He didn't reply until late on Friday night telling her to come and meet him for drinks.

She ignored it. It was almost midnight and she was already in her pajamas with Patti snuggled next to her. Now, with something to plan and focus on, Jazzy wasn't so lonely. And she didn't need a half-hearted invitation from someone who obviously didn't really want to make the effort to be her friend.

Or at least, she could be in denial about the loneliness, which suited her just fine.

She would find a real friend someday. But for now, it was finally time to meet the band she'd helped to put together for her Lowenstein's show, and she couldn't wait. She applied a deep red lipstick, slipped her feet into her favorite black boots, and pushed her large, dark sunglasses up her nose. With her black t-shirt and moto jacket, she looked and felt like she was ready to kick some ass. In the mirror, she caught herself grinning.

"I'm going to *work*, Patti." She turned to open the door, picking up her keys from the little table next to the club chair. "Don't get into any trouble when I'm gone, okay?"

Patti glanced up from the paw she was licking as if to say *oh please, lady*.

Jazzy chuckled, closed and locked the door, and headed down to SoHo.

§

"Jazzy Summers, as I live and breathe!" Toby Anderson pulled her into his loft, a beautiful, open space with exposed brick walls and minimalist furniture. The kitchen gleamed with stainless steel and a sleek concrete countertop. A baby grand piano stood in a corner backed by shelves and shelves of music and books. Gigantic floor to ceiling windows lined one side of the place, with curtains as tall as trees to keep the sun out. It was the perfect artist abode.

"Toby, it's so good to see you." She hadn't seen him in ages, not since she'd auditioned for *On Her Own*. She was thrilled the talented composer had agreed to take on her little cabaret show. "Thank you so much for agreeing to do this."

"For you, and that voice, anything." Toby pulled her into a hug and squeezed tightly.

"That's very kind." She kissed his cheek on her way out of the hug.

"Come in, come in," he sang, as he waved her into the apartment. "Can I get you something to drink?"

Jazzy pulled her water bottle out of her bag. "I'm all set for now, thank you."

"Well, at the end of this, it'll be past five and maybe we could open a little bubbly to celebrate." He winked at her.

Jazzy snickered and followed Toby into the vast apartment. Sitting on the black leather couches surrounding an enormous natural wood coffee table laden with books about musical theater, were four other people who all stood to greet her with various handshakes and hugs. Everyone settled onto the couch.

"Now I know you know everyone, but we might not all know each other," Toby said. He gestured to a woman with short, spiky blonde hair wearing leather leggings. "This is Sam, our drummer. She's one of the best percussionists I've ever worked with."

"I'd love to do some rock and roll, if you're interested, Jazzy," Sam said.

"And I'm Marcy, the bassist. Sam and I came up in the punk scene together." Marci swung her long black hair behind her shoulder and placed a hand on Sam's knee. Sam beamed at her and laced their fingers together. "We've also been married for four years."

"It only took twenty to figure out we should be." Sam laughed boisterously and Marci joined her.

Jazzy smiled and noted how easy they were with each other. She'd worked with them both on a show in her early twenties but hadn't seen them since then, and it was lovely that they'd gotten together. They fit. She wondered briefly how they knew they were meant to be after so many years of friendship. As Sam toyed with

Marcy's hair in an offhand but familiar way, she wondered if there was anyone in her past that she would open her heart to like that.

Not very likely.

"And this is Andrew, our guitarist."

Very much a rock star with long, shaggy brown hair, and a full sleeve of tattoos up and down his left arm, Andrew also had a wide smile and kind blue eyes. "I played in the pit for *Something Blue* for a week or so. You were a marvel," he said warmly.

"Thank you very much. Too bad you aren't a reviewer." Their laughter at her good-natured joke filled her with warmth. She could feel a connection forming.

"It is terrible that audiences won't get to see you on a Broadway stage for a while, and that's why I'm glad that we're doing this. I was honored you asked for me. Oh, and I'm the pianist, Toby."

"Hello, Toby," they all intoned in unison, collapsing into surprised laughter. Jazzy knew she was part of a team now.

Toby shifted and captured Jazzy's hand. "You know we all think you're marvelous. So let's give Lowenstein's what for!"

Marcy began to clap and Andrew joined in with a "Whoop!"

Everyone turned to Jazzy expectantly.

A little thrill ran up her spine. Time to work. "I am so glad you are all lending me your talents and so thankful you agreed to work with me on this. Toby asked me what I wanted this show to be, and all I want it to be is *fun*. I want audiences to know the songs, and I definitely want to do some of the ones I'm known for. I just want them to walk away having forgotten about their lives and felt a little something for an evening, you know?"

Sam and Marcy nodded appreciatively. Andrew looked pleased.

"Well then," said Toby. "Let's get started, shall we?"

Throughout the afternoon and into the evening, when they did pour that champagne, Jazzy and the assembled band talked through the show. Everyone threw out ideas, gave opinions, made changes, and worked together wonderfully. Sam was already tapping on the coffee table and Andrew strummed Toby's acoustic guitar. As they sang a little melody, Jazzy's relief at working again was palpable to her. She felt a settling in her chest she hadn't felt in weeks.

As the sky turned pink outside, with the help of the champagne, the little group seemed to meld and at the end of the evening, the bones of the show had come together. They made plans to rehearse at a space on 42nd Street in two days. Jazzy walked home from the train lighter than air, still hiccoughing a little from the bubbles. Even Patti giving her the cold shoulder for a late dinner couldn't bring her down.

The next morning, she went to H&H Bagels again, intending to write out some stories she wanted to tell between songs. With her head in the clouds, she didn't notice the handsome stranger until she'd almost bumped into him on the sidewalk just under the awning of the shop.

"Hi again, Jazzy Summers."

Oof, that voice. He could read the phone book and she would listen. If they still had phone books, which she wasn't sure they did. No one wanted to list their cell phone numbers, and who even had a landline anymore?

She realized she was just staring up at him like the big weirdo she apparently was around him. But he was like a stun gun. And not just because of his smile and general gorgeousness, but he projected this ease and comfort and charisma—

"Mateo. Remember me?" His voice rang with amusement, his lips pulling into a grin. "What are you thinking about?"

Jazzy shook her head, determined to be normal. "Phone books," she said as though that should be obvious.

He laughed aloud, genuinely, and started to say something else when he was interrupted.

"Mateo! Really, get in the car!" The same woman from the other day stood next to a black Mercedes, tapping her foot.

He waved to her then turned back to Jazzy, still looking amused, but also . . . disappointed? "Duty calls, again. Let me know where you come down on phone books," he said as he backed away from her, coffee cup in hand. "For? Against?"

49

"I . . . Yeah . . . " There weren't any words in her brain. Cool. She was either a basket case or a blithering fool around him. *Top notch humaning, Jazzy. Well done.*

Clearly amused at her inability to be a person, he said, "See you later, I hope." He turned to the car idling on Columbus Avenue and folded himself inside, giving her a grin that sent her heart on a little rollercoaster.

Inside the shop, only a few people sat eating bagels and sipping lattes while writing the next great American novel. Jazzy was grateful for the solitude.

Over the noise of the grinder, she shouted, "Hi, Kara."

Kara looked up, then her face lit up with joy. "Oh my gosh, he was just in here again. Did you see him?"

Jazzy chuckled and propped her elbows onto the counter. "I ran into him outside. And he has me totally tongue-tied. I keep behaving like a clown around him. Or a mime."

"Oh man, so sayeth we all." Today Kara had her hair up in two buns on top of her head. Her nose ring with a single sapphire stone on it sparkled. Jazzy bet with herself that at least one of Shakespeare's plays was in her backpack, heavily annotated.

Kara's big brown eyes took on a dreamlike quality. "Did you talk to him?"

"Kind of?" Jazzy winced. "He talked. I acted like I was new. To earth."

"Oh my god, if you guys get together, can I come to the wedding?"

A surprised laugh leapt out of her throat. "Let's not get ahead of ourselves. We've barely spoken."

"What a dream." Kara placed her elbows on the counter and looked at Jazzy with her big doe eyes. "Do you want a coffee?"

"Oh, yes, please. A large." Jazzy dug in her bag for her wallet.

Kara messed with the touch screen and Jazzy put her card in the slot. She tipped Kara five bucks for making her feel like a friend for a few minutes.

The girl beamed at her and poured her coffee.

A few minutes later, Jazzy sat with her laptop open and a blank document staring at her, cursor blinking. She had been so ready to write some stories down for her show, but right now, the fizziness in her chest wouldn't settle. Too distracted by Patti after their first encounter, she hadn't Googled him. Then she'd been having too much fun in her daydreams to want to know what the internet said about him. But now, she navigated to a web browser and typed in 'Mateo Williams'.

Whoa. Hundreds of thousands of hits. Jazzy realized that she wouldn't be writing much today as she began to sift through. She started with his Wikipedia page.

Mateo had been sixteen when his first single made him Beatles-level famous. His first record went gold in about thirty seconds, and each single that came off of it shot to the top of the pop charts. Kara had been right; he was a fixture on the late-nineties early-aughts MTV show, "Total Request Live". He was even on the very last episode. She put her headphones on and clicked on a video. When Mateo appeared, she had to lower the volume when the screams of his fans erupted.

In what seemed like overnight, Mateo was everywhere. She hadn't noticed at the time, not really. She was in her first Broadway show during the height of his fame, carrying a principle role at fifteen years old. She didn't focus on much but homeschooling and performing, but she vaguely remembered a gigantic billboard in Times Square with his face on it.

In the "Early Life" section of his Wikipedia, she learned that his mother had moved to New York from Puerto Rico to attend Columbia University for marketing. She had always wanted a child but remained without a partner, or anyone she wanted to have one with. So at forty-one, she went through IVF. She had called Mateo, named after her father, her little miracle. Marisol raised Mateo on her own in Inwood, a neighborhood at the northern tip of Manhattan, and he'd later described his life with his mother as idyllic.

He'd begun performing in grade school while Marisol worked at a PR firm in Midtown. He was discovered by a record executive at an open mic night at a coffee shop near her offices, and the rest was history. After a Best New Artist Grammy nomination, he joined the ranks of the pop superstars, doing a duet with Britney and opening for the Backstreet Boys on tour before his album dropped.

Jazzy was fascinated. She watched a couple of music videos and was charmed to death with how of-the-time they were. Leather jackets and tight t-shirts, standing in shallow infinity pools and pointing a lot. Young Mateo was adorable, vulnerable and sweet and charismatic. She read on.

And wrinkled her nose.

By the time he was twenty, his second album had gone double platinum, and he was a millionaire many, many times over. Mateo was constantly seen buying extravagant things: a Maserati, houses in L.A., a movie theater. His episode of MTV's "Cribs" showed off an ostentatious, completely unnecessary, palatial estate, just for him and his mother in Beverly Hills. And then he was seen about town, partying too hard, staying out all night.

And that didn't bother Jazzy. People could party and still be good people. Hell, she'd worked with many of them. But then the rumors began to swirl that he didn't want to work anymore. That he was throwing fits in the studio, that he was not showing up to scheduled interviews. That, after she started saying bizarre things to the press, he had fired his mom from being his manager. It seemed she was never seen again. He went on a disastrous tour and was almost always late to the stage, sometimes performing only six or seven songs before dropping the mic and leaving. The industry began to blacklist him.

When his third album flopped completely—barely hitting five hundred thousand sold—he took up with

Ariel Star, a former Disney Channel child star, who was also making all the wrong choices. She and Mateo were seen out clubbing every night, at first canoodling, followed by very publicly fighting and making up. Mateo proposed on top of a mountain with a seven-carat engagement ring. Of course, that was followed by the inevitable breakup in front of the cameras.

He hadn't been seen in L.A. since. He'd sold the palatial estate and moved back to New York City. Paparazzi eventually lost interest in chasing him down outside of the building he rarely left, and he essentially disappeared.

He had no social media presence himself, but there were lots of fan pages that posted old photos, videos, interviews, and, on occasion, rare sightings. Other than that, it seemed that Jazzy was the only one who'd spoken to him in about a decade.

She sat back and huffed out a breath.

Well.

That was a journey.

It seemed that her handsome stranger was just a totally spoiled former pop diva who didn't really do anything now but hang out in his Upper West Side penthouse. And make Jazzy feel foolish, now that she thought about it. Of course, he could have changed in a decade. Who hasn't? But Mateo seemed too casual, too noncommittal, to have changed much. His manner was just so . . . easy. Not a care in the world.

Jazzy didn't have time for unserious people. So she wrote off her thrilling encounters as just that. As hot as he was, Mateo was a slacker, and Jazzy could never be compatible with a person like him. Her daydreams about him disappeared with a palpable *poof*. She was nothing if not a realistic daydreamer.

How disappointing. How boring.

How utterly predictable.

# Five ♫

"I legitimately cannot believe that voice is real. Incredible. I think we're ready, kids!" Toby said to Jazzy and the rest of the band. He played a little trill on the piano.

The week after her second encounter with Mateo had been filled with rehearsals with the band, looking for her next project, and playing with Patti. She barely noticed that not a single former castmate had tried to get in touch. Not once.

And that was *fine*. Because she had Toby and Sam and Marcy and Andrew, and now, even a sax and a trumpet, and she was ready to blow the lid off of Lowenstein's. She was ready with the stories and the songs. All of it had come together in the magical way that some things do. Excitement zinged around the room.

Bring it on.

The two weekends of shows had sold out in minutes, reminding Jazzy that she was, indeed, a Broadway star. It stunned her, even now, fifteen years after becoming Jazzy Summers, that anyone cared to hear her sing. She pictured herself in a Barbie-like doll box, posed with a mic and wearing all black with character shoes. *Jazzy Summers: kind of a loner who talks to herself. Now with cat!*

In the dinky Lowenstein's basement dressing room on opening weekend, she took a long look in the mirror. She wore a black crop top and high-waisted leather leggings. Her voice was already warm, thanks to Toby and his piano. She was feeling confident and, for the first time since the closing night of *Something Blue*, happy. Grinning at herself in the mirror, she shook out her long blonde waves and stood.

She heard the call for places, and she made her way upstairs, past signed photos of all the legends who'd performed here before her. She could hear the diners finishing their meals, the clank of plates against cutlery as they were being cleared. As she quickly ran through all the stories she wanted to tell in her head, she stretched her arms up and then bounced on her feet.

Finally, "Please welcome to the stage, Jazzy Summers!"

Smiling widely, she strode onto the stage, confident and excited. The audience was on its feet as she stepped to the mic, beaming out across the room. Jazzy loved how intimate this room was, with the cabaret tables mere feet from the edge of the stage. She could make out faces and outfits and individual cheers. The stage had just enough room for her and the band to perform.

Toby gave her a note and she started the show with a bang: "The Wizard and I" from *Wicked*. At twenty, she'd gotten to slip into Elphaba's green makeup, and it still thrilled her to sing this song.

"Thank you, thank you so much!" she said into the mic over the cheering after the song. "I'm so glad to see all of you. My goodness, I can't believe you all came out to see me."

The audience cheered again, and she saw some familiar faces in the crowd. A director she'd worked with, a few cast members from another show, some other colleagues in the industry. No one from *Something Blue*, notably, but she didn't let that get her down.

"This next song is from the very first show I ever did. I was a little tiny thing when I did *The Music Man*, but even at seven, I would stop what I was doing backstage every night just to listen to it."

Jazzy began to sing "'Til There Was You", modified by the band so it sounded a little more Beatles and less August Wilson, but it still tugged at her heartstrings. And when she finished, she noticed one woman wipe a tear from her eye, a small smile on her face.

Jazzy felt the same.

After letting the feeling linger for a few moments, Jazzy turned and introduced her band. Andrew waved, Marcy beamed, Sam saluted from behind the drums, and the horns players raised their instruments, smiling. Toby, of course, got a huge round of applause.

From there, she sang two of her favorite funny showtunes: "Right Hand Man" from *Something Rotten* and "Summer in Ohio" from *The Last Five Years*. Then she pulled out the stool and sang the ballad that had gotten her famous, from her very first Broadway show, *After All*, and the audience went wild.

At intermission, she sipped water and joked around with the band and she felt like she was flying. The audience was still right there with her when they returned to the stage. With Toby on the piano and singing the part of Jonathan, they sang "Therapy" from *tick . . . tick . . . BOOM* which had the audience rolling with laughter. There were two more classics after that, "The Sound of Music" and "Finishing the Hat" and then the more contemporary "A Way Back to Then" from *[title of show]*. After that Jazzy was ready to get a little goofy.

"Now, I know that we in this room are all total musical theater nerds," she said into the mic as she pulled it from its stand. Cheers and whoops rang out through the room. She chuckled and moved the mic stand out of the way. "That's right. So I ask you, fellow nerds, how many times have you been alone in the car trying to sing all of the parts in 'One Day More'?"

Everyone laughed and she heard *absolutely* and *obviously* and *hell yeah* from various tables as nearly everyone in the audience nodded.

"I thought so. Now, I've always been pretty ambitious. I've always heard 'you can't do that' and said 'yes the hell I can' so . . . I'm gonna do it. I'm gonna sing every part in this song."

The laughter and cheering reached into her chest and curled around her heart, fulfilling her.

"But I might need your help, so feel free to chime in. Here we go. Toby, if you please!" Already laughing, she signaled to Toby. She sang through the song as best she could with the audience chiming in at the competing parts then joining her in the big finale ending. She turned the mic out to them and pretended to conduct as they all sang "one day more" and held the last note for what felt like an eternity.

Joy coursed through her, filling her with energy in a way that nothing else could.

"Now that is a *song*! Well done. Thank you all for playing along." The power in the room as the applause went on was palpable, joyful, upbeat. She had made people laugh and gotten them to sing, and that is all she really wanted for her life.

And she wanted to end the evening on a high note. Literally.

"My heart is so full. Thank you all so much for coming out tonight. I have had so much fun with all of you. I can't tell you what it means to me that you've left your homes and your Netflix behind and brought your beautiful energy here. This is my happy place."

For a moment, Jazzy simply beamed out at the audience, searing the memory into her brain, not wanting to lose a moment.

"Now, if you'll indulge me, I have always, always wanted to sing this for a crowd. I hope you enjoy this last song of the evening. Thank you so much!"

Toby began those few iconic chords, and Jazzy ended her show with "Don't Rain On My Parade" from *Funny Girl*. Everyone began cheering as she held the last note, as she thanked her band, as she left the stage, and they didn't stop until she reached her dressing room downstairs.

That weekend and the next went much the same way. Jazzy felt like an emotional vampire, feeding off the energy the audience brought each night. Though she hadn't expected it to go badly, she didn't know that "One Day More" would be such a hit. The audience went nuts for it every night, standing and singing and waving their napkins like flags. But then she realized: one hundred and fifty people all singing together in one room, that was prayer. That was community.

If she could have that, she could sacrifice close friends and even a life-changing love. If that's what it took to feel like this.

So when the last show ended, it was with tears in her eyes that she left the stage, arm draped around Toby.

They walked down the stairs like that together until they got to her dressing room.

"You're just a dream, Jazzy. You should be so proud. Thank you for letting me be a part of it." Toby kissed her temple when she hugged him.

"No, thank you. I couldn't have done it without you. Give me a few minutes, I'll be right out." She smiled at him and went into her dressing room and closed the door. Feeling satisfied, she tilted her head back against it and grinned to the ceiling. After she came down from her applause-fueled high, she changed her shirt and touched up her face. She gathered the gifts from the shelf next to the mirror, picked up her bag, and went to the green room.

There, in the concrete walled space painted a garish green, she found the band and various guests who were allowed backstage. She gave the band her gifts—leather-bound journals of blank staff paper and fancy pens with handwritten thank you notes—and chatted with them and a few other guests and acquaintances until she felt a tiredness seep all the way to her bones. She began to make her goodbyes.

When Jazzy turned to leave, her jaw dropped.

Mateo Williams stood chatting with Toby, at complete ease, his shoulders relaxed and his unreal smile beaming.

He seemed to feel her stare because he turned that mega wattage smile onto her.

She was frozen, not quite believing what she was seeing.

"Hey, Summers. Excellent show." Mateo ambled over to her, slow and easy, and opened his arms for a hug. Jazzy, still stunned, stepped into his arms and let his scent wash over her, masculine and potent and summery. Her heart hammered and she felt his beneath his chest. In the few seconds he held her, she was nearly overcome by his physical presence.

"Thank you," she said, stepping back, still a bit tongue-tied. Big surprise. "Thank you for coming."

"When I saw you were doing this, I knew I had to make the time." Mateo relaxed back against the counter, all easy smiles and sunshine.

"I . . . uh . . . " Jazzy shook her head briefly, which felt empty around him, as always. "Where were you sitting?"

"In the back. I didn't want to freak you out or anything."

Though he was joking, Jazzy suddenly remembered all of the things she'd read about him. They weren't flattering, and despite his overwhelming, well, *everything*, his presumed attitude was quite a turn-off. And did he just say she would have been thrown off by his being there?

"Ah, well. I don't think that would have happened." Her tone was a bit chilly.

Mateo seemed to notice. "Sorry, no, that's not . . . I didn't mean it like that. Just . . . I didn't want you to think

I was a stalker or anything. Again." He stood up straighter, his brown eyes plaintive.

"No, it's cool. Thanks again for being here." She crossed her arms in front of her chest and silence descended for a moment.

"You're incredible. I was totally enchanted. You're like an angel or . . . Something . . . less lame." Mateo ran a hand over his hair, glancing at her a bit awkwardly.

Now who couldn't speak? Jazzy let a small smile sneak across her face. The tables had turned. "Thanks, I think."

Mateo swooped his hand down his face. "I'm cooler than I sound, I swear."

She turned and picked up her heavy show bag. "I have no doubt you are. But I'm really tired, so . . . "

"Here, let me get that for you." Mateo reached for her bag and Jazzy stepped back.

"I've got it."

"Yeah, no, yeah, of course you do. I'm sorry. I'm really not used to being, um . . . out. Man, I can't say or do the right thing at all, can I?" He grinned sheepishly.

"You can so. You came to my show. That was very nice of yo—"

"Can I get you a drink? I mean, can we go get a drink?" Mateo blurted. He looked flummoxed, which Jazzy kind of enjoyed. She smiled kindly.

"I'm really beat. But thank you for the offer."

"Oh. Yeah, of course. I totally understand.

Maybe . . . Maybe another time?" He had shoved his hands in his pockets and was angled toward her, eager and hopeful.

No matter how attractive he was, or how much she was drawn to him, Jazzy was not going to let herself get involved with Mateo. She knew exactly what would happen. She'd been through it before with other men who didn't understand or share her work ethic. If drinks turned into something more, he would eventually get more and more upset with how much time she devoted to her career. And then the fighting would come, then the inevitable break-up.

It was easier just to let it go, even if he may have changed since his disappearance.

She stepped a little closer to him. "I don't really get drinks, Mateo. Or date. Or do much of anything but work. So, probably not. But I'll see you around H&H, yeah?"

Mateo nodded, barely concealing his disappointment. "Yeah, for sure."

"Okay. See you next time." Jazzy turned to say her goodbyes to the band, noting Mateo's expression had changed from one of perpetual contentment to a little bit sad. She watched as he rolled his shoulders a bit, then he caught her eye and grinned fully.

"Good night, Jazzy. Great show." He loped past her and out of the room, and she marveled at how fast he'd shaken off rejection. That kind of proved she wasn't wrong. It could never work. And as far as she knew, he was still a recluse, other than his coffee runs.

And tonight, she supposed.

Other than tonight . . . Just to see her.

# *Six* ♫

Six weeks passed in the blink of an eye. She watched the city turn into Spring, the most magical time in New York for her. For some people, it was the fall, but Jazzy loved the cherry blossoms and the scent of lilacs. It felt like promise and expectation. She sat on the fire escape outside of her window and read or prepped for auditions as Patti lounged behind her on the cat tree. It was very peaceful, and she didn't even get itchy for work too often.

Stop the presses: Jazzy Summers was almost enjoying a bit of time off, though that didn't mean she wasn't working. Calls with her team became routine as she looked for her next project. She auditioned for a few commercials, because if one of them went national, she would be free and easy to do whatever she liked while knowing her bills would be paid for the year. She did get one in which she had to wear a wedding dress and mascara smeared down her face, inexplicably for a national chain of auto shops.

After that, she auditioned for and got a one-off part on a popular half-hour comedy. Those two things plus the Lowenstein's show made her feel better. She wouldn't have to blow through any of her savings while on this unintended hiatus. She and the team nixed the idea of a national tour when that offer came. She didn't really want to travel now that she had Patti. But she kept up with voice lessons, ready for a call at any time.

Regularly, she went to H&H Bagels where Kara was eager to update her on Mateo sightings, but there weren't any. Jazzy couldn't help but think that might have something to do with her rejection of him but brushed that off as perhaps a little too egotistical. Occasionally, she still thought about his smile, but was certain she'd made the right decision. She couldn't be with someone who didn't take work seriously, and she highly doubted he actually did anything with his days. It's not like he had a work-from-home job. What for? He was still worth millions.

One afternoon, as she breathed in the beautiful spring air and sipped a chamomile tea, her phone rang.

"Hi, Joshua." She rested against the window frame, loving the feel of the warm breeze on her cheeks, the city below, blossoming. "Whatcha got?"

"You sound exceedingly relaxed."

"Trust me, I am antsy to get my hands dirty. But I do not mind my afternoon tea-and-stare-out-the-window thing."

"Sounds lovely. I hate to break the habit."

Jazzy slapped her mug down so hard on the marble island that she nearly cracked it. "I'm dying. Please tell me it's a solid job."

Joshua laughed at this change of tune. "There's my girl. And it is."

"Yes!" Jazzy pumped her fist in the air and spun in a circle, then kissed Patti's furry head. "What is it?"

"Have you heard about *Bridges That Burn*?"

"Of course. They called me in for it, remember? That was years ago now."

"Ah, yes, I remember now. They really wanted you, but *Something Blue* was moving faster and we decided not to go with another new show."

Jazzy snorted. "And that turned out—"

"Hey, it was the right move. You got six months on Broadway and you did great work," Joshua interjected.

"You're right, you're right," she conceded.

"Anyway, *Bridges That Burn* just finished its out-of-town tryout in Seattle. And it got some great initial reviews, definitely picked up for Broadway. I know they're still looking for a house, but it's going for sure."

Jazzy felt a fizzing in her chest, an excitement that meant something good was coming. "Is the whole cast moving to—"

"No. That's why I'm calling."

She couldn't help the grin that spread wide across her face.

"The two leads are leaving. Lucas Samuels just found out that he and his partner are finally getting a baby. They've been trying to adopt for years, I guess, and it's finally happening for them."

"Aww, that's wonderful. I'm so glad to hear it." Jazzy knew Lucas and made a mental note to send a congratulatory text.

"And Annie Parsons, who played Amelia, just got cast in the next Marvel movie."

"Whoa, good for her. But wait . . . " Jazzy braced a palm against the island.

"Yes. They want you."

Her heart pounded and she jumped up and down a little. "Me?"

"Absolutely. Annie was wonderful and they loved her, but you were the first choice. Seems like fate, doesn't it?" She could hear the smile in his voice.

"I can't believe it. When do I start?"

Joshua chuckled. "The first table reads are in two weeks, they're looking to open this season. The rest of the cast is moving, so they just need you and a Cole."

"Who is playing opposite me?"

"Well, we'll need to clear your schedule this week. They want you to come in for chem reads with the guys they're considering."

Jazzy nodded. She loved chemistry reads, finding the compatibility with the right person who would be her partner in a show. When she and Neil first read for *Something Blue* together, she knew it was lightning in a bottle. She was eager to find that with someone else.

"I can't wait."

§

"Jazzy, we're thrilled that you're here. We know your Amelia is going to be fantastic." Sasha Marsden, her trademark red curls wild around her head, was all warmth and crisp consonants. The Tony-award-winning director smiled widely.

It was two days later and, after brief negotiations, Jazzy's new contract was signed and she was in a Midtown rehearsal studio, facing a long row of mirrors in front of which the production team sat at a folding table.

Sasha, wrapped in a paisley caftan, sat at the center. Reid, the stage manager, sat at the end of the table, a binder with the full book and score open in front of him, the black hood of his sweatshirt pulled over his head. Jazzy knew the suits at the other end as a couple of producers. The wiry but imposing man in thick black glasses next to Sasha was Drew Masters, the choreographer. The woman with cornrows and bright brown eyes on the other side of Sasha was Catherine Spots, the assistant director. The others down the table, dressed in what Jazzy referred to as the artist uniform of skinny jeans and leather jackets, were likely production assistants.

The table was covered with scripts and sides, open laptops, and a few headshots and resumes; in other words, controlled chaos. Jazzy had spent the last two days watching clips of the show from Seattle and reviewing the script and score. She was excited to work with everyone seated in front of her.

"Thank you. I'm honored to be here. This is such a wonderful show and I can't wait to see who we get to play Cole."

"We're excited, too." Sasha smiled indulgently at her. Jazzy was so excited to work with the woman who'd brought *Fully Engaged*, which had won four Tonys, to the stage.

"Our first of four prospects will be here in just a few minutes. Do you know Daniel Moore?"

"I do. He'd be wonderful." Of course Daniel was coming in. He'd come out of Chicago and took over for Gunner Collins in *Fully Engaged*, taking the small Broadway community by storm. Jazzy wasn't surprised that Sasha wanted to bring in the star she'd discovered. Daniel was a powerhouse with a beautiful baritone. Jazzy had been very impressed with his performances but wasn't sure if his voice was right for the part.

"Great. You'll be reading the last scene of act two, right before the duet, and then singing through 'All Hearts Fall Once'. We'll do that with each actor, and then we'll all have a chat about what we think. Sound good?"

"Sounds great." She nodded enthusiastically, looking down at the binder that held her script. She'd already begun to memorize her lines but flipped to the correct scene to familiarize herself with it.

A diminutive blonde woman poked her head into the studio. "Sasha, Daniel Moore is here."

Sasha smiled. "Great. Jazzy?"

"Ready!"

Nodding to the woman, Sasha said, "Send him in, please."

Daniel Moore walked in the room, all earned confidence and a big smile. He was tall, much taller than Jazzy, with a buzz cut and striking hazel eyes. A wedding ring glinted on his left hand. He was lanky in a way that wasn't awkward, long-limbed and lithe. Graceful. Jazzy imagined he'd be a wonderful dance partner.

"Hello, everyone. Thank you so much for seeing me today. It's a pleasure to finally meet you, Jazzy."

"You too, Daniel." They shook hands.

"Daniel, we're going to read through the sides you have, then sing through the duet. Sound good?"

"Sounds great." Daniel grinned at Jazzy, and she loved his energy. He seemed like the kind of person you could rely on, who made you feel at ease in any situation.

This could work.

But it didn't. Daniel was wonderful. He had clearly worked on the scene and got the beats. They read through it, took some notes from Sasha, and then read it again. There was a kiss in the scene that they merely mimed, and all of it was . . . fine. But then they sang through the duet, and Jazzy knew Daniel wasn't it. The song was too high for his smooth baritone. They needed a tenor. Jazzy hugged Daniel when Sasha thanked and dismissed him. She really did like his vibe.

Gunner Collins came next, a completely different energy. He was nervous, and it showed, at first. He and Jazzy had known each other for a long time, so she squeezed his hand as Sasha gave them direction. Gunner relaxed a bit.

"There's a kiss in the scene, is that okay to play?" he asked Jazzy.

"Sure, I'm fine with that," Jazzy said.

"If you're both comfortable, go right ahead." Sasha put her chin in her hands and gave them a generous smile. "Whenever you're ready."

The scene was good. Gunner was great in it, despite his nervousness. And the kiss was nice. Jazzy just felt a bit awkward with him, and he with her. Their chemistry simply wasn't there.

As the production team chatted a bit after his dismissal, he kissed her cheek and whispered, "Good luck."

Jazzy knew that he knew it wasn't him.

Dion Hart was next, and he was perfect. He was a Taye Diggs lookalike with an even sunnier personality, and he had a beautiful tenor that gave Jazzy chills. When the kiss was supposed to happen, he held her gaze so intently instead of kissing her that she nearly did fall in love with him.

"That was wonderful, Dion. Let's sing through the song again, shall we?" Sasha asked at the end of their reading.

Dion looked over at Jazzy, a hopeful smile on his face, which she returned. Their voices blended in harmony beautifully. Dion was a pro who'd been working for years but hadn't yet had a shot at a principle role. Jazzy thought it was definitely time.

They kept Dion for a bit longer, running through the scene again, then he was dismissed. As he walked out the door, out of sight of the production team, he turned and gave Jazzy a thumbs up and a gigantic grin.

She nodded and smiled back. Dion would be wonderful as Cole. She turned to the table. "I thought Dion—"

"We have someone rather exciting next!" Sasha said before Jazzy could finish her sentence.

"Oh! How wonderful." Jazzy was pretty sold on Dion but was absolutely willing to give someone else a shot.

"This is someone who has never worked on Broadway at all but is very interested in a career move.

He's got quite the voice, we're told, and would be a good name to pull in ticket sales."

Jazzy tried to hide a grimace. She didn't particularly want to work with someone who saw Broadway as a hobby to tout on their Instagram, a celebrity who wasn't going to take it seriously. Stunt casting. Ugh. Who would it be? A Disney Channel kid? Or worse, a viral TikTok star?

"That sounds—"

Sasha seemed to note her uneasiness and chuckled a little. "I know, it could be a disaster. But if it doesn't work, it doesn't work. Daniel, Gunner, and Dion were all great choices and we can debate about them."

Jazzy let her shoulders relax a little. "Sounds good to me. Who is it?"

"Do you remember a pop star named Mateo Williams?"

# Seven

Jazzy's heartbeat hastened and she hardly knew what to say. "I . . . Yes. I do."

"Oh, great! He'll be here in—" Sasha was interrupted by a knock on the door. "Well, right now, I guess. Send him in, Sarah, thanks!"

Mateo Williams walked through the door, every bit as handsome as she remembered. Jazzy hardly had a moment to collect herself before his energy consumed the room. He was smiling widely with his sides in his hand. The papers were rumpled, as if he'd been twisting them together.

Jazzy could hardly believe he was nervous. This was the kid who got whatever he wanted his whole life until he ruined that all on his own. He probably thought the part was his already.

Mateo shook the hands of everybody at the table and then turned to Jazzy. When his eyes met hers, she couldn't help but feel her breath catch. He really was beautiful.

But beauty didn't mean talent.

He'd have to prove himself first.

Mateo stepped toward her, his walk easy, confident, his eyes ablaze. "Nice to see you again, Summers." He moved in for a hug, but Jazzy, ever the professional, stuck out her hand.

"Good to see you, too."

Mateo, with an amused expression, took it. His hands were large, warm and smooth. He held her gaze a beat longer than necessary and Jazzy couldn't help but be taken under his spell, just a bit.

"We're eager to see what you've got for us today, Mateo. We'll be starting with the scene, then we'll give some notes, and we'll see that again. Then we'll move on to the duet." Even Sasha had stars in her eyes looking at him. "Do you have any questions?"

"I do, if that's okay?"

"Of course!"

Mateo chuckled a little, patting his hand on his chest. "Sorry, I have to catch my breath. I'm a little nervous. I've never been on a full Broadway audition."

The panel, each and every one of them, gave Mateo a smile or nod, encouraging the newcomer.

Jazzy kept her expression friendly but neutral, but she did melt a little bit inside at his show of vulnerability. Maybe he had changed. She hoped to be proven wrong.

"Are we supposed to . . . There's a kiss? Do we, um, do that?"

Everyone laughed a bit, including Mateo, and Jazzy snickered too. The tension in the air eased.

"If Jazzy is okay with it, yes, you can do the kiss. But no, it is absolutely not required."

Mateo looked at Jazzy, his deep brown eyes penetrating. "Um, we don't have to."

"No, it's okay. Good to see how the chemistry works. We can kiss." She smiled shyly at him. She'd stage kissed hundreds of times. It never meant anything.

He looked a little sheepish when he said, "Are you sure?"

"I'm sure." She smiled and nodded encouragingly at him. Though she thought Dion was the one to play Cole, she didn't want him to feel uncomfortable or think she wasn't giving him her best. If he had the wherewithal to pull this off, he deserved a chance.

"Okay then. Whenever you're ready, you may start." Sasha wrote something on a piece of paper and slid it over to Catherine. Catherine glanced at the paper, looked up, and nodded, also starry-eyed.

Mateo hadn't noticed. Jazzy watched as he blew out a breath, glanced down at the sides in his hand, and then rolled his shoulders. He met her gaze and that brilliant smile hit her like the spring breeze she enjoyed from her open window.

She nodded at him and he took another deep breath. His were the first lines.

Mateo looked up from his pages, straight into her eyes. The vulnerability was gone, replaced by pain and confusion. "I don't know what to do with that. I don't know what I'm supposed to say."

Jazzy folded her arms across her chest. "I can't tell you what to do, Cole."

"You can. I know you can. It's been like this your whole life, Amelia. Please. Decide." Mateo stepped toward her, his eyes blazing with passion and want.

She took a deep breath. "I can't do that. You know I can't." She unfolded her arms and took a deep breath. "If River doesn't finish the program, we're going to lose everything. The house, my father— And that's all I can handle thinking about right now."

Mateo kept glancing down at the script. Though he seemed to be in the scene with her, she was bothered that he had to keep looking down. A little preparation could have helped him. They continued the scene until at last, the heat in the room was palpable. This was the most romantic moment of the show, when Amelia finally admitted that she echoed Cole's long-held feelings for her.

Jazzy was surprised to find that her eyes pricked with tears. She hadn't been this emotional with any of the other actors.

Mateo stepped toward her once again, finally not looking down at his script. His voice strained. His eyes now danced with expectation. At this point, Cole knew he had Amelia.

"Tell me. Tell me what you want, Amelia!" He was commanding, unstoppable.

Jazzy turned to face him, letting her arms down at her side, feeling Amelia give in to her love for the man who was right in front of her the whole time, the boy from the wrong side of the tracks who was there for her no matter what.

"You!" she nearly shouted. "I want *you*, Cole!"

And then something happened that hadn't with the other actors. There was a beat, a moment, the kind that you cannot bottle or manufacture. Jazzy and Mateo gazed into each other's eyes and Jazzy saw his chest rise and fall quickly. His eyes sparkled at her, intense, wanting. The nape of her neck prickled in anticipation and she felt the tension in the room become taut until finally, Mateo took two long strides to her. He placed his palm on the side of her face and pressed his lips to hers.

Starlight seemed to burst behind Jazzy's eyes. This sweet kiss was lemonade and promises and nights under a summer sky. It was chaste, by most standards, as an audition stage kiss should be, but still, she felt her knees go a bit weak and she clutched Mateo's waist to steady herself.

Mateo stroked a thumb on her cheek tenderly. The three seconds she had with his soft lips on hers made her forget everything around her.

Instead of stepping back after the kiss and saying the last line as the other actors had, Mateo stayed right where he was, dropping his hand to the curve of Jazzy's neck. His gaze seemed to bore into hers, powerful and tender all at once.

"I've been wanting to do that my whole life," he nearly whispered.

Another heated beat passed and then Jazzy and Mateo stepped apart. They both turned to the panel.

Sasha sat open-mouthed, her hands clasped to her heart. "And . . . scene," she said a bit breathlessly.

The rest of the team seemed equally bewildered, and Drew, next to the stunned Sasha, began to clap. That led to the whole table giving them a round of applause.

Jazzy had a feeling she was going to have to fight for Dion, despite the intensity that Mateo had brought to the scene. Even if he had changed from the person in his twenties who had made terrible choices, he was barely prepared enough today to look up from his script, despite claiming how excited he was. And that told her all she needed to know.

Sasha glanced around at the rest of the panel. "Does anyone need to see that again? I don't believe that I do."

Mateo glanced over at Jazzy, eyebrows furrowed. She knew that he must have been wondering if not going through the scene again was a bad thing. In her experience, it was not.

The panel all agreed to move on to the song, and Jazzy was not surprised that it suited Mateo's tenor beautifully. She wasn't as prepared for their voices to blend so well together, but still, she and Dion had sounded just as good.

Once they'd sung through the song a couple of times, Sasha seemed quite satisfied and so did the rest of the panel. "I think that's all we need to see, Mateo. Thank you very much for coming in today."

"No, thank you, truly. It was an honor just to get the chance to perform for you all today." Mateo picked up his bag from where he'd discarded it on a chair and slung it over his broad shoulders. "I appreciate all of you. Thanks again. See you around, Jazzy."

As he walked out of the door, he winked her way. She couldn't help but return his smile. "See you around."

Mateo's presence, sunshine and light, faded moments after he had left. Reid brought Jazzy a blue plastic chair and she joined the panel around the table. She grinned at them all. "That was fun."

"That was fun. How do you feel?" Sasha folded her hands under her chin, clearly eager to get Jazzy's thoughts.

Jazzy wanted to remain neutral until the panel weighed in. "I think all of them had high points."

Sasha nodded and glanced at Drew.

Drew glanced down at his notes. "I know Daniel can move. He's a beautiful dancer, and he was wonderful in the scene, but for me, all three of the others sang better."

"I agree. I think we can eliminate Daniel right off the bat. A shame, but we need a tenor. Jazzy?"

She nodded. "I'd love to work with him someday, but this is not the project."

"Moving on. Gunner. A little nervous today. I haven't seen that from him in a long time." Sasha glanced at Catherine.

"He was like that right before that New Year's Eve concert at Carnegie Hall, when his wife was about to give birth. I think they're about to have number two," Catherine chimed in.

"Oh, how wonderful. And I know that's a very big personal life change, but, well, he just wasn't great today."

"He was, and I mean this in all sense of the word, fine," Drew said.

Jazzy had never been in on these kinds of meetings and while she wasn't surprised by how cutthroat they were, it was still unnerving. She wondered what had been said about her in all the years that she'd been auditioning, what all the reasons she'd been rejected were.

"Jazzy?" Sasha looked at her expectantly.

"Oh, well. I would agree that I didn't feel the chemistry with Gunner. And we've worked together before. But today wasn't right. Maybe he's just having an off day."

"Okay, he is in the no pile." Sasha moved his headshot on top of Daniel's.

Jazzy was uncomfortable with this much power. She just wanted to perform with someone who would be there for her.

"I really liked reading with Dion," she offered.

Drew nodded, pulling Dion's headshot in front of him. "He is very talented. And he has the *What's Next* fanbase. Though if we're choosing someone from that cast, I would have rather had Ethan Carter in."

"Mmm. He would have been good, but he's still doing his Netflix show," Sasha said as she contemplated Dion's headshot.

Jazzy sat on her hands to keep them from nervously playing with her hair. This was absolutely nerve-wracking.

"Dion is a star. And he has a featured actor Tony. We'd have a nominee—" Sasha paused and grinned at Jazzy, who'd been nominated for her first role and never since. "—and a winner headlining. That would certainly bring people in."

"Jazzy, say more about what you liked about him." Catherine tapped her lips with her fingertip.

Her eyebrows shot up. "Well . . . He has an ease about him. He was very prepared, and that makes me feel good about what kind of scene partner he would be. I felt safe with him. Did you notice how he mirrored my blocking? I think that says a lot about how we would work together."

"Would he be your choice?" Drew asked.

"We haven't talked about Mateo, she doesn't need to choose yet," Sasha quickly cut in.

Drew didn't back down. "I would argue that you could say the same things about Mateo."

"Dion would be a fine choice, so let's move on to Mateo. To be honest, I was surprised at his performance. He was wonderful." Sasha pulled Mateo's headshot out of a folder.

"And there's a lot to be said for charisma. It oozes out of him, doesn't it?" Catherine said almost reverently, looking at Mateo's headshot.

"That's an understatement." Drew also seemed taken. "And I would say that the chemistry between them, the tension . . . You could cut it with a knife. And he's danced in stadiums all over the world, so we know he can take choreography."

Drew, Catherine, and Sasha all turned to look at Jazzy as one.

She bit her lip, her left hand starting to go numb under her thigh. "I was impressed as well. More impressed than I thought I would be, if we're being honest. And I thought he did well in the scene, and he can obviously sing and dance. But if we're talking about who I trust, just going off gut instinct, for me, it's Dion over Mateo."

She also didn't think that Mateo should just be able to come in and say, "Me, please!" when Dion had worked so hard for so long and deserved it. Jazzy knew that's not how it really worked, but that is what she was feeling, however uncharitably. But she wasn't about to admit that out loud.

"How would you feel with Mateo as a partner?" Sasha said.

"Well—"

"I think you're missing a crucial thing, here." One of the suits at the end of table rapped it with a pen. All of their heads swiveled toward him.

"Mateo would bring in his fans. A comeback story? From fallen pop artist to a Broadway star? People love that shit. Obviously, it's important that Jazzy feel safe, but come on. The show would make money, and the show would *run*. And that's the end goal, right? To be successful?"

Jazzy chewed her lower lip again. This was not a conversation she wanted to be a part of. Every part of her body was screaming at her to run out of the room.

Sasha merely stared at the suit, a white-haired man with large hands, and then looked at her. "Jazzy? How would you feel with Mateo playing opposite you?"

She thought it through. Dion was a safer choice in her mind. Something inside of her was irritated at the fact that Mateo simply didn't deserve it. Not yet. Let him climb the ranks, too, in a different show, in a smaller part. Even after her first show, she'd had to work her ass off to keep getting cast. And there was the matter of his unpreparedness. She did not want to be in a rehearsal room, fully off-book, lines memorized, while the person with whom she had the most scenes fumbled about with his script.

She knew it was impossible to predict exactly how Mateo would work, how the show would work with him. But Dion felt like the better choice for her.

Inwardly, she winced. That was a selfish thought. The producer was right, as gross as it made her feel. Mateo was still incredibly popular, if the fan pages on Instagram were any indication. And with the promise of a comeback story and a chance to get to see a pop star, they could sell tickets for years. Jazzy thought of everyone that might affect: costumers, stage managers, set designers, front-of-house folks. She had the chance to almost guarantee a long, secure job for literally hundreds of people.

Mateo made her feel something. Okay, a lot of things. He had been great in the scene. If this worked out, she would have to lay down the law about the drink he'd asked her out on. She did not do showmances, and would not tolerate him pestering her after she'd said no.

It had been clear he wanted this, and whatever annoyances would come, she could deal with that. As long as he was prepared.

She was a professional.

She was Jazzy freaking Summers, and she wanted to do the best job she could.

After a deep breath, she said, "While I feel safest with Dion, I know Mateo would be a great choice, too. I would be very happy to work with him on his Broadway debut."

# Eight ♫

The energy from Times Square just a block away hit Jazzy as she emerged from the building. The cries of street vendors and noise of the tourists interrupted her thoughts of *Bridges That Burn*.

"Jazzy! Jazzy, hey." Mateo jogged up to her.

She was surprised by his dynamic presence and once again couldn't seem to find words. "Hey. Hi. Great job today."

His face lit up with joy. "You really think so?"

"I mean, I don't think I'm allowed to say anything, so let's just say your chances are more than zero." She gave him a half-smile.

Mateo looked ready to burst with happiness, his eyes bright. "I'm gonna keep it chill on the outside, but I need you to know that that is some of the best news I have ever gotten in my life."

Jazzy let her half-smile turn into a full grin. "That's lovely, but yeah, please do keep it chill." She turned toward 7th Avenue and began walking to the subway. He fell into step beside her.

"Where are you headed?" Energy was coming off him in waves, kinetic and enticing. "I know I should wait and I could be setting myself up for disappointment, but do you want to get a coffee or something? I don't want to go home."

Jazzy stopped and let a woman with a tiny, prancing poodle on a leash pass her by. She pursed her lips and turned to Mateo, one eyebrow raised.

"Just as friends! I'm sorry I asked you out after your show. I totally respect your wishes. I know better than to press my luck. But if we might be getting to work together, I'd love to get to know you better." He grinned at her, sheepish but confident.

My, he was disarming. "Listen, Mateo, we can definitely sit down together if—"

"When," he interrupted cheekily.

Jazzy rolled her eyes but smiled. "When then, *when* you get the part. I'd like to get to know you, too. But you need to know right now, I do not do showmances. There will be nothing but professionalism between us. Okay?"

He held up his hands. "Of course. Absolutely. But just professionalism? Or can we be friends?"

She gazed at him for a moment, at his eager expression, all open and honest. "Let's see how it goes, okay? We may have the cart before the horse. Maybe they're bringing in a ringer and they'll surprise us both." She began walking toward the subway again.

"Funny, I thought *I* was the ringer." He skipped a little as he joked, falling into step beside her once again.

Was he ever serious? Jazzy couldn't help but be charmed. "Are you always this egotistical?"

"Only when I'm feeling this confident." Mateo turned and began walking backwards, grinning goofily at Jazzy. "So you really don't want to get a coffee? You've been heard loud and clear. Just friends."

Jazzy gazed at his sweet, open face, a little of the vulnerability that he'd demonstrated as Cole coming through. "I will be happy to get to know you, but let's wait for the bonding to begin when we know you've got the part."

The tiniest bit of disappointment crossed his expression, but then he brightened. He glanced behind himself quickly, still walking backwards, but then turned his smile onto Jazzy. "You said when."

"I'm not the decision-maker." She held up her hands, giving nothing away.

He almost bumped into a trash can at the corner of 7th and 42nd. He righted himself as she chuckled. "Okay, okay, I give. Have a good day."

"You, too." She grinned and started toward the subway stairs, then turned back. "By the way, I adopted a cat."

His expression landed between wonderment and surprise. "You took my advice."

Jazzy just nodded, still smiling, and turned away again.

"Hey, Summers!"

She turned, brushing a strand of hair that whipped across her face in the spring breeze.

"I forgot to say: you were marvelous in there. It's no wonder you're a star." He slipped his hands in his jeans pockets, and leaned against the lamppost on the corner, wearing that smile of his that warmed her heart.

"Thank you. See you soon."

He raised his hand in goodbye.

She made her way down to the train, with his contagious energy fizzing inside of her all the way home to Patti.

# MATEO WILLIAMS SCORES ROLE IN NEW MUSICAL

An *OMGCeleb* Exclusive
by Roger Smallwell

Can the troubled star redeem himself as a leading man on the Great White Way?

Kittens, we were right! When Mateo Williams was coming out of the Equity Office some months ago, it was to secure his place in the union because—drumroll please—he will be starring in B*ridges That Burn*, coming to Broadway soon!

Once headed up by Lucas Samuels and Annie Parsons, the production had to search for two new principles. Jazzy Summers was a no-brainer. The Broadway superstar just got a closing notice for Something Blue (you know how we felt about that one), so *Bridges That Burn* scooped her up immediately.

This intrepid reporter learned that in the running for the role of Cole was Daniel Moore, Gunner Collins, and Dion Hart, all of whom would have been fantastic. The Broadway community is up in arms that a failed pop star is now doing the trendy thing of moving to the stage. Mateo has big shoes to fill—Lucas Samuels is nearly six-four, you know—and he'll be itching to prove himself. Let's hope his reported shoddy work ethic doesn't drive the meticulous and talented Summers to an early grave.

The cast is rounded out with Simone Baxter as River. Simone will be the first trans woman who could be up for a Tony nomination for Featured Actress in a Musical. The rest of the cast from the Seattle production is also making the transition to Broadway.

Stay tuned and visit *OMGCeleb* early and often for reports about Mateo's rehearsal behavior. And you bet we'll be there opening night.

The regular press release from the *Bridges That Burn*'s PR team was far more professional, but Jazzy did want to know what the gossip set was saying. *OMGCeleb* was always the place to go for that. The train rattled on and she looked up from her screen. In just a few stops, she would get off and walk into the rehearsal studio for the first table read with the new cast of *Bridges That Burn*.

On the crowded subway car, she could feel her excitement zinging around her chest. A new show family was exactly what she needed. She loved chatting with Patti, but the conversations were just so one-sided. Her weekly FaceTime with her parents did not a social life make. The *Something Blue* group text thread had been quiet for ages. And as always happened when she started feeling actual loneliness, she alleviated it by way of a guy named Brian.

Every once in a while, this Brian guy would text her. Or she him. It had been on and off since about three years ago, Jazzy had caught his eye in a bar. He was handsome and funny and most importantly, had never seen a musical in his life. His last name was probably something boring like Smith or Johnson, and he probably did something in advertising or marketing, but Jazzy didn't really care. He was a good distraction on lonely nights. She would bring ice cream and they would pretend to choose a movie to watch, but it always ended up in his bed.

It was, she realized sadly, her most satisfying relationship.

But now, she would have people around her who, for as long as the show ran, would be her friends.

And just maybe, this would be the time that one of them stuck around after the ghost light went on.

She got off at the 42nd Street station and made her way to the building where the studio was located. Glancing down at her phone, she realized that, true to form, she was almost twenty minutes early. She entered anyway, looking forward to beginning the work.

On the seventh floor, Sasha was at the vending machine. "There's our star!" she said when the elevator doors closed behind Jazzy. "Are you ready for this, my friend?"

"I am more than ready, Sasha. I can't wait."

Sasha put her acquired water bottle in her boho bag. Today's caftan was a bright pink with yellow stripes. Jazzy felt a bit drab in comparison in her black sleeveless jumpsuit. Sasha linked her arm through Jazzy's and began walking with her to the studio. "I can't either. You're going to be amazing. This whole cast is going to be amazing."

"I agree."

"Even Mateo." Sasha squeezed her arm and gave her a knowing look.

Jazzy bit back a smile. "I'm eager to see what he can do."

They entered the room, occupied at the moment only by Reid and Catherine at a long table in front of the mirrors again. This studio was different: no floor-to-ceiling windows, just sound-proofing on the walls. In the vast space, long white folding tables had been arranged in a square with the blue plastic chairs around it. Each chair had a tented name card in front of it. At the top of the square sat the production team. At the opposite end, Jazzy, Mateo, and Simone had assigned seats with Jazzy in the middle. The rest of the ensemble's names rounded it out around the sides.

It was a small show with a small cast. Each of the ensemble members would be playing multiple roles, bits of costume delineating each character. Amelia, Cole, and River were the only ones who didn't change. The twelve actors in the ensemble had the hardest jobs—almost all of them would be onstage the whole time. Through most of her career, Jazzy had performed in larger musicals, period pieces, with a giant cast of dancers and spectacular sets. This was a departure for her, and she was excited— not nervous, her stomach was *fine*—to begin.

Reid stood and brought a binder over to Jazzy. "There've been a few changes since the last time you saw the score. I've put Post-its on those pages. And the schedule and contact sheet for the cast is at the front."

"Thank you." Jazzy flipped a bit through the binder. At first glance, the changes were easy and made the show better. Her perusing was interrupted by the rest of the cast beginning to trickle in, chattering and calling hello. She set her binder at her spot at the table, then hugged those she knew and introduced herself to the people playing all of the various ensemble roles.

Simone Baxter swanned in, there was no other way to describe it. She was gorgeous, at least six-three, in towering combat boots paired with a swishy coral skirt and a white t-shirt that made her ebony skin glow. She hugged all of her castmates from the Seattle show, imposing and graceful and long-limbed, then turned her bright gaze onto Jazzy.

Jazzy had watched Simone's star rise over the years. The dynamo had gone from school at AMDA straight to a tour of *Rent* where she played Angel. After several more successful tours, she made her way to ensembles on Broadway, and then up to smaller parts. Finally, she was asked to step into Elphaba's shoes in *Wicked* just a few years after Jazzy had played her. Simone's voice soared over the seats of the Gershwin Theater. She was a fan favorite. Jazzy felt lucky to be included in the club of "green girls" with her. She was not at all surprised that Simone had been asked to originate the role of River.

She felt suddenly shy. Simone's energy was electric, like Mateo's, but less easy and more dynamic. This was a person you simply wanted to look at, no matter what she was doing. Star power in the flesh.

"Jazzy Summers, this is a long time coming. It's such a pleasure." Warmth emanated from Simone's entire being and she held out her hand as if to be kissed, the other on her hip.

Stymied, Jazzy didn't know what do. Did she kiss the hand? She just stared in amused shock.

And then Simone seemed to realize what she'd done. She pulled her hand back and placed it over her heart. "Oh my god, I swear I didn't even mean to do that." Her laugh was infectious, loud and brash, unafraid to be heard.

Jazzy laughed along. "Well, you seem like royalty to me. It's only fitting."

"It is nice to meet me, isn't it?" Simone laughed at herself again, tickled at her outrageousness.

"It really is."

Simone stopped laughing, and she said kindly, "And it's equally nice to meet you. I'm so excited to get to know you, Jazzy. This is the beginning of a beautiful friendship."

Jazzy felt something stir in her, a familiar longing. Was it possible to have a friend-crush? Because that is exactly what she was beginning to have on Simone.

As she chatted with the cast and the clock ticked forward, Jazzy was not impressed that Mateo was not at the studio yet. As her dad always said, being on time is late, and five minutes early is being on time.

Finally, one minute to ten o'clock, Mateo strode through the doorway, looking like he wanted to throw up. He caught Jazzy's eye and his nervous grin widened as he raised his hand to her in greeting. The other members of the ensemble were eyeing him with curiosity, and he turned his smile on them as he made his way to his seat.

Sasha stood up from her seat at the table. "Welcome, cast of *Bridges That Burn*!"

Whooping resounded throughout the room. Simone slung her arm around Jazzy's shoulders as the two of them cheered together.

Mateo smiled and applauded as well, but Jazzy could see the nervous twitch of his lips. Not that she was looking at them or anything.

"Please take your assigned seats. Let's put on a show, shall we?"

They all chatted as they made their way to their chairs. Jazzy took her seat next to Mateo. His leg bounced up and down and he faced the production table like a deer in headlights.

"You're gonna do great," Jazzy said under her breath. She put her hand on his arm to help ease the tension and smiled softly. His skin was warm and she felt as though an electric current flowed from him, lighting up her insides as he turned his head.

He looked down at her hand on his arm, then raised his gaze slowly to hers. In that instant, it seemed like everything fell away from her. Simone, the ensemble, the tables. Her breathing slowed as she gazed into the rich color of Mateo's eyes, which were like windows to his every emotion.

He put his hand over hers. "Thanks," he said softly.

Sasha clapped three times loudly, snapping the tension between them. They both faced forward quickly and Jazzy could feel Simone staring at her.

"Okay," Simone said under her breath, chuckling.

Jazzy shot her a pointed glare, amused. "Shh. We're starting."

"Don't think we're not gonna talk about that later, missy."

Jazzy snorted as Sasha began to speak.

"My darlings. I am so glad to see all of you, and I am so excited to welcome Jazzy Summers and Mateo Williams to the cast of *Bridges That Burn.*"

More applause broke out and Mateo grinned at the rest of the cast, casting his spell on all of them. Jazzy waved and smiled as well, feeling warm all over.

"I think it would be nice if we very quickly introduced ourselves and our parts," Sasha said, pointing at a tall blonde woman at the end of the table next to Simone. "Parker, why don't you start?"

The blonde called Parker smiled at Jazzy and Mateo and introduced her characters. Next came Carson, vivacious and loud, and the quieter Blane, who seemed to be a calming presence. Jason had a swagger Jazzy knew well; it had almost worked on her once at a cast party. Almost. Julian, Mateo's understudy, had a smile as wide as Mateo's and a magnetic presence. Jazzy's understudy, Casey, had a serious look in her eyes. The rest of the cast was rounded out by three other women and four other men. Jazzy did her best to note their names. *DariaMaxStephenColbyMeredithBaxterJen* she repeated in her head several times. Their swings and understudies had the biggest jobs to do, covering multiple roles, ready to step into the show at a moment's notice.

And then they came to Simone.

"Hi, I'm Simone Baxter and I play River, the extraordinary scientific genius who is going to save the town of Rutherford, and Amelia's best friend. In regular life I am just extraordinary, and Jazzy's best friend."

"Oh?" Jazzy asked through a laugh.

"Inevitably, honey." Simone declared it as fact. Jazzy believed her.

Sasha turned expectantly to Jazzy.

"Hi, all. I'm Jazzy Summers and I am so glad to be here with you. I know some of you and I'm so happy to see you and work with you again. And for those of you I don't know, I can't wait to get to know you and play. This is such a wonderful show with wonderful music, and I think we're going to be magical. Thank you for inviting me along." Jazzy and the cast turned eagerly to Mateo.

His eyes widened. "Oh! Me. Okay, um, hi everyone." His pause was long enough that some of the jokers in the cast called "Hi, Mateo" making everyone laugh, including him.

Jazzy watched his shoulders relax as he realized he was among friends now. "Wow. I really can't— I'm nervous as hell, y'all. This is something I've wanted for so long, and I haven't even really . . . Well, I'm just going to be honest with all of you, because that's what it's all about, right? So here goes. I haven't really left my house much for a decade. And I've missed performing like crazy. And I respect the hell out of all of you, and I'm so impressed that you do what you do. But I am a novice, and I'm a nervous one. If I'm doing something wrong, please tell me—"

"That's called 'shove with love', sweetie," called Carson from the middle of the table on the left.

Blane, who sat to Carson's left, shoved his shoulder into Carson's. "Just don't *shove* anyone into the pit again." Snickers all around.

"I did not *shove* you—" Carson began to protest.

"Boys." Sasha said it with affection, but with just that one word quiet settled again.

"Ha, well, yeah, shove with love then, please, just preferably not into the pit?" Mateo continued.

The cast tittered and Jazzy could see that they were all under his spell already.

"I want you all to know that I am going to prove myself worthy to be on stage with you. I am going to do my best, and I am going to do right by you. All of you." He looked pointedly at Jazzy. There was a loaded beat.

"Well then, let's get started," Sasha said. A great shuffling commenced as everyone opened their binders.

Jazzy kept her eyes on Mateo as she thumbed through the first few pages of her script. The corners of his lips twitched upward.

"Pay attention, Summers."

"How *very* dare you. I *am* paying attention."

His smile grew. So did hers.

# *Nine* ♫

The first read-through went relatively well. Though Mateo was a little stiff, Jazzy chalked that up to his anxiety at meeting new people and having to perform in front of them, especially after such a long time not being around anyone. And the rest of the cast knew most of their material, so that was an added layer of anxiety. Jazzy was certain that he would warm up.

For the next couple of rehearsals, just the two of them were called in to go over their music. When Mateo sang his solo "I want" song, he was stunning. His voice soared around the rehearsal room, bright and clear with just a bit of gruffness, giving the music a gravitas that even Dion hadn't. Jazzy knew they'd made the right choice. The next day was spent on their blocking notes without the rest of the cast since they weren't changing much from the Seattle run. Mateo listened and took his notes in a chicken scratch handwriting that Jazzy couldn't help but chuckle at.

She helped Mateo make his illegible notes and reminded him that upstage and downstage meant almost the opposite of what you thought. He took it all in stride, but the fact that so much attention was on him when it was just the two of them seemed to make him even more nervous. He wasn't joking as much, and the heat that had passed between them at the read-through didn't return.

That suited Jazzy just fine. She was there to work and wanted to build Mateo up to be the best partner she could have. She threw herself into the role of the headstrong and stubborn Amelia, loving her character arc. Mateo seemed to understand Cole, though it was early days. He was doing everything on the surface, and Jazzy was eager to see how deep he could dig. They were getting used to each other, tentative at first but growing stronger with each passing day.

At the end of the first week of rehearsals, the whole cast was called again. The studio was cleared now, just one long table for the production team at the front. The blue chairs lined the walls, and black painted wooden blocks and doorways stood in as set pieces.

"Hello, gorgeous!" Simone sauntered over to Jazzy. Today's look was a pink tank top layered over a stretchy black jumpsuit, with the same combat boots on her feet.

"Hi, Simone." Jazzy smiled widely at her, not too surprised to find that she'd missed her presence.

Simone set her bag down on the floor and flopped into the next chair. "How's our boy doing?" Her tone was conspiratorial.

"He's doing great. A little nervous, but I think he'll pick it up."

"Tell me something . . . " Simone scooted closer, ready for a gossip. "Has he told you anything about why he disappeared? I never bought the diva-pop-star thing. He seemed too sweet. Seemed like tabloid rumors to me."

"No, he's never said. And I wouldn't want to pry."

"Me neither, but that doesn't stop me being curious." Simone raised her eyebrows once, her dark eyes dancing.

Jazzy turned to her, whispering so the rest of the cast couldn't hear. "I really don't buy it either. He seems so down to earth. But maybe that's who he was then. We can all change in a decade."

Simone laughed. "Tell me!"

At ten o'clock on the dot, Sasha stood up from the table and called the cast to attention. "Hello, everyone. Quiet please. Today, we're going to run through all the scenes with Cole and Amelia so that you can join. We spent the last few days blocking them, and Jazzy and

Mateo put in a lot of hard work. So I hope you haven't forgotten too much since Seattle."

Snickers rose all around.

Sasha smirked. "There are some changes to go over, so this will be stop and start. I'm going to go through some of them now, then we'll begin." She looked down at the notebook in her hand and read through some of the changes for a while.

Jazzy flipped diligently through her notes as Sasha talked. Hers matched perfectly. She was excited to get started with the whole cast.

Twenty minutes later, Sasha closed her notebook with a satisfying slap. "Okay then, ready? Act one, scene two."

"Places, please!" Reid called from his corner of the table.

The cast shuffled about the room and Jazzy took her place.

Mateo was not beside her. Everyone began murmuring. Jazzy hadn't realized he hadn't arrived yet.

Reid looked down at his sign-in sheet, frowning. "Oh, apologies. We don't seem to have Mateo ye—"

The door of the studio was flung open. Mateo barreled in, looking frazzled, and dropped his bag on the nearest chair. "I'm so sorry everyone, I didn't mean—"

"Don't worry about it, just take your place, please," Sasha said, not unkindly, but definitely with a hint of frustration.

Mateo pulled his binder out of his bag and went to stand next to Jazzy. The whole cast eyed him, not out of malice, but out of curiosity. Jazzy knew they were all wondering the same thing, what she and Simone had just discussed. Was Mateo really just the spoiled pop star everyone said he was ten years ago?

"I'm sorry, again, I—"

"Richard, if you please." Sasha ignored Mateo and motioned to the pianist.

Jazzy was quietly fuming and trying very hard not to. This is not the look she'd wanted to present to the rest of the cast after their first few days of rehearsals. Mateo couldn't be bothered to show up on time and now he was studying his binder like he hadn't looked at it since the day before. Every night, Jazzy had been memorizing and singing through their songs, but he apparently could not be bothered.

"I'm really sorry, Jazz," he whispered as the ensemble began marking the scene's first number.

"It's fine." She stared straight ahead but felt him looking at her. She caught his expression in her peripheral vision. He looked almost panicked.

The stumble-through of their scenes with the ensemble went on in that vein for the next six hours. Jazzy avoided Mateo at the breaks, though it was clear he wanted to talk to her. But she was not feeling entirely charitable, which in turn bothered her all the more. She knew she should not see Mateo being late once as a ding on his character, but she couldn't help it. Being late to work showed that he didn't care about other people's time, and she felt disrespected.

On top of that, Mateo got confused and had to consult his notes often. Jazzy was surprised by how different it was working with a novice to stage acting, and she didn't blame him for that, but she longed for the days when she could dive in with a scene partner who knew what they were doing. This was not the satisfying return she had hoped for and she couldn't help feeling disappointed. After Sasha dismissed them, Jazzy moodily packed her binder in her bag and headed to the door.

Mateo had high-tailed it out of the room with barely a goodbye after a quiet exchange with Sasha. Jazzy had watched him go and felt a little badly, but not enough to go after him. She waved to Parker and Blane on her way out, and then a shadow fell across her path.

"Are you doing anything this weekend?" Simone's eyes were full of mischief.

"I don't know. Memorizing lines, ordering takeout, playing with Patti."

"Oooh, what's 'patti' code for?" Simone smiled wickedly.

Jazzy's mood brightened considerably. "Nothing *that* exciting. My cat."

"Aw, cute! Can I come meet her?"

Startled, Jazzy paused, gazing into Simone's eager expression. "You want to come to my apartment? And hang out with my cat?"

"Um, duh." Simone shifted her bag higher on her shoulder.

"Oh." Jazzy was a bit stunned at Simone's forwardness and felt her heart warm.

Simone pursed her lips. "Not if you don't want me to, though."

Panicked, Jazzy exclaimed, "I do! Oh, I would love that, yes please. Come over. Anytime. I'll be there."

Simone chuckled, giving Jazzy an affectionate pat on the arm. "Okay, girl, damn. It's just a hang."

"I know. Can't wait." Jazzy supposed she was a bit overenthusiastic.

Simone tapped the binder in the crook of her arm. "Your cell is in here? I'll text you."

Jazzy nodded and Simone kissed her cheek before sauntering toward the elevator.

"Hey, Simone," Jazzy called after her. "Are we friends?"

Simone rolled her eyes magnificently. "Yeah, duh. I already told you. We're best friends."

As frustrating as the day was, Jazzy was grinning as she followed Simone to the elevator and out of the building. The early evening sun had turned New York's sky pink and Jazzy breathed in the fresh air, feeling brighter.

"Jazzy." Mateo was leaning against the building, the perfect light turning his brown eyes into deep pools of gold.

Simone gave her A Look and a deeply suggestive wave as she walked toward the subway.

Jazzy rolled her eyes and turned to Mateo. Around them, 7th Avenue was alive. Friday afternoon commuters were on the move, heading to drinks, an early dinner, a show. A cab idled on the curb and then honked at a golden retriever who stepped in front of it, taking its owner on a walk, tongue lolling.

Mateo came to where Jazzy stood near the curb. Not willing to say the not-so-nice things she wanted to, she scuffed the sidewalk with the toe of her boot, unable to meet his eyes.

"I really want to apologize for today. I was horrible."

Jazzy tried to soften but crossed her arms over her chest. "You weren't . . . horrible."

"I just— Something came up this morning and I had to take care of it, and . . . and I was only a little bit late?" He rubbed his hand over his hair, his brow furrowed in a way that made him look very young.

Jazzy turned her face away from him. "I get it."

"It feels like you don't." Now his arms were crossed in front of his chest.

Jazzy's patience gave out after the taxing week and the words rushed out of her before she could stop them. "Okay, fine. I don't. I've been doing this for a long time, and the people who have lasting careers are the ones who respect everyone's time. The ones who respect how many people count on them. And I'm sorry, but being late—*twenty* minutes late—is disrespectful."

Mateo's face fell and his eyes held a flash of anger. "It wasn't twen— I waited out here to apologize to you." He seemed to be gritting his teeth.

She shrugged. "I don't like excuses, either."

His eyes met hers, anger glinting in them. "Well . . . I . . . " He threw his hands up. "Sorry we can't all be perfect like you."

She took a step back. "Exc*use* me?"

His frustration seemed to boil over and the next words came tumbling out. "You're a perfectionist! It's difficult to be around someone so perfect all the time. We're *rehearsing*, Jazzy, that's what this is for. Figuring it out. It's fucking intimidating being around someone who seemingly needs no rehearsal." The last words came out clipped and he bit his lip, like he wished he could take them back.

Jazzy shook her head, stung. "The rest of the cast already knows their parts. We need to catch up quickly, and I'm more than willing to give you the time to figure it out. That's what the beginning of this week was for. The problem is, I can't do that if you're not *there*."

His eyes bored into hers and she saw something like a decision happen across his face. This was not the sunny person she'd met at H&H. "Okay, wow. Fine. It won't happen again." He stepped away from her, frustration leaking out of him and catching up with hers. Shoulders rounded, he began to walk toward a sleek black car parked on the curb.

Jazzy couldn't believe he was leaving in the middle of their conversation. That he took a town car to and from rehearsal bothered her too, even though she knew it shouldn't, but *ugh*. "And for the record," she continued, unable to stop herself from following him, "why is it that women are labeled difficult, or perfectionists, when we're just trying to do a good job? That's not fair. I'm *good* at what I do." She couldn't believe she felt tears prick at her eyes. It had been a long, exhausting week but she would not cry in front of this man.

Mateo had opened the back door of the car and he put his elbows on top of it, facing her. His expression was regretful, his words sincere but rushed. "I'm sorry. That was uncalled for. And I won't be late again. Have a good weekend."

"Wait—" Jazzy stepped forward, now wanting to apologize for her outburst, but he'd folded himself into the backseat and closed the door. As the car pulled away, she stood on the curb, chewing her lip, and biting back the tears that threatened.

Still feeling edgy when she got home, Jazzy stomped down the hallway, unlocked her door, and flung it open. She placed her bag on the club chair as the cat jumped off of the couch with a chirp. She slid off her boots, her feet aching from being in character shoes all week.

"Hi Patti." Grumpy, that's how she sounded. Her dust-up with Mateo had left her with a sour taste in her mouth. She kicked herself for not being more forgiving, for always holding everyone at arm's length instead of offering to help. "I had a fight."

Patti circled around her legs. Jazzy scooped her up and let the purring calm her down. She made her way to the window and slid it open, the warm breeze and the softness of Patti making everything seem a little lighter. Jazzy gazed down at her city, at the cabs and the children playing and the new leaves on the trees that lined 85th Street.

From her bag, her phone chirped with a text. Jazzy was so unused to the sound—her parents only texted in the mornings—that she nearly dropped Patti when setting her down. An unknown number had texted her:

Hey girl! Tomorrow, 1:00? Can I come over?

While Jazzy began a response, another text came through.

This is Simone, by the way.

And another.

Obviously.

Jazzy's heart leapt and she couldn't keep the grin off her face. A friend was coming over. She texted Simone back and gave her the address just in case it was wrong on the contact list. Simone sent her a GIF of RuPaul blowing a kiss.

"You're going to make a friend, Patti!" Jazzy scooped the cat up again. Patti squirmed; she had clearly had enough of this. Smooching the cat's furry face, Jazzy said, "And I am, too."

The next day, at precisely one o'clock, her buzzer buzzed. Jazzy scooted the tray of hummus an inch to the left before she walked to the buzzer and let Simone upstairs. A minute later, there was a knock on her door. Jazzy smoothed her black t-shirt over her jeans then opened it.

Simone, wearing a red and blue maxi dress, took her sunglasses off and looked down at Jazzy with an open-mouthed smile. "I told you we'd be best friends!"

Jazzy opened the door wider, unaccustomed to such enthusiasm. "Come on in, please."

Simone stepped in, looking around as if she were at a fascinating museum. "Shoes off or on?"

"Oh, I don't mind. Whatever is more comfortable for you." Jazzy stood with her hands clasped behind her back at the end of the bed, like she was a cadet hoping to pass muster on the bunk inspection. It had been a long time since someone had been inside her home.

Simone walked to the middle of the large studio and turned on the spot, taking in the carefully arranged décor, the meticulously curated furniture, the gleaming surfaces Jazzy had spent all of the previous evening cleaning, even though they barely needed it.

"Looks to me like off is the best idea." Simone's energy filled the whole room with a buzzy excitement. Jazzy hurried forward and took her bag, letting Simone lean on her shoulder as she slipped off her blue wedges. Jazzy placed the bag on the club chair next to her own, the shoes underneath, which Simone watched, amused.

"And is this the little miss?" Patti had never had a visitor and was peering out from underneath the pink couch. Simone bent down. "Hello, angelface. I'm your Auntie Simone. Come out whenever you're ready."

Jazzy just kept grinning until she realized that she'd barely said a word. "Do you want something to drink?"

Simone gave her a mischievous look and shimmied her shoulders. "Do you have any bubbles?"

Jazzy opened her mouth in surprise. She didn't drink that often, and certainly not on a Saturday afternoon. But they didn't have rehearsal until Monday. Of course tomorrow she wanted to spend some time memorizing her lines and she couldn't do that with a hangover—

"Jazzy. Hello? Okay, young lady, come here." Simone took her arm and dragged her over to the bed where they landed together on the plush comforter, the bangles on Simone's wrist jangling. "Ooh! The luxury. This is nice. But I won't get distracted by your beautiful home. Jazzy Antoinette Summers, I am going to crack open this pretty professional shell, and I am going to make you have some fun."

Jazzy giggled. "My middle name is Lynn."

Simone sighed dramatically.

"And my real first name is Jessica."

"Jessica. Lynn. Oh my god. Jazzy was the right choice. Listen, I was at your show at Lowenstein's. I have been watching you perform for years, and I have a confession. Shawn is a good friend of mine. And he told me when you were cast in my show that we should be friends. That you . . . Well, frankly that you needed one, especially with *Something Blue* closing. And here's the thing. I think you're wonderful, but there is a hard little candy shell around all this talent. I saw it this week, and I *know* what you're thinking in that room. You're the leader, Mateo is new, and you can't screw up. Well, I am here to tell you that you can. You can loosen up, and you can joke around, and you can have fun. You have my permission. *Capisce*?"

Jazzy felt a rush of emotion for Simone, some kind of love, and in a moment of abandon, threw her arms around her. "*Capisce*. And thank you."

Simone's grip was tight. "And you know what? I could use a friend, too. My bestie just moved to L.A. like a jerk. And I don't let my guard down much, either. I feel we're kindred spirits, and we're playing best friends, so we might as well be them."

Jazzy pulled back and stuck out her hand. "It's a deal."

They shook.

"Now." Simone stood and straightened her dress. "Do. You have. Champagne." Each word was punctuated by a very serious eyebrow raise.

Laughing, Jazzy went to the fridge where she procured the bottle she'd bought to celebrate something ages ago but never opened. She pulled vintage champagne coupes out of the cabinet above the fridge.

"Ooh, we are fancy. I love these. I feel like Jay Gatsby." Simone set the coupe down gently and grabbed the bottle. She fought a bit with the gold foil and the wire, then the cork popped and they both shrieked with delight.

As Jazzy poured she asked, "Do you like to read?"

"My childhood bedroom is practically a library. I used to read Gatsby every summer."

"That's a perfect summer read. I've just recently discovered my love of books again." Jazzy handed Simone a glass.

"I've got a million recommendations if you want them."

Jazzy smiled and clinked her glass against Simone's. "To new friends."

"Forever friends."

They drank, eyes locked, and Jazzy somehow knew that this was it. Maybe her weirdo loner days were over. Maybe she could dive into a friendship right in the middle, without all of her walls and rules. Settling into her couch, the champagne went down easy as she and Simone chatted their way through *Singin' in the Rain*.

"Oh my god, I love that movie. Like, where do you even start with Gene Kelly? What a delicious man. Good morning, indeed." Simone tipped her head back against

119

the couch from where she sat on the floor. She reached for the bottle and topped up the glasses of champagne, then scratched Patti under her chin. Patti had decided that Simone was okay. She was lazing next to her on the floor, purring.

"Did you know he married a thirty-year-old when he was seventy-seven?" Jazzy said from where she was sprawled on the couch.

"So there's hope for you yet!" Simone cackled at her own joke.

Jazzy glared at her. "Very funny. Hilarious. Someone call . . . someone call . . . Who's the oldest guy on Broadway?"

"You are a lightweight." Simone chuckled.

Jazzy sat up and brushed her hair out of her eyes. "I told you I don't drink much."

"But it's fun, right?"

Jazzy grinned lazily. "I'm having a great time."

"So what's with you and Mateo?"

Jazzy glanced around, pretending to be stunned. "That came from nowhere."

"I've been dying to ask since you had that heated little exchange at the read through. So you see, I have an endgame." Simone caught the fluffy white pillow Jazzy threw at her.

"I get it now. You just want gossip." Jazzy took another sip.

Simone climbed up onto the couch next to her, tucking her legs up underneath. "No seriously, that was a moment. Or was I wrong? Keep in mind that I'm rarely wrong."

"It was—" Jazzy sighed, feeling loose. "I don't know what it was. Every time I've met him, he was so . . . magnetic. And I liked him and all. But you know, his past and everything. It seems complicated so I—" Jazzy decided not to mention that he'd asked her out. "So I was surprised to see him at the chem reads."

"You'd met him before?" Simone raised an eyebrow, coupe at her lips.

"A couple times. Sort of. He must live around here because he goes to my coffee shop. Anyway, we had a weird conversation yesterday and he probably hates me and like, it didn't even matter anyway even though he hurt my feelings. He's going to show up when he shows up and people are going to see the show because he's in it and that's the point. Right?" Jazzy could tell she was slurring just a bit, but it felt good to get this out. "And for the record, I do not do showmances. Ever. They only spell disaster." She suddenly scooped up all of her hair, piled it on her head, and pulled the hair tie off her wrist. Twisting it around her hair, she glanced at Simone, who was staring at her open-mouthed.

She looked like she wanted to say something else, but she didn't. "I've never heard you speak that much before but— Duly noted. I won't push. But I will say, even I could feel that heat." Simone took another sip as her phone lit up on the coffee table.

Jazzy rolled her eyes. She could feel the heat too, but that didn't mean anything real. Just because Mateo was warm and beautiful and funny, and kind of clumsy, and—

"Blane and Carson want to come over, and they'll bring Chinese. Are you in?"

Jazzy's head snapped up, Mateo's face poofing away in her mind. "Really?"

"Three friends in one day? Who are you all of the sudden?" Simone teased.

Jazzy grinned wide and nodded. "Yes, please."

Simone stayed with Patti while Jazzy ran down to the bodega on the corner for more booze. Blane and Carson arrived an hour later bringing egg rolls and noodles and a playlist of pop music. Both boys had come from a jazz class and were dressed in casual dance clothes. Carson, short and lithe and full of energy, cooed over Patti who immediately took to him. His dirty blonde curls fell in his face as he stroked her head. Blane, tall and well-muscled with neat corn rows, steered clear of Patti. He exuded calm. They fit together, Carson's exuberance balancing out Blane's peaceful demeanor.

Over the rest of the evening, they watched *Dreamgirls* and the boys asked Jazzy about ten thousand questions. They discussed what theater *Bridges That Burn* would run in, since they still didn't have one, and which would bode the best for the run of the show. She learned that Blane and Carson had been dating for years and had never done a show together, and that

Simone had just gone through a break-up on top of her best friend leaving town.

Toward the end of the evening, Simone talked them into playing Never Have I Ever and Jazzy learned things about these three people that she definitely wouldn't have otherwise. They learned about her sometimes-hookup, Brian, and shrieked with delight when Simone told them she'd once had sex in the basement of the Gershwin Theater.

When they all finally left, carrying the empty Chinese containers and bottles of wine, blowing air kisses and promising to do it again, Jazzy closed the door gratefully. She was a little unsteady as she glanced around her normally pristine apartment. Blankets were mussed, the coffee table was shoved out of the way, her bed had been lain upon by Simone when she'd pretended to get the vapors over one of Blane's "I nevers".

Jazzy somehow didn't mind the mess. It seemed like mess meant a night well spent with good friends and lots of laughs. She could do with more of those.

And from the fullness she felt in her heart, she was sure that she would get them.

# Ten ♪

On Monday morning, as Jazzy walked down the hallway to the studio, she felt a bit apprehensive. As always, she was about fifteen minutes early in order to stretch and chat with Sasha if necessary. She hoped Mateo would give her at least a few minutes to talk and make things normal again so they wouldn't be awkward all day. While she didn't mind speaking the truth, she felt badly for being so harsh. There were certainly gentler ways to have handled her frustration.

To her very great surprise, Mateo was already sitting on one of the chairs lining the perimeter of the room, poring over his script. Sasha and the team were at their usual table, quietly chatting. Mateo looked up when Jazzy walked in and she gave him what she hoped was an apologetic smile. He returned it.

She gingerly took the seat next to him and crossed her arms over her chest. "Hi."

"Hi." He closed his binder and turned to look at her. "I'm here."

"Early." She nudged him with her elbow, a smile tugging the corners of her mouth.

Mateo's grin lit up. "Early, even. Listen, I'm really sorry about Friday."

"Me too. Very." She let out a deep breath and stuck out her hand. "Friends?"

Mateo nodded and shook it. "Friends."

She ignored the butterflies in her stomach and nodded to his binder. "How's the memorization going?"

"Oof." He tossed the binder on the bag by his feet next to hers and leaned back, scrubbing one hand down his face. "I don't know. It's hard. I know you don't think it's hard, but it's hard."

Jazzy was mildly offended. Eyes downcast, she muttered, "Hey."

"Sorry. I'm sorry." He gave her puppy dog eyes.

She rolled her own and conceded that they worked. "Do you want to run lines?"

"That would really help, yes."

For the next ten minutes, Jazzy and Mateo sat facing each other on the floor, stretching as they ran their lines together. Though he had to refer to the script often,

Jazzy could already see how he embodied Cole, smart and idealistic, passionate and proud. If Mateo could pull this off, he'd be nominated for a Tony in a heartbeat.

Upon his arrival, Carson ran to where Jazzy and Mateo sat and threw his arms around her shoulders then flopped next to her. "Oh em gee, how hungover were you yesterday?"

Mateo looked from one to the other. "Did y'all go out this weekend?"

"Worse. We stayed in. So the booze was free and we just kept drinking it." Carson nudged Mateo's outstretched leg with his foot. "You should join us next time."

Jazzy chuckled. "I don't think I can make a habit of that." She waved at Blane from across the room, and then Simone filled the doorway with her presence. All four of them shared secret looks.

"I'd like to," Mateo said, catching Jazzy's gaze. "Hang out with y'all, I mean."

"We would love that." Carson stood and held his hand out to Mateo, who took it and stood. In turn, he held his hand out to Jazzy.

His eyes didn't leave hers as he pulled her up and she felt a little burst of pleasure run through her body. "You should. Next time." Jazzy couldn't see what was wrong with getting to know her co-star socially. It didn't mean anything other than what they just said. They were friends.

Mateo grinned as Sasha called them all to attention.

"Okay, folks! Let's get started. I want to run through as much of Act One as possible today. Jazzy and Mateo are blocked, and we'll just mark through the songs for now until we get through their dance rehearsals in the next two days."

"Places," Reid called in his deep baritone.

Jazzy and Mateo moved upstage right where they would be entering. He held his binder in his hand and they began.

A total disaster ensued. When Mateo couldn't remember his lines, or even what they might be about, he got flustered and also forgot his blocking. His face was constantly buried in his binder. Jazzy tried to be gentle, tried to remember that it had only been a week, but it was as if Mateo wasn't doing any sort of preparation outside of the studio. He was like a kid who hadn't studied but thought he'd ace the test anyway, and she found that so damn *annoying*. What was he *doing* at home?

Dion would have remembered his lines.

As the day wore on, Jazzy hid in the bathroom during union breaks to avoid Mateo and ran out with Simone for lunch. She didn't want to fight again or pretend she wasn't frustrated. The afternoon dragged as they slogged through the rest of Act One, stopping and starting often. Though it was normal to be stumbling along at this stage for a regular musical, the cast had already been together for a year and the tension in the air grew until it felt like it might burst.

127

Jazzy was frustrated. Mateo seemed exasperated. The rest of the cast was trying to be kind, but their annoyance boiled over, too. The production team was nearly silent at the end of the day. Sasha dismissed them with barely a wave.

Jazzy watched Mateo slink into the bathroom and was glad he wouldn't be outside to fight with her again, because she wasn't sure she could be so forgiving this time. He'd had the weekend to at least try and prepare. But today had been like his first rehearsal, as if he couldn't be bothered at all to improve.

With very deep breaths and more patience than she realized she had, the next two days were better: dance rehearsals in a different studio, just the two of them, to learn their choreography. Drew Masters had two Tonys, and though he cracked a whip, he had a sunny personality that matched Mateo's.

This is where Mateo shined. The man could *dance*. Jazzy floated along in his arms through a waltz, watched as he smoothly soft-shoed through his solo, and felt so safe when he held her. The mirrors along the wall reflected a couple perfectly in sync with each other. Mateo's large hand was warm on the small of her back, guiding her expertly. His deep brown eyes bored into her as they crossed the springy wood of the dance floor.

Effortlessly, he swooped her up around the waist and she rested on his hips. Her right leg stretched out in front of her, toes pointed, while her left crooked behind her.

And they spun and spun and spun, gazes locked. Together.

This is what it was supposed to be like, this was partnership. He would never drop her.

Those two days of choreography rehearsal gave her hope. Mateo could do this. If he could learn a complicated Broadway routine in two days and need no notes, the rest would come.

But it didn't.

"Stop, stop please. Mateo you are supposed to be on stage right." Sasha took her glasses off and rubbed her eyes, her red curls bouncing with her frustration.

Blane slowly set Carson down from a lift. The ensemble pulled out of their poses. Simone stopped rushing across the floor. Jazzy, at stage right, crossed her arms over her chest and looked at the floor, quietly fuming.

Mateo had never sounded more upset. "I'm so—"

"Sorry. Yes, we know. Reid?"

Startled, Reid looked up from his binder then looked at his watch. "What? Oh, sure. Let's take a ten."

The cast faded away around the room and Jazzy stood still. Mateo started to approach the production table but was waved away by Reid. Sasha, Drew, and Catherine were deep in conversation. Mateo hesitated a moment and then slunk out of the room.

Jazzy finally moved. She walked to her pile of stuff in a chair near the door, picked up her water bottle, and took a long drink. Slapping the lid back in place, she collapsed into her chair.

"I know you're frustrated, but we gotta get through today, okay?" Simone sat down beside her.

Jazzy nodded mutely, her jaw clenched.

"It's only been a week. Let's give him some grace." Simone was being gentle.

Jazzy was too frustrated for gentle. "Almost two weeks. And I know that. But he's clearly not doing any work outside of this room, and that is unacceptable when *this* is his performance. Something has to give, Simone. Dion would have at least *tried*."

Simone gave a sharp intake of breath as she looked over Jazzy's shoulder.

Jazzy turned to see Mateo standing in the doorway, his face stricken. Before she could say anything, Reid called them back. They stumbled through the rest of the day with nothing improving and Jazzy wracked with guilt. Mateo wouldn't even look at her when he didn't have to.

She had never behaved that way before and was so angry at herself and the entire situation. Her uncharacteristic outburst is why she always kept a distance, why she kept everything professional. Friends made you let your guard down. Not that she was regretting letting Simone into her life. Just that . . . *augh*!

This time, she was the one to wait for him after rehearsal. He had stayed behind to talk with Sasha and

Jazzy waited until he walked out of the building, shoulders drooping.

"Mateo."

"Don't." His expression was like a storm cloud.

"Please, I'm so sorry. Emotions run high in rehearsal, you know? I feel awful. And I didn't mean it."

Mateo wheeled around to face her. "Didn't you? Listen, I know what you think of me, okay? I know you think I'm some spoiled, shallow, no-talent pop star who has no business being on your turf."

"That's not true, I can see how wonderful you—"

"Stop, Jazzy! Just stop. Because for the record, I think you're uptight and stuck-up. So neither one of us likes each other. You don't have to try anymore, okay? You don't have to be nice to me, or tell your friends to invite me to things—

"I didn't—" Jazzy was too shocked to go on. And she couldn't believe they were fighting on the street again. They were *thirty*.

"We *don't* have to be friends. I just need you to be my partner in the room. That's all."

Mateo met her eyes, and the anger she saw there almost made her back away a step, but not quite. Instead, she stepped closer to him, feeling a fire within her that she didn't try to settle.

Mateo took another step toward her, his face now inches from hers. She could feel the heat of him, could imagine the solid muscle of his chest. She was distracted by his full lips for a moment, but then she looked up and met his gaze. The anger wasn't gone, but it had turned to something else.

Passion. Or hatred.

Or both.

"We're not friends, Jazzy." His voice was almost hoarse, lower than usual.

"Fine," she spat.

"Fine," he said with just as much vitriol. Mateo stood for another moment, breathing out through his nose. Then, inexplicably, he let his hand brush down her bare arm, sending a shiver through her all the way down to her toes. Abruptly, he turned and got into his waiting car.

Jazzy stood still as commuters marched around her and yellow cabs sped by. Her heart pounded and her skin burned with the memory of his touch.

§

Unsurprisingly after that, the week did not improve. Mateo continued to act like it was the first day of rehearsal. Jazzy continued to act like she was neutral about it. They stumbled through pieces of the show each day, adding in choreography, marking their blocking, and then, blessedly, Friday came. A music rehearsal. Everyone sat and sang through the show with their music on the stands in front of them. Mateo couldn't forget anything with his score right there, which was a relief to everyone. Jazzy sat next to him and tried to stay unaffected by his voice, but that was very difficult. There was a reason that Mateo had filled stadiums.

He was sensational.

Seeming buoyed by the approving looks on the faces of the cast and crew after Friday's rehearsal, Mateo approached Jazzy as she gathered her things. "Hey."

Jazzy zipped her bag and slung it over her shoulder. "Hey." They'd been friendly for the rest of the week. Or, at least, cordial. She had tried not to openly seethe when his performance didn't improve, he had tried not to openly hate her, and Friday's music rehearsal had made her feel much better about him.

Him in the role. *Not* him in general.

She didn't care about Mateo. Just Cole.

That's all.

"First real scenes on Monday." He scuffed the toe of his Chuck Taylor against the floor near her feet.

"Yep." Her eyes met his, and his expression was friendlier than she was expecting.

"You wouldn't want to run lines with me this weekend, would you?"

Jazzy hesitated. The thought of a long, hot shower and a weekend alone was heavenly after the heightened emotions of this trying week. She was hoping to relax, go for a long run, watch movies with Patti . . .

"Never mind," Mateo said quickly. He seemed to sense her hesitation and presume it was a no. He stepped back, frowning. "It's fine. I can run lines with—"

"No, I can—"

133

"No, it's fine. Don't worry about it."

"Mateo." Jazzy stepped closer to him. "Please. You just caught me off guard." She put her hand on his forearm, felt his muscles become taut.

He glanced down at her hand on his bare skin, then back up into her face. She watched as his gaze lingered on her lips then traveled up to meet hers. His lips parted and his chest moved up and down a fraction faster. As he gazed at her, she saw a thousand words he wasn't saying and felt they were entering a dangerous territory. She removed her hand.

Finally, after several beats, Mateo said, "No. It's fine. Like I said. Don't worry about it." Then he turned on his heel and walked away, leaving Jazzy to stare after him wondering what had just happened.

§

"Folks, let's do this!" Sasha stood up from the table the next Monday, her black and white caftan swishing. "I want to see scenes four and five of Act One today, and I want them full out. No marking— Yes, Mateo?"

"Sorry, full out? Does that mean no calling line?"

Somehow, despite the past weeks, the cast burst out into laughter at this. Even Jazzy managed a smile.

Sasha smiled at him indulgently. "You may call line or use your script. We aren't off-book until next week."

Jazzy, already almost off-book, chanced a glance at Mateo. He was smirking at her, seeming to say *See? I have until next week.*

Ignoring him, she tugged her tank down over her black leggings and knelt down to strap on her character shoes. She felt a presence next to her and turned her head up to see Mateo.

"So . . . um . . . the kiss?"

"Yes?" She finished buckling and straightened.

"We're going to kiss, right? That's what full out means? Full out dancing, full out blocking, full out kissing?"

She snickered in spite of herself. "Yes. We kiss. You cool with that?" She put her hands on her hips and stepped closer to him.

He cocked an eyebrow, a smile twitching on his lips. "Yup."

The morning scenes went rather okay. Better. Mateo still carried his script but did seem to have studied over the weekend. Jazzy felt electrified when they danced together in the party scene. After the lunch break, they came back to do the scene they'd performed for the audition. Jazzy tried to tamp down the memory of what Mateo's lips felt like on hers, anticipating his thumb grazing the softness of her cheek.

As Amelia and Cole fought through the scene, Jazzy noticed the rest of the cast sitting around the perimeter of the room, some with mouths hanging open, almost entirely still. The tension created by their passionate fighting was palpable.

As Amelia, she finally admitted her feelings and Jazzy felt the most vulnerable she ever had onstage, almost as though she were doing it herself.

"Tell me. Tell me what you want, Amelia!" Mateo said forcefully, his features twisted in pain and desire.

Jazzy let her arms drop to her sides and nearly shouted, "You! I want *you*, Cole!"

Mateo's binder hit the floor with a thud as he took three long strides toward her and pulled her into his arms. He took a beat as she wrapped her arms around his neck to look into her eyes, his own blazing with satisfaction. Finally, he crushed his lips to hers and Jazzy felt starlight burst inside of her once again.

His lips were as soft as they looked and the stars were rocketing around inside of her, though she told herself it was just stage chemistry. He tightened his grip on her waist and she let her fingers slide up his neck. His skin was hot to the touch. Finally, Mateo pulled back, keeping his arm tight around her, his right hand on her upstage cheek.

Jazzy felt well and thoroughly kissed.

Mateo's gaze was steady as he said the last line of the scene. "I've been wanting to do that my whole life."

Here, Jazzy knew that music would swell and they would sing their duet and kiss again as the lights went down, but now, a beat of silence followed. Mateo slowly took his arm from Jazzy's waist and they separated. She glanced around the room.

No one was on their phone or thumbing through a script. Simone's mouth was agape. Blane and Carson, arms and legs draped around each other on the floor, stared wide-eyed at her and Mateo. Parker had one arm in and one arm out of a sweatshirt. Everyone seemed enraptured by what had taken place.

And then Sasha spoke. "Yeah, well. Now see . . . *that*. That was a *scene*."

# Eleven ♫

"You absolutely cannot deny it, Jazzygirl."

Jazzy wrinkled her nose at this nickname.

"Don't give me that face." Simone sat back after another bite of her breakfast burrito.

Jazzy dipped her quesadilla into the ramekin full of guacamole. She and Simone were having brunch the day after The Kiss, and she was trying to deny that it meant anything at all. They sat outside a trendy Upper East Side taqueria, sipping Bloody Marys and watching a New York City summer day play out in front of them.

"Can we please talk about anything else? Tell me more about your brothers."

Simone pursed her lips. "You're lucky you landed on one of my favorite subjects. But don't get comfortable. We're not done with Mateo yet." For the next few minutes, Simone had Jazzy laughing over the ways she and her two brothers would torture each other as children. The fake snakes they would leave for the others to find, the wiffle ball bats they would use on anything that wasn't a wiffle ball, including each other.

"They're both married now. I have three nieces and a nephew and I adore them. Just like you. Adore. Mateo."

"That was an impressive segue." Jazzy made the face again. "It's just stage chemistry. If he could remember anything, he'd be an excellent partner."

Simone rolled her eyes. "Please. We all felt that explosion."

"It wasn't an explosion." Jazzy said through a mouthful of cheese and tortilla, while replaying the definite explosion in her mind. She swallowed. "It's the scene. It's passionately written and we were both in it. That's all."

Simone sipped from the straw in her Bloody Mary while she stared at Jazzy incredulously.

"Besides," Jazzy said in response to the stare, "he's impossible. He's hot and cold. One minute he wants to be friends, the next he's mad because I'm frustrated that he isn't doing the work."

"Mhmm."

"And I don't even really know him. He doesn't talk about his life. So what I do know is what the tabloids said ten years ago, and he's not doing a very good job of disputing those rumors. He's late, he's unprepared, he's—"

"Gorgeous, he's magnetic, he's going to get it eventually . . . "

"Is he though? I mean, sure, he's a brilliant dancer, and he's picked up the choreo well. But if that's all we can say after three weeks of work, come on. He's supposed to be a professional. How can I know I'm going to be able to rely on him whenever they figure out when the show is going to run?"

"Was he not better this week?" Simone popped a stray bean into her mouth.

Jazzy thought through the previous week. After The Kiss, the rest of the week had seemed tame. Mateo had tried a couple of scenes without his binder but Sasha had him retrieve it when he'd called 'Line!' too many times. He was getting better at remembering the blocking, though Jazzy had to liberally 'shove with love'. She conceded.

"Fine. Yes, he's been better."

"You're in denial." Simone pointed a fork right at her face. "And he feels it too, that much is obvious."

Jazzy remembered something, and she stared off into space briefly. "He asked me out," she blurted.

"*What?*" Simone's eyes widened to the size of saucers. "What? When?"

Jazzy kept her stare fixed on the bustle of the sidewalk beyond them as the memories of Mateo pre-*Bridges That Burn* came flooding back. When he was just a handsome stranger. Before she met him. "After my Lowenstein's show. Closing night. He asked me to get a drink and I told him no. I had no idea he was coming in for chem reads then. He was just this guy I'd seen at the coffee shop a couple of times. He— Oh, that's right. He knew who I was."

"Holy shit." Simone leaned back to let the server clear their plates and stared at Jazzy, who was staring at nothing.

In an almost dreamy voice, she went on. "Yeah, I had just Googled him because my barista is obsessed and told me about his past. I was curious. And I found all of the rumors about him before he disappeared, so . . . So I said no . . . " She shook her head, before looking back to Simone's dumbfounded expression. "Which was clearly the right decision, because not only was I right about the work ethic, I don't do showmances."

Simone shook her head slowly. "I'm stuck on the fact that he asked you out before."

Jazzy shrugged and reached for her bag, pulling out her wallet.

"He came to your show. He's a *fan*."

"He is not."

"He came. To. Your show." Simone punctuated each word with a slap on the table.

"Okay, so he knew of me. Maybe he knew he was already coming in for the readings and I was cast. Maybe he was trying to manipulate me!"

"That boy doesn't have a manipulative bone in his body." Simone handed the server the check folder with their cards inside.

"You don't know that."

"You're right, I don't. But you know what I do know?" Simone leaned forward, her gaze steady.

Jazzy leveled her gaze at Simone, feeling like she was about to hear a truth she didn't want to. While Simone let the silence linger, a bus rumbled by, a woman called for a cab, and a group of children on skateboards crossed the street just beyond where they sat.

Finally, Jazzy gave in. "Fine, what. What do you know."

"I know that we just sat here for an hour and—" Simone checked her watch. "—fifteen minutes. And you haven't talked about anything but Mateo Williams."

"So?" She could feel a blush creep up her cheeks. "He's my co-star."

"You've got it bad, Summers." Simone was grinning like the Cheshire Cat as she stood and swung her bag over her shoulder.

"I do *not*."

Simone just looked at her with an eyebrow raised until Jazzy finally gave up and stood as well. She tilted her chin up in defiance. "I don't."

"Sure you don't. Let's go shopping. I'll buy you something pretty if you admit you love him."

Rolling her eyes but smiling ear to ear, Jazzy said, "Even though you're wrong, thank you for bullying me into this friendship."

Simone just swung her arm around Jazzy's shoulders and they sauntered over to Fifth Avenue.

§

Jazzy escaped the bustle of Times Square by entering the nondescript building next to the Lyric Theater on 43rd Street. Instead of rehearsal that Tuesday morning, she was meeting with a representative of Cahill & Brown. The fact that *Bridges That Burn* had hired the biggest Broadway PR firm to represent it elated her. That meant the producers had a ton of faith in the production and it would go far.

Fingers crossed, anyway.

The foyer of the sleek, modern offices on the fifth floor was all white walls and fresh lilies. A low black couch and two chairs sat in front of a wall on which hung dozens of musical posters, shows the firm had represented.

"Hi, I'm Jazzy Summers. I'm here to meet with Keith Lyons?"

The receptionist, a short, middle-aged woman with incredibly kind eyes, smiled widely at her. "Wonderful to see you, Jazzy. He's just finishing up with Mateo. Then I'll send you in."

"Great, thank you." Jazzy made to turn to the wall to study the posters.

The receptionist stood. "I know you won't remember me, but I've been here for ages, and we did the work on *After All*."

"Really?" Jazzy turned back to her, smiling wide. "What's your name?"

"Andrea. You were just the sweetest kid, so wide-eyed and fresh. We loved working with you, and it's been a joy to watch your career."

"Wow. That's so nice to hear. Thank you." Jazzy reached across the desk and shook Andrea's warm hand.

"I can't wait to see *Bridges That Burn*. I bet you and Mateo will just shine." Andrea patted Jazzy's hand just as her computer made a 'ping'. She glanced over at it. "Oh, you can head on back. Keith is ready for you."

"Thank you, Andrea. See you soon."

Andrea motioned for her to go through the glass doors behind her where an open plan office buzzed with energy. "Go all the way to the back. Keith's is the second office to the right."

Jazzy made her way through the bright office toward the closed row of doors at the back. As she approached Keith's office, the door opened slowly. She couldn't help overhearing.

"And can I just say, I've been on the board of BC/EFA for years, and I am so floored that you're donating your salary to us. I will only ask once, but would you let us do a press release about it? You can't imagine what good PR that is. I do understand if you don't want to."

Mateo's voice was smooth as silk when he answered. "Thank you, but no. I really want to keep that anonymous."

A jovial man in a striped navy button down appeared in the doorway with Mateo right behind as the door swung open fully. "Absolutely. And we thank you."

"My pleasure."

The man noticed Jazzy standing just down the hall. "Ms. Summers! Welcome to Cahill & Brown. I'm Keith, and I think you know my guest."

Jazzy, who had been trying to process what she just heard, shook her head slightly and smiled widely. "Nice to meet you, Keith. Hi, Mateo."

Mateo had frozen in the doorway, seeming to know that she'd overheard that he was donating his entire salary to Broadway Cares/Equity Fights Aids, the philanthropic heart of the Broadway community.

"Hey, Jazz." He nodded to her, then stuck out his hand to Keith who took it and shook it warmly. "Very nice to meet you, sir. I look forward to working with you."

"And you. Thanks for coming. Jazzy, come on in."

Jazzy walked toward the office and Mateo moved toward the exit. Just before he passed her, he placed a hand gently on her arm. Her nerve endings fired at his soft touch.

"Please don't say anything," he whispered.

She looked up into his sparkling eyes, lighter today, and filled with a plea. All she could do was nod. He squeezed her arm gently and walked past her.

Jazzy was still buzzing from Mateo's presence as she followed Keith into his office which was filled with cushy furniture and warm lighting.

"I should have kept the door closed to ask him that. He really doesn't want anyone to know." Keith took his seat behind the large, mahogany desk which suited his frame.

"I won't say anything."

Keith ran a hand over his bald head. "Kid just wants to be on Broadway. There's something very pure about that."

Jazzy merely nodded, still thrown by the news. Mateo's salary, if anything like hers, was not insignificant. What a generous gesture. "I like your office," she said to change the subject.

"Well, thank you. All this minimalist, modern nonsense. I much prefer an office with warmth. Now, let's talk strategy. I always meet with my leads separately because I want them to be free to tell me how they see PR going. So I have some questions for you, then we'll move on to the strategy I've drawn up. Sound good?"

"Sounds great."

An hour later, Jazzy had a grasp on the firm's expectations of her: what she would be posting on social media, interviews they were lining up, podcast recordings she'd be doing, the commercial shoot for the tri-state area. Outside, the early July sun was warm on her face and she was looking forward to the long weekend ahead. Checking her watch, she decided she had plenty of time for lunch before heading to rehearsal for the afternoon. She ate a salad at a café near the studio, enjoying watching the people passing on 42$^{nd}$ Street. Then she strolled over to the studio and caught up with Blane, who was just returning from his lunch break.

"Hey, beauty, how was the PR man?" he asked her as they waited for the elevator.

"Really smart. Very kind. I think we're going to have fun with him."

The elevator doors pinged open and they heard a voice cry out behind them. "Wait! Hold the doors, please." Mateo, out of breath, scooted into the elevator, sweat on his brow. "Sorry, thank you."

Blane pressed the call button and stepped back, raising an eyebrow in Jazzy's direction. "No problem."

"Where'd you go? We were only a block away." She eyed him curiously.

"I just . . . I had to run home for something."

Jazzy took in his lack of bag, of anything he might have brought from home. "Don't you have a car?"

Mateo turned to her, his expression telling her to drop it. Then he quickly turned away. "Traffic was

147

backed up, it was faster to get out and run. Wouldn't want to be *late*."

Jazzy, unsure why he was being so prickly, didn't know her eyes could roll that hard. "Okay. Well. Glad you made it." Her gaze reached his, and she caught something like pain pass over his face. He gave her a withering look when the elevator doors opened and loped off into the studio before she could say anything else.

"What was that about?" Blane asked her.

She startled. She'd forgotten he was in the elevator with them. Collecting herself, she said, "I don't know."

§

"Thank you, thank you for all your work today, my lovelies." A few hours later, Sasha paced in front of the cast, today's caftan long and white. They were piled on the floor in front of her, draped around each other, stretching and sipping from water bottles, exhausted. Parker had begun a braid in Carson's hair. Jason was massaging Blane's calf with strong hands, the muscles of his arms on full display in his tank top. Max and Jen assisted each other in a stretch while Daria splayed out next to them, touching her toes.

Jazzy sat next to Mateo, her legs flat out in front of her, gripping the bottoms of her feet. He sat cross-legged, looking exhausted but happy. He hadn't forgotten anything today.

"We have two more days of rehearsal this week, and then it is my understanding that you have rented a boat together for the holiday?"

A cheer went up from the cast. They had indeed rented themselves a small yacht, all pitching in a bit of money to celebrate the Fourth of July on the Hudson River. Nothing like day drinking on a boat to bond a group of people together.

"Well, I suggest you party it up this weekend, because when we come back from the holiday, we will have a lot of work to do. People," she paused dramatically, "we have a theater and an opening date."

More cheers began and the energy in the room ramped up. Jazzy looked at Mateo, the tense elevator ride forgotten with this news. And for once, there was no animosity between them as they beamed at each other.

"Get ready to have your work cut out for you. You will be hearing this from your agents and teams this week, but I wanted to be the first to tell you. We will have four more weeks of rehearsal with two weeks of previews that will start in August. Our opening date is August twentieth."

Whoops and hollers rang out around the room. Sasha let the cast celebrate some more until Carson called, "What theater?"

She smiled and paused, letting the drama sink in, the tension build. Finally, she said reverently, "The Schubert."

"No way," Parker breathed. Silence descended suddenly, moments passing as if they all held their breath.

"I assure you. Way." Sasha beamed at all of them and this time, everyone rose to their feet and began hugging and shrieking and jumping around the studio. Jazzy and Simone were in the middle of a celebratory dance when Jazzy saw Mateo looking around, happy but confused, in a group hug with several others. She approached him and he disentangled himself.

"What am I missing?" he said, his eyes bright. "This is obviously good news, but I don't get it."

Jazzy smiled up at him and took his hands, elated. "*A Chorus Line. Chicago. Gypsy.* "

Mateo just looked down into her face, still mystified.

"Mateo." She squeezed his hands and felt him squeeze back. "Schubert shows *run.*"

# Twelve ♫

The Fourth of July was humid and warm. A perfect day for boating. The cast of *Bridges That Burn* had met for a rowdy, celebratory breakfast in Chelsea. At noon, they'd walked over to Pier 62 and boarded the small luxury yacht they'd rented for the day. Their captain, a no-nonsense man named Rick, had walked them through safety protocols and then they were free to party. The boat rental included drinks, lunch, and dinner and they'd all immediately converged on the bar before climbing to an upper deck to enjoy the sunshine.

Carson had compiled a playlist for the whole day. He plugged his tablet into the yacht's sound system and turned up the bass. Jazzy felt like a wild thing. She shook her hips and held on to whoever was closest to her. Simone, resplendent in a white bikini, led them in line dances, and after Blane poured shots, the dancing got wilder. Parker was the first in the hot tub on the top deck, and Jazzy denied that she felt a twinge of jealousy when Mateo joined her.

Mateo, who once must have felt like an outsider, was the life of the party as the cast cemented their bond. He made sure everyone had a drink who wanted one, and when a song from his pop star days came on, he took it in stride and performed the whole dance with a gin and tonic in his hand. Jazzy felt her heart swell watching these people who were now her show family. No.

Her family.

Everyone was dressed in their yachting best: short shorts and tank tops, bikinis and speedos. Simone gave choreography orders like a queen to Blane and Carson, who performed for her, laughing until Carson had to lean over the side of the boat. Parker, who was still in the hot tub cuddling up to Jason, called Jazzy over to join them.

Jazzy climbed in and chatted with Colby and Meredith, ensemble members with whom she hadn't yet had a real conversation. They played a round of Never Have I Ever, laughing uproariously, until Carson pulled her out of the hot tub to join him as Mateo's backup dancers.

As she mimicked Carson's choreography, she felt a rush of joy. These were her people, and she counted herself so lucky to be a part of them. What a tribe.

Twilight. The lights of the city dazzled her as the cover-up over her red and white bikini blew in the breeze. The yacht was idle on the river. Jazzy had taken a moment away, not used to having so many people around her who wanted to hang out with her. As she leaned over the stern, she was smiling secretly to herself at how her life had changed in just a month. The laughter from her cast drifted over to her from inside, where they were lingering over the luxurious dinner. For the moment, she was alone.

But not for long. She heard footsteps behind her and turned to see Mateo approaching.

"I'm not disturbing you, am I?" The tight white t-shirt he'd put on over his blue board shorts accentuated the muscles of his arms and chest.

Jazzy had had just enough to drink to blatantly stare. She turned back out to the water to stop herself. "Not at all."

Behind her, she felt Mateo approach and watched as he placed his hands on the railing on either side of her. She could feel the heat of his chest just inches from her back. Even so, she gave a shiver.

Then she realized what he was doing.

"Don't do it, Mateo." It was an order.

He chuckled behind her, his breath hot on her neck. "But Jazzy, I have to. I think it's legally required."

153

"I will think you're incredibly lame."

"I don't care." He took a deep breath and she watched the taut muscles of his forearms tense as he tilted back and screamed, "I'm king of the world!"

Jazzy laughed out loud despite her warning. Mateo screamed it again and she turned around to face him. His expression was exuberant and his eyes were full of humor.

"You know, he's not with Rose when he screams that. He finds her there later." Jazzy couldn't help smiling up at him.

Mateo didn't take his arms from the railing. He faced her now, his lips parted for a moment as he stared into her eyes. "So what, do you have *Titanic* memorized?"

"Yes, obviously. I was a teenage girl once." Jazzy's laugh didn't quite make it out of her chest as Mateo stepped an inch closer to her, his intense gaze lingering on her lips. Inexplicably, or perhaps not, she wanted to wrap her arms around him, touch her lips to his, make that starlight burst inside of her again.

"Are you saying that you're Rose, and I'm Jack?" Mateo scooted his hands closer together on the railing and his arms brushed against hers.

Jazzy swallowed with difficulty. No, she didn't do showmances. She didn't. And Mateo's lips were always soft and inviting and nothing was different about them in this moment. "I hope not. Jack dies."

"So you wouldn't move over on the door for me? You'd let me sink to the bottom of the ocean?" He licked his lips slowly.

In that moment, Jazzy would have done anything for him. But she absolutely could not say that out loud. "I would never let you sink." She tilted her face up to his, just tipsy enough to be this bold.

Mateo moved a fraction closer, his eyes on hers, and then a sudden burst of laughter from inside broke the spell. Jazzy felt the heat dissipate around them. Mateo removed his hands from the railing as they listened to their castmates leave the dining room and start the music again on the back of the boat.

The sky was turning purple and Jazzy knew they would soon be in inky darkness, the lights of Manhattan winking at them. The fireworks were due to start soon.

Mateo moved next to her, seeming to understand the moment had passed, and propped his forearms on the railing. "Do you ever think . . . "

Jazzy mirrored his pose right next to him, her arm brushing his. "What?"

Mateo looked deep in thought, his brow furrowed, a slight frown on his face. "Just . . . You and I, we were both famous when we were really young. Do you ever think that we're just . . . inextricably broken?" He turned his face to hers, eyebrows hitched, eyes wide with vulnerability.

Jazzy looked out to the water and took a deep breath, surprised at the turn in conversation. She pondered for a

155

few moments. "Sometimes I wonder. I wonder what it would have been like to go to a normal high school and go off to college and come home on winter breaks. I wonder what it would be like to have a normal job and maybe have met someone, maybe have a kid."

"Me too." He smiled softly. "A place in a burb somewhere, grilling on the weekends. Taking the kids to soccer."

Jazzy chuckled. "And we might be intensely bored of it all in a year. I can't pretend to know what it was like to be as famous as you, very few people can. But having expectations put on me at such a young age probably had some effect on my psyche. I'm happy with my life. I love performing. I don't think I could do anything else. So do I think maybe it was hard? Sure. But I don't think we're broken."

Mateo nodded, facing forward. "I'm not so sure." Jazzy let his uncertainty linger for a moment.

"Mateo, why did you disappear?" she asked gently.

He looked sharply at her, a modicum of shock crossing his expression.

"Sorry, never mind. None of my business."

Mateo turned away to look at the water again. "It's just . . . complicated. I just—"

"Okay."

A heavy silence settled over them as the boat gently swayed. The laughter and shouting from their castmates along with the other boats on the river swirled along the warm and comforting breeze.

"So what brought all this on?" Jazzy asked after a while. Her voice was soft but she knew he could hear over the wind.

The corner of his mouth twitched up. "I switched to vodka. I get philosophical on vodka."

"Oh? And what are you on gin?"

He turned to face her. "You saw me. Dance pants."

A few moments passed as Jazzy lost herself in his sweet expression. He turned back out to the water, the levity dissolving and she knew he was still thinking about his question. She reached out and put her hand on his wrist lightly.

"I don't think you're broken, Mateo." The starlight she felt inside of her when they kissed during rehearsal sparkled at this simple touch.

Mateo gazed down at her hand then slowly turned his upward to capture it. He laced their fingers together and ran his thumb over her knuckles. Slowly, he raised his eyes to hers and straightened. He pulled Jazzy's hand up to his chest right over his heart and wrapped his other arm around her waist. She stepped closer to him without hesitating, her body perfectly fitting into his, just as it had in rehearsal. But this was different. The air around them shifted as she wrapped her other arm around him, her fingers tracing the nape of his neck.

The cries and laughter of their castmates at the back of the boat were barely audible, and Jazzy stopped hearing them. At the moment, Mateo was the only other person in the world. His heart hammered beneath her hand on his chest and she felt her own speed up considerably.

Mateo gazed down at her, as if drinking in the curve of her cheek, the fullness of her lips. His hand grazed across her waist until it met the small of her back and gently pulled her closer. She met him halfway, anticipation flowing through her body, every nerve ending standing on edge, desperate for him to brush his lips on hers, to feel that starlight again.

His lips parted and his breath hitched when she tilted her face up to his, a silent assent. When his lips finally touched hers, Jazzy felt her whole body sway, either from the boat, or because she had never been kissed like this. She pulled her hand off of his chest and wrapped it around his neck.

His free hand moved to the soft skin of her cheek. He cupped her face gently but boldly, cradling her like she was something delicate to be cherished.

Jazzy hadn't let herself dream that his kiss would make her feel so treasured. But here they were, in a moment that felt, somehow, inevitable.

Being in his arms felt exactly right.

Outside of the confines of a stage kiss, his lips were tender but insistent, parting hers, until she could feel his breath, met his tongue with hers. His hand on her back steadied her. It seemed he would always steady her. Her skin warmed under his touch as he pulled her closer, until she could feel every part of her touching every part of him.

She was not about to let this moment go. She'd wanted it, unconsciously or not, for far too long. Rising up on her tiptoes, she drew his bottom lip between her teeth. His moan of pleasure sent shock waves down her spine. His arms tightened around her and he deepened the kiss, his tongue sweeping across hers, the hitch of his breath sending a tingling through her stomach. The world fell away as she lost herself and he kissed her and kissed her.

This wasn't starlight.

This was a super nova.

Jazzy's body was aflame as his lips traced the gentle curve of her jaw to her earlobe where his breath was hot and he whispered her name. She tightened her hold on him, desperate to stay in this perfect moment for as long as possible. He brushed his lips on hers again, claiming her. And oh, she was his.

A resounding boom seemed to shake the boat. Surprised, they broke the kiss and pulled away from one another, gazing upwards. As they did, he caught her hand in his. Jazzy couldn't seem to find the words as they met each other's eyes once again. Mateo was breathing heavily, gazing down at her in awe.

Another firework went off above them and Jazzy heard their castmates cheering at the back of the boat. She tipped her face to the sky where the red and gold glittered above them.

"Well, that's appropriate," she said into the sky.

Then she watched as Mateo's expression changed, his mouth falling open, his eyes widening. "Jazzy, I'm so sorry."

"What?" Her blood ran cold when he dropped her hand.

"That was so unprofessional of me. I shouldn't have done that. I said I would respect you and I do, I think you're one of the greatest—"

"Mateo, it's fine. I started it. I wouldn't have kissed you if I didn't want—" She took a step closer to him, but he stepped back. Her heart slammed against her chest. She was suddenly very sober.

"It doesn't matter, this shouldn't have happened. I shouldn't have followed you out here. Or had another vodka. I'm so sorry. Let's just— We can just forget it. Let's go back to the party. Fuck. I'm sorry." His words seemed to tumble out without his thinking and he scrubbed a hand down his face.

"I am so sorry for that, and I am so sorry I'm having trouble with rehearsal and that you're so frustrated. I'm just sorry that everything isn't working. Everything I'm doing isn't working. I just—"

"Mateo, please. It's okay. You'll get it, I know you will." She stepped toward him, her hand out.

He shrugged in frustration and threw up his hands. "Easy for you to say. Everything comes easy to you."

Jazzy took a step back, desperate to get the last few moments back, trying to ignore how much his words hurt. Trying to conflate this moment with the one just before, when they were so entwined, Jazzy nearly burst. "I don't— I've given up so mu— I work *really* hard, Mateo."

Panic etched all over his face. "Shit. I know, that's not what I meant—"

On second thought, she didn't care what he meant. Whoever that Mateo was who'd kissed her, he didn't really exist. Apparently, he could turn it on and off easily. And if he could, so could she. She took a deep breath and then deliberately draped ice all over her words. "No, it is. I get it. It's fine. You're right. Let's go back to the party."

"I . . . wait . . . "

Jazzy turned on her heel, not waiting for him to follow, and began walking to the back of the boat. "Come on. I'll make you another gin and tonic."

"Jazzy, wait!" But whatever else he said was lost in another round of fireworks and the breeze off the river.

Jazzy tried to enjoy the rest of the party, but her mind kept drifting back to Mateo and his lips, his breath against her ear. It had upended her, but he was right. It wasn't professional, she didn't do showmances, and the best thing to do was ignore it.

Even though it had awakened something in her that she hadn't known was sleeping.

But no matter. That was that. At eleven o'clock, the boat docked and the cast disembarked. Most were going on to another bar, but Jazzy begged off, finding another reason why adopting Patti was a great idea. Her cat needed her. Simone had rolled her eyes, seeing right through Jazzy, but let her go without a fight. She strutted off after the rest of the cast as Jazzy called a car.

Carson and Blane had Mateo between them, arm in arm, as they loped off to their next adventure. Jazzy watched out of the corner of her eye as he said something to them both and then jogged back to her. She checked the map on her phone, willing her Lyft to hurry up.

"Jazzy, listen—"

"It's okay, Mateo."

"It's not. I feel like I really screwed up. The . . . you know . . . kiss, and the— I didn't mean it the way it came out. I know how hard you work."

Jazzy crossed her arms over her chest, standing her ground. "You think I'm stuck up, you think this is all easy for me, and yeah, I don't deny that I've been lucky. But I do work really hard, and I know. I *know*. That's not what you meant."

She held up a hand at his expression. He clearly wanted to defend himself. She went on, in a gentle but firm voice. "But intention doesn't matter when the words have already been said out loud. I accept your apology. Mateo, it's fine. I like working with you, when you know what you're doing, and I think you're going to be wonderful in the show. But if you want to forget the kiss happened, fine. It didn't. Poof." She made a little explosion motion with her hand.

Mateo's lips were parted and his eyes bored into hers. "I don't—"

"Jazzy?" A blue sedan pulled up next to them and she checked the license plate, then waved to the driver through the open window.

"That's me." She opened the door and got in.

Mateo hung onto the door handle until she was settled. He looked resigned and a little sad. He swallowed hard and his words were clipped. "Okay. Poof. I'll see you Monday. We're good?"

Jazzy gave him a sad smile. "We're good."

He let go and she closed the door. She watched as he met Carson and Blane half a block up. They resumed their walk to wherever they were going, laughing and joking. Jazzy's stomach felt like a ball of lead. She watched for a moment and then, just like that, the car turned a corner, the night was over, and the kiss had never happened.

Poof.

# Thirteen ♫

If fighting with Mateo was maddening, pretending that the kiss hadn't happened was much worse. Jazzy tapped her foot against the studio floor, trying to push down the frustration and the fact that she wanted to grab Mateo and kiss the exasperated look off of his face. Or yell at him.

Or both.

Oh, help.

"Mateo, did you party too hard this weekend? You had this last week." Sasha rubbed her eyes.

Mateo glanced at Jazzy and his eyes burned at her momentarily. "I'm sorry. Sorry, everyone. I mixed this up with scene three."

"It's okay. This is the first week off-book. We're bound to get confused. I will remind everyone that Mateo and Jazzy are stepping in. They haven't run the show yet. So let's move on with grace." Sasha swept back behind the table and took a seat, her sunny yellow caftan settling around her.

Jazzy thought that was generous of her. But the day went on in much the same manner. She knew that this week would be tough without the security blanket of her binder in her hands, so she had studied all weekend after the party. It was her happy place to cook a meal from her favorite delivery kit and sing through her songs with her rehearsal recordings. Then she would sit down with a delicious sweet potato salad or chicken and broccoli and go over her lines again and again.

And if it had distracted her from memories of the searing kiss, well, good.

By the Sunday night after the party, she was fairly certain that she would be just fine.

Mateo, not so much. He had clearly not done any work after the party and for the rest of the weekend. Jazzy left rehearsal irritated again, not only because Mateo couldn't seem to get it together, but because every time they kissed, just the stage kiss, it lit her up inside. She had never, ever had such a confusing rehearsal experience.

165

She stomped down the block, sour faced and crabby and alone, having practically run out of the rehearsal room. Simone had called to her, but she took the stairs. She couldn't face any questions about what had happened on Friday night when she and Mateo had disappeared.

Through her grumpy haze, Jazzy noticed a gaggle of women on her way to the corner. They stared at the entrance to the studio's building, holding up phones. Mateo's fans had started staking out the place once the *Bridges That Burn* official Instagram started posting teasers. It wasn't hard to figure out where they were rehearsing, and this group of gals, who looked to be in their late twenties, weren't even hiding it. And they didn't even notice her.

Jazzy's scowl grew deeper as she marched past. That was another thing. Even if she *did* do showmances and *did* have feelings for Mateo, which she obviously and completely did not, he was still incredibly famous and could have anyone he wanted. Why would he want an introverted workaholic who couldn't remember the last time she'd been kissed like that? Who'd never, actually, been kissed like that?

Wait, no. There was never a kiss.

Poof.

As she waited for the light to change, she heard a collective gasp from the group of fans behind her.

"Jazz, hold up. Wait." Mateo jogged toward her, ignoring his fans, who started unabashedly snapping photos. He stopped in front of her and seemed to note her stormy eyes and mouth set in a line. He hesitated a moment before saying, "I feel like a broken record at this point."

"I swear to god, Mateo, if you apologize to me one more time, I will freaking lose it." Jazzy turned away from him.

"I get it. I do. I'm so—"

"Just do the work! Please. Go home and study. Could you do that for me?" She tilted her head, turning to face him.

For a moment he looked wounded, but then he crossed his arms over his chest. "That's kind of patronizing."

"I . . . uggghhh . . . " The light changed and Jazzy stomped across 43rd Street.

Mateo followed her and matched her stride and her exasperation. "I'm trying. I am. You know, you don't leave any room for mistakes."

"I do *so*."

"You do *not*."

After stepping up onto the curb, Jazzy wheeled around, facing him. "Are we *three*?"

She'd never seen him scowl before, but he was now. "Now you're comparing me to a toddler?"

"Can we not?" Jazzy said through clenched teeth. She tried to disguise a gesture to the women across the street.

Mateo gave them a sideways glance, noting their phones. He rolled his eyes upward and sighed heavily.

"Fine. I'll see you tomorrow." He turned heel and walked back to the fans, saying hello. They fell out over him and his beaming smile. Of course they did.

Jazzy, angered at how easily he could turn off and on his emotions, continued stomping to the subway and rode it home, scowling the whole way.

# *BRIDGES THAT BURN* OVER TROUBLED WATERS!

The much-anticipated new Broadway musical is set to open this August, but will its stars quit fighting before it does?

Kittens, you absolutely heard this from me. There are rumors going around that Mateo Williams, who stepped into the role of Cole in the new musical, *Bridges That Burn*, is having serious problems in rehearsal. Remnants of his hashtag diva life?

The musical is set in modern-day Ohio where the town of Rutherford needs to save its water supply from an evil corporation. The cast is only fifteen people, and each of them play several roles: the mayor, the gym teacher, the grocery store owner, with the exception of three. The aptly named River (Simone Baxter) is the scientist who is going to save the day.

Mateo plays Cole, the love interest, naturally, who has been in love with Amelia his whole life. Amelia is the mayor's daughter who turns on her father and finally admits she loves Cole too at the end of Act One. She is played by the powerhouse Broadway star Jazzy Summers. And of course River, with Amelia and Cole's help, saves the town. This blogger saw the show in Seattle and loved it.

But Jazzy and Mateo? Not so much! See below for some photos of the two of them having a tiff on the street. Such little hooligans! We don't know what they were saying, but they are undeniably having some strong words. Here's hoping this production isn't brought down by Mateo's ego!

Keith finished reading aloud and looked up at them. In front of Keith's desk, Mateo sat with his hands folded in his lap, his head down. Jazzy stood behind him, against the wall next to the door, jaw tensely set and hands fisted.

"This isn't good, kids."

Jazzy chewed the inside of her cheek.

"I'm really sorry, Keith." Mateo looked up at Keith as Jazzy shot daggers at the back of his head.

"Me too," she said contritely.

"Jazzy, take a seat." Keith gestured to the chair next to Mateo, which she reluctantly slumped into. She'd never been in trouble like this before. Her fury at Mateo was as yet unmatched today.

"Now, listen. First off, we can fix this. Secondly, I need you to tell me if there is anything sensitive here that we need to discuss. Anything personal."

Jazzy and Mateo stared, stone faced.

Keith sighed, clearly not fooled. "Anything that could spark a rumor like this."

Jazzy shook her head, hands clenched on her lap.

Mateo looked over at her.

Keith raised an eyebrow in Mateo's direction then looked to Jazzy.

She threw her hands up in frustration then crossed her arms. "There's nothing. I got frustrated that he's not prepared."

"And I think she's not giving *me* the room to rehearse. Which is what we're doing. Rehearsing." The last word came out in a hiss.

Jazzy started to respond when Keith held up his hand. Her mouth snapped shut.

"Okay. Okay. So this is all just work stuff. No personal issues?"

Mateo blew out a breath.

"If there *were* any personal issues, we've decided that there aren't," Jazzy said, and crossed one leg over the other. "We're friends. Friendly, at least. And for the record, I like working with him, when he's on top of it."

Mateo nodded. "Ditto. I agree."

"Really?" Keith was skeptical and had a right to be.

"Really." Mateo, seeming resigned, crossed his heart. "Really."

Jazzy nodded.

Keith seemed to decide to trust them, even though it was clear he knew they were full of shit. He scheduled a takeover of the *Bridges That Burn* Instagram and TikTok accounts. The two of them would manage the feeds for a whole day in the next week, and Keith would hype it up until then. Jazzy groaned, but Mateo seemed excited. He'd never really used social media before.

"This is a fake-it-til-you-make-it situation, okay? You post videos of you going about your day. What you're rehearsing, but make it goofy, too. Down-to-earth. Friendly. Understood?"

Mateo nodded and stood. Jazzy followed his lead. "Thank you, Keith. No more fighting on the street. Promise."

"Good. Now get outta here. Go put on a play." He smiled at them both, but there was a warning in his eyes. They picked up their bags and left the office.

Mateo didn't say a word and Jazzy wouldn't give him the satisfaction as they walked toward reception. They said goodbye to Andrea and took the elevator downstairs, silent the whole way, staring up at the ceiling or down at the floor, but definitely not at each other.

At the door to 43$^{rd}$ Street, Mateo stopped suddenly before the revolving door. He turned to her, took a very deep breath, and stuck out his hand.

Jazzy regarded him for a moment, the hopeful smile playing on his lips, the light in his eyes. She couldn't help a tiny grin from tugging at the corners of her mouth.

Fine. A new start.

She took his hand and shook it, ignoring the sparkles that lit up inside her as his full Mateo grin beamed out at her.

§

"Not bad, huh?" Mateo was crouched on the floor over their pile of stuff that had somehow jumbled together over the rehearsal day. He shoved his binder in his shoulder bag, smiling up at Jazzy.

She knelt down and stowed her binder away, too. Though they hadn't really talked, it seemed to Jazzy that they both had come to a tacit understanding: they were a team. "Not at all bad."

Mateo had made it through the rest of the week calling line only a few times, and only forgetting an entrance twice. Jazzy was pretty proud, and they'd both happily endured the good-natured teasing of their castmates about the *OMGCeleb* article.

"What are we doing this weekend, kids?" Simone had pulled on a black jersey dress, paired with sky-high blue sandals. "Wanna get a drink?"

Jazzy stood and slung her bag over her shoulder. "I could be up to hang later this weekend. But I'm just going to relax tonight."

"Done. Sunday, picnic in Central Park." Simone gave Jazzy no choice, which was fine by her. She turned to Mateo, grinning wide. "What about you, handsome? Drinks? Carson and Parker and a bunch of others are coming."

Mateo returned her smile. "Not tonight, thanks. I gotta get home." He glanced at his phone. "Oh man, yeah, I gotta go. See y'all Monday!" Mateo called as he hurried out of the studio.

"You two aren't fucking are you?" Simone asked in a low, conspiratorial voice.

"Simone!" Jazzy was only slightly offended and laughed. "No!"

Simone stared after Mateo. "Okay, but you want to, right?"

"Oh my god." Jazzy felt a blush creep up her cheeks all the way to her hairline.

"Oh, you *do*. I am *here* for it. Has he said anything? Have you said anything? Has anything happened?" Simone was chattering like an overexcited squirrel. "Wait a minute, we haven't really talked since the party. You're avoiding me. Something happened. Tell me. Now."

Jazzy was thankfully saved from answering by Jason, who was waiting in the doorway at the studio entrance. His well-muscled arms were, as always, on full display in his tank top. "Simone! You coming?"

Jazzy tilted her head. "I thought Jason was hooking up with Parker."

Simone waved a dismissive hand. "Oh please, that was last week."

Jazzy pursed her lips. "You know, no one ever talks about how slutty theater people are." She draped her arm through Simone's and they made their way to the door.

"Good. Drama clubs the country over would be overrun with wannabes if we did." They laughed all the way to the subway.

§

"Hi, Patti," Jazzy said as she closed and locked her apartment door and slipped off her sandals. She looked forward to her routine of making a meal and going over her script with all the notes she'd made that week. The cat hopped off the bed and Jazzy scooped her up and kissed her neck. "Did you have a good day? I missed you. Did you miss me?"

Patti responded by jumping free and walking over to her food bowl, where she sat and stared.

"Message received." After feeding the cat, she went over to her bag to retrieve her binder and begin her routine. "Well, shit."

The binder wasn't hers. Instead of her neat, color-coded and highlighted notes, Mateo's ridiculous scrawl went all through it. "No wonder he can't keep anything straight." She flipped to the front of the binder where the contact sheet was and found Mateo's address.

"Oh wow, Patti. Mateo's our neighbor. Did we know that?"

Patti blinked at her.

Jazzy looked out the window in the direction of Mateo's building, wondering if they'd ever talked about it. "Hm. Maybe not. Or he didn't want me to share his fancy car." She pushed that thought away. Mateo would have absolutely offered her a ride if he'd known.

"I'll be right back, okay?" Patti, who hadn't moved from her food dish the whole time, merely flicked her tail.

Jazzy rolled her eyes and slipped on her sandals again.

The building on 86th Street was very *nouveau riche*, all marbled floors and muted colors. Ferns and new money.

175

Fancy. That's the only word Jazzy had for it. With the binder under her arm, she walked through the door the uniformed doorman held for her and approached the security desk.

"Hello, I need to see Mateo Williams? I have something of his."

The no-nonsense woman behind the desk, whose name tag read 'Susan', smirked. "Sure you do, love. Mr. Williams doesn't see unexpected guests."

"Oh, of course. He's got stalkers, I bet."

Susan pursed her lips in response.

"I'm not one, I promise. I guess I could have texted him. My name is Jazzy Summers; I'm doing a show with Mateo. I play Amelia. In *Bridges That Burn*? It's a new musical."

Susan's face remained stoic.

"He plays Cole. He's getting really good. Look, see?"

Susan's expression hadn't changed so Jazzy opened the binder to the front where the contact sheet was. She pointed to Mateo's name and her own. Susan took a cursory look, then looked a little closer.

Jazzy plucked her ID from her bag and handed it over.

Susan took a hard look at it and seemed satisfied. "I'm sorry about that. You know how it is." She shrugged. "Pop stars."

"Of course. Good lookin' out." Jazzy winked.

Susan picked up the phone. "You said your name was . . . "

Susan had needed a key card in order to press the button for floor thirty-five, once Mateo had approved her entrance. When Jazzy stepped out of the elevator, she gasped at the most magnificent apartment she had ever seen

Stretching before her was an immense great room. To her left, a gigantic gray sectional sofa was facing the wall where a television the size of a movie screen was mounted. In front of her, four low, modern club chairs sat in a circle surrounding a cement coffee table on which a bowl of fresh lilies sat. On the wall opposite the sofa hung several framed gold records surrounded by various plaques and awards. A grand piano, its surface polished black, stood on a raised platform in front of the wall. Several guitars sat on a stand next to it.

Beyond the living area, a long driftwood dining table surrounded by plush white chairs sat in front of floor to ceiling windows. It was the best view of Manhattan that Jazzy had ever seen. A hallway led off to the left of the dining table. Opening up to the right was a gigantic, restaurant-grade kitchen. The cabinets were a soft dove gray, the giant island was made of white marble, and the stainless-steel appliances gleamed. Another hallway led off to the right of this great living space. Jazzy presumed more grand rooms were waiting just beyond.

She stood near the edge of the sectional, a bit dazed.

"Hey, Jazz. What are you doing here?" Mateo was coming out of the kitchen, wiping his hands on a dish towel and looking extremely pleased to see her. "Welcome."

"Are you kidding me with this place?" Jazzy was absolutely starstruck.

Mateo smiled. "Is that a compliment?"

"I'm not entirely sure." Jazzy shook herself physically and held out the binder. "I suppose you haven't yet opened your bag. But we got our binders switched."

Mateo's expression seemed to falter for a second, some kind of hope dropping out of his eyes. "Ah, she's all business. Of course. Come on in."

Jazzy followed him through the vast living room, unable to tear her eyes from the floor-to-ceiling windows. The kitchen seemed larger than her entire apartment. Something was simmering on the stove and she sniffed the delicious aroma.

Mateo smiled and tweaked her nose. "My Uncle Gus' *asopao de pollo*. He died before my mom had me and left his secret recipe book to her. Best you'll ever have off the island." He tossed the dish towel down and reached into his bag on one of the cushy stools circled around the vast island. He flipped through the binder. "Yep, this is definitely yours. Color coded Post-its?" He held it out to her, his eyes dancing with humor.

"And yours is the barely discernible scribble, right?" Jazzy teased back. They switched. Jazzy flipped through her binder, making sure nothing was out of place, when she felt Mateo's eyes on her.

He leaned back against the counter of the island, his arms crossed and his vibe a little intense. He was staring at her in a way that made her feel nude. Like he truly saw every part of her. She closed the binder and almost took a step closer to him.

His eyes squinted and he sucked his teeth. Then, "Jazzy, I've never really done this with anyone. But would you like a tour?"

She set her binder on the counter, desperate to see the rest of this palace. "Are you kidding? I would love one. Yes, please."

Mateo first took her to the wing off the kitchen where he showed her his private recording studio ("You can use it anytime you want."), his movie theater ("Couldn't help myself."), and a library. ("I read a lot. Mostly fiction and biographies. Don't look so *surprised*.")

The wing off the dining area was more domestic. His bedroom was enormous and had an inviting king-sized bed facing a gigantic TV. A desk sat next to the windows with stacks of paper and what seemed like Mateo's trademark disorganization. Directly in front of the floor to ceiling windows was a gray couch and blue coffee table, littered with a few mugs with tea bags still in them. His furniture was all deep grays and blues, and the whole room had a calming effect. It seemed like a haven for him.

Mateo guided her down the hall where there were several just-as-impeccably decorated guest bedrooms and bathrooms. Jazzy had been in plenty of fancy New

York apartments, but this penthouse took the cake. What kind of place has *wings*?

Finally, after showing her the door to the rooftop deck, they reached the end of the hall where Mateo paused at the door. He tapped his index finger on the doorknob lightly, avoiding her gaze, seeming to decide something.

Jazzy stood behind him, a bit confused.

He turned to her, his expression soft, and he asked in a low voice, "Would you like to meet my mother?"

"Your moth—" Jazzy was startled. He couldn't live with his mother. She'd disappeared years ago, after he fired her. What? "Of . . . of course I would."

Smiling softly, Mateo motioned her forward and opened the door. This room was no different from the others, filled with windows and light. Twilight had turned the sky outside a rosy purple. A plush white carpet whispered beneath Jazzy's feet as she moved inside and took in what she was seeing. A wall lined with bookshelves filled to the brim, an entertainment center on another wall, holding lovely little knick-knacks and three shelves of VHS tapes. A pleasant sitting area faced one of the windows.

And in the middle of it all, a hospital bed. It looked to be state of the art, and very plush, but a hospital bed nonetheless. Next to the bed was a cushy beige armchair with a blanket folded neatly on the seat.

Tucked lovingly under the covers on the bed was a diminutive woman whose eyes were closed and whose face was peaceful as machines beeped by her bedside.

Mateo nodded to the nurse in blue scrubs who Jazzy hadn't noticed standing near the door to a private bathroom. She was the same red-haired woman he had brought to the coffee shop. "*Gracias*, Judith. This is my friend Jazzy. See you tomorrow."

Judith pulled on a cardigan, a fleeting look of confusion on her face before she smiled at Jazzy. "Nice to meet you. Goodnight, Mateo." She glanced at the machines quickly before patting Mateo's shoulder and leaving the room.

Mateo put his hand on the small of Jazzy's back and guided her toward the bed. "Jazzy, this is my mother, Marisol."

# Fourteen ♫

"It's dementia." Mateo stood next to the bed, where his hand brushed against Jazzy's. With his other hand, he took Marisol's.

Marisol's hand was so small that Jazzy couldn't see it underneath his. She flashed back to the photos of Mateo's mother that she had found in her research. The tiny, vivacious firecracker had been with him every step of the way, until she started saying outlandish things and he'd seemingly fired her. It was hard to believe the woman who'd dyed her hair orange for an album release party was the same one shrinking in this posh hospital bed.

When Jazzy glanced at Mateo, she saw his face was crumpled in pain. "Oh, Mateo." She put her arm around him and squeezed.

He turned and wrapped his arms around her, pulling her head to rest against his shoulder.

She fit perfectly into the crook of his neck.

They stood that way for a long while. Jazzy stroked his back as she felt his chest shudder. She let him be, let him cry, as she tried to process the situation.

He'd been all alone.

Eventually Mateo stepped back. He pulled up his t-shirt and swiped it down his face. "Sorry about that. Didn't see that coming. You're the only person I've ever—"

Jazzy just picked up his hand. "Stop apologizing to me. I'm here."

Mateo nudged her forward to the bed again. "*Mami*, hi. It was a pretty good day today. I remembered all my lines." He nudged Jazzy, his mouth upturned in a small grin.

Jazzy chuckled. The machine beeped on.

"This is *mi amiga*, Jazzy Summers. I think you'll really like her. She's strong and opinionated, just like you."

In a gentle tone, Jazzy said, "It's nice to meet you, Ms. Williams."

Marisol didn't stir. Mateo took a seat gently at the end of the bed and gestured for Jazzy to sit in the armchair. He took his mother's hand again and gazed at her, his expression naked with devotion. "Judith said she had a good day. The day nurse. She was a little lucid this morning but has been sleeping the rest of the day."

Jazzy was unsure how to deal with any of this, so she thought it would be best just to listen.

"That's why I have to keep running home. Why I'm sometimes late. There have been a bunch of doctors in and out, new diagnoses . . . Things have gotten more complicated." He took a shuddering breath. "I figured it was time that you knew, so you showing up here tonight was good timing."

Jazzy turned her gaze toward Marisol. "I'm feeling a little stunned."

"I'm sure." Mateo gazed into her eyes when she looked over to him. "I'm sorry I didn't tell you about my mom. I should have."

"It's all right. Really. I'm sorry I've been such an asshole."

Mateo laughed out loud. "Not an asshole. I withheld pretty pertinent information. That's on me."

"*¡Hola, Mateo!*" The cheery words came from down the hall.

"*Hola, Julissa. Nosotros estamos en el dormitorio. ¿Como estas?*"

"*Bien, bien. ¿Como esta Marisol?*" A short brunette in pink scrubs bustled into the room. She stopped short when she noticed Jazzy. "Oh, hello."

"Hello." Jazzy tried to smile but was feeling outside of herself. So much information was swimming in her head.

"This is my friend Jazzy, Julissa. Julissa is our night nurse, Jazzy. She's an angel on earth."

Julissa seemed to unfreeze. "Oh hush, you. He's such a flirt, isn't he?"

Jazzy snickered, remembering meeting Mateo in the coffee shop for the first time. "That's for sure."

"Why don't you two get out of here so I can check on Ms. Marisol, *sí*?" Julissa began fussing with something on the monitor.

Mateo stood and helped Jazzy get to her feet. "Are you hungry? I made a ton of *asopao*."

Jazzy thought of the meal kit in her refrigerator, her lovely nightly routine . . . of this new and deep information. "Um, I think I should get going soon."

"Oh, okay." Mateo's face fell and he turned to walk out of the room.

"But I wouldn't say no to a cookie."

Mateo's smile lit up his face when he turned and pointed at her. "She's got a sweet tooth. Good, so do I. I'm gonna hit the bathroom. Meet you in the kitchen." He loped off down the hall.

Jazzy turned away from the bed. "Nice to meet you, Julissa."

"We don't get many visitors." Julissa gave Jazzy an appraising look. "That boy. He won't leave her side, you know. He sits in that chair every night, playing old videos for her, reading to her, and telling her about his day. He's the most devoted son on earth."

"That doesn't surprise me." They exchanged knowing smiles, and then Jazzy made her way back to the kitchen.

§

"It was so weird. That whole year when I was fucking up? So was she. Saying weird shit to the press, acting out on my tour, a complete one-eighty from who she'd been. She was always professional and calm, and all of the sudden, it was like we were in a competition to see who could be wilder."

Jazzy broke off a piece of her cookie and ate it, nodding along as Mateo continued his story. He had warmed the cookies in the microwave and the chocolate chips were melty and delicious.

His story had poured out of him quickly, like a river after a storm, unstoppable once he started. He'd obviously had no one to talk to all these years.

Jazzy's heart broke a little for him as he went on.

"Then one day, she got lost in the neighborhood. I was totally frantic because she'd never just disappeared. We had just bought this place to be bicoastal." Mateo rolled his eyes. "And then I found her purse and phone in her room and got really worried. I was about to call the police when I had this idea that maybe she'd gone up to Inwood, to our old place. So I drove like a bat out of hell and it was like a miracle. I found her in front of our old building and she asked me if I wanted to go in and watch a movie, but she couldn't find her keys. Couldn't get into the building."

"God, Mateo, that must have been so scary."

"It was."

"I can't even imagine." Jazzy wanted to comfort him with a touch, but the weight of all of his grief stopped her. She felt completely out of her depth.

"I called my team and cancelled everything to get her to a doctor. They did about a billion tests and it was conclusive. Early onset frontotemporal dementia. All the signs were there, you know? Saying nutty shit, the mood swings, forgetting words. And now this. So I set her up here and she pretty much stayed in this place. And I went a little nuts."

"The partying."

"Yeah. And Ariel. God, that was a mess. It started to get pretty bad, with the press and the idiotic choices I was making. Most days, Mom was completely lucid but knew she should stay in. She had started forgetting so much *so* quickly. So when I broke off the 'engagement'— biggest air quotes ever—I decided to make this place a palace and I . . . " Mateo paused, his eyes fixed on something faraway.

"You disappeared."

"Yeah." He finished his cookie.

"Why didn't you tell anyone? Or say anything?"

187

Mateo shrugged, and then looked into her eyes. "She was adamant that nobody know. She didn't want anyone to think she was weak, and begged me to keep it quiet. And I— I just felt like it was nobody's business. We don't have any family, and my entourage—" He spoke the word with disdain. "—were all fake anyway. I didn't have anyone real around. No one but her. So I respected her wishes. I didn't say a word. It just became a habit after that. To keep her secret."

"I'm so sorry, Mateo."

He gave her a small smile. "Thank you. It feels good to tell someone."

So it hadn't been his work ethic after all. All this time, he had just been a worried son.

"This year, in January . . . " His voice broke a little. "She had a stroke. She'd been—" A deep shuddering breath.

"She'd been on the decline for a little while. And the stroke made things much worse."

Jazzy let him have a moment, her heart aching for him.

He let out another shaky breath. "But before that? She told me to find my bliss. To start getting out of the house. And my first love had always been theater. So her doctors, her nurses, my therapist, everyone encouraged me to pursue it—"

"You have a therapist?" Jazzy couldn't keep the surprise out of her voice.

Mateo chuckled. "Yeah, of course, don't you?"

"No. Should I?"

"Child star? Workaholic? You might look into it."
Mateo was teasing her, clearly needing a moment of
levity. He swiped the last bite of her cookie.

"Hey! My cookie." Jazzy feigned a pout.

He just grinned, his sunny disposition showing and
hiding as he spoke about his mom.

She couldn't stop herself from grinning back, happy
to see him smile. She plucked another cookie off the
platter and broke off a piece. "So you've just been in this
palace for ten years with your mom?"

"We went to Sweden for a while a few years back for
some experimental treatment. And I go out for coffee
sometimes obviously. And the occasional show. But
basically, yeah." Mateo's mood abruptly changed again.
His eyes fixed on the counter and he went very still.

They were sitting at the corner of the island in the
white expanse of the kitchen. Jazzy finally gave in to her
impulse and put a hand on Mateo's knee. "What is it?"

Mateo raised his eyes to the ceiling. "She doesn't have
long, Jazzy. I've been trying to deny it, but—"

"Oh, love," Jazzy breathed. She immediately stepped
down from the stool and wrapped her arms around him,
drawing him close.

He buried his face in her neck, and she held him fast
and stroked his back. They stayed that way, breathing in
sync, until Mateo's heart rate slowed a bit and she felt his
grip slacken.

He pulled back and placed his forehead against hers. "I've been lucky to get ten years."

Jazzy nodded slightly.

"Thank you for being here. Thank you for listening."

She was at a loss for words again. "I'm so sorry you've been alone for so long with all of this. I'm honored to be your friend. To be here for you."

"Right." Mateo sat back a bit, his gaze meeting hers, a hint of fire back behind his eyes. "Friend."

She couldn't resist looking at his lips.

*Bad idea bad idea bad idea.*

Mateo seemed to be thinking the same thing. He stilled for a moment, obviously letting her take the lead. And she wanted nothing more than to kiss him, to stay, to talk to him for hours, to hold his hand and comfort him. She saw him clearly now, saw the kind, loyal man beneath all the gossip.

But Jazzy Summers didn't do showmances. And she was much too close to breaking her own rule. Before she gave in to herself, she said, "I should go. Let you have your time with Marisol."

"Right," Mateo whispered as he nodded. He let his hands fall from her waist.

She slowly backed away and picked up her script from the counter. After stowing it in her bag, she followed Mateo to the elevator. "Have a good night. I'll see you Monday."

He pressed the call button and turned to her, his gaze lingering on her face. He didn't say a word but reached out and caressed her cheek with a featherlight touch. He took a deep breath, searching her eyes. His lips were parted.

Jazzy's heartbeat sped up. She nearly stepped toward him.

The elevator dinged open. She jumped, startled, back to reality. "Goodnight, Mateo." She stepped onto the elevator.

Before the doors closed, Mateo spoke again. "Please don't tell anyone about my mom?"

She nodded and made a *my lips are sealed* motion.

How one person could wear their many emotions so nakedly, she didn't know. But she didn't think she would ever forget the grateful, sad, hopeful look on his face.

# Fifteen ♫

"So he is taking forever to get the condom from the bathroom, right? And I'm like, what could he possibly be doing? So I go knock, and I kid you not, Jazz, he was jerking off before we even started hooking up! While I'm in his apartment! He claimed it was because he'd be too fast, and I'm just like, right, I could have helped. And clearly he wouldn't have been too fast because he'd been gone for fifteen minutes! I put my clothes on and left because that is just too weird."

Jazzy lolled against the soft blanket, laughing. She and Simone were in the middle of Central Park near the duck pond, having their promised picnic and swapping embarrassing dating stories. Jazzy didn't have too many to contribute as she rarely dated, but Simone had enough for both of them.

She was still reeling from Friday evening. She'd spent the whole of Saturday in a daze, trying to meld this new Mateo with the one she had been so wrong about, and trying to forget his lips.

Which she couldn't.

"Excuse me young lady, focus! I'm giving you my best stuff here." Simone snapped her fingers at Jazzy.

"Sorry, sorry!" Jazzy shook her head and took another sip from her seltzer. "I'm here. Tell me . . . Tell me about your ex."

"Oof."

"Only if you want to, of course."

Simone toyed with the hem of her sundress, deep in thought. She pulled it off and laid back on the blanket. Her eyes were hidden behind her big sunglasses. "Mathieu."

She'd put a little bit of a French accent behind his name. Jazzy drew her knees up to her chest. "Big love?"

"Big, big love." Simone sighed. "Five years. He'd been with me through all of it. My career, my mom beating cancer, my nieces and nephew being born." She paused. "It was a big love with a small ending. He needed to go back to France. I couldn't follow him."

Jazzy placed her hand on Simone's and squeezed. "Do you think he'll come back?"

"I can't think that. Or I won't live. So, no. It was a beautiful thing we had. But we can't get that back."

"I'm sorry."

"Thank you."

Silence fell for a bit. Music played from a nearby Bluetooth speaker. Dogs barked and children laughed. Bicycle bells rang and an ice cream vendor shouted. Summer in New York. Jazzy wasn't really seeing any of it, though. She was thinking about big, big love.

"I'm not sure I'm ready for a rebound, but Jason in those jeans—"

Simone sat up on her elbows, clearly seeing that Jazzy was not paying attention.

"Lady, are you going to be present with me or are you going to keep daydreaming about Mateo?"

Jazzy snapped her attention back to Simone who was giving her a look between amusement and exasperation. "I'm not daydreaming about Mateo."

"Okay, sure. What were you thinking about then?"

Jazzy just took another drink.

Simone chuckled. "He loves you, you know."

"Oh, please." It was Jazzy's turn to roll her eyes. "He barely knows me."

"What happened on the boat, Jazzy." Good lord, this woman could be commanding.

"Nothing happened on the boat, Simone."

"Liar."

"Nosy."

"Aha! So something did happen." She propped herself up on one elbow, looking like a panther ready to pounce.

Jazzy glanced sideways, wondering how much to give. Obviously, she wouldn't betray Mateo's trust, but having someone to help sort through her feelings would be helpful. "This stays between us?"

Simone shot up and sat at attention. "Pinky swear."

Jazzy linked her pinky with Simone's and told her everything about the Fourth of July party, including the fight afterward leading to the gossip column and the PR strategy.

Simone's mouth hung open. "Okay, number one? I told you so."

Jazzy gave a surprised laugh and let her have that one.

"Number two, what do you feel?"

"What does that matter?" Jazzy flashed back to the kiss that almost was in Mateo's swanky penthouse. "It's not going to happen. I don't do showmances. And I don't do co-stars. And he's all hot and cold, too. Like there was the moment—the *moment*—we had on the boat and then it was over in an instant. Like he flipped a switch." She snapped her fingers.

"Maybe to you. But the rest of us see the way he looks at you, girl, and *wooooeeee!* The heat."

Jazzy rolled her eyes. "Okay, calm down."

"All right. How about this. How do you actually feel about him?" Simone tipped her face up to the sun.

Jazzy slipped her sundress off, revealing her black, fifties-inspired two-piece suit, and joined Simone in lying back. "I like him."

"Are you attracted to him?"

"Aren't *you*?"

Simone laughed. "Okay, wrong question. Are you attracted to him outside of the physical realm? Are you drawn to him? Can you feel his presence in the room even when you can't see him?"

"That's deep." Jazzy turned to face Simone and pulled her sunglasses down so she could look into her eyes.

Simone looked right back at her. "I have many layers. Answer me."

Jazzy grunted, not used to laying herself so bare. "Okay, yes. I am drawn to him, I have been since I met him. He seems to . . . to know me somehow. But I also really really hate him sometimes. He's the most frustrating man I've ever known. And of course I can feel him when he's around. He's Mateo Williams. Can't you?"

"No, babe. That's all you." Simone sat up again, taking a generous swig of her seltzer. "I think you're falling for each oth— Don't you roll your eyes at me!"

"I am wearing sunglasses." Her voice was a dry as a desert.

"Mhm. Did you roll your eyes?"

"Shut up." Jazzy flung her arms over her face.

"I think you both have it bad and I think if you don't do anything about it soon, something is going to happen that you haven't thought through. And if I have learned anything about you, an unplanned something big happening will send you spinning."

Jazzy groaned her assent. "Nothing is going to happen though. Showmances. Don't do 'em. And he's—" She searched for a negative to Mateo's personality. "—annoying."

"You don't actually believe that." Simone finished her seltzer and cracked another.

"Yes I *do*."

"I like when you're petulant because it means I'm right."

Jazzy sat up quickly and glared at Simone, before finishing her own seltzer.

Simone just laughed at the look on her face and tossed her another can.

"Can we talk about your love life now?" The *crack fizz* of the can opening was starting to sound like summer.

The best thing about Simone was that she knew when to stop pushing. "A long and storied history. Settle in, babe. When I was on tour in Ohio, we were at this seedy little bar . . . "

§

Monday, the day after the picnic, Jazzy left the studio late after talking with Sasha about a scene. Mateo had been a gem all day. He was getting better, though still having to call line, but she could see improvements. And now that she knew why he was the way he was, she found it easier to give him grace. And the whole cast could sense the shift. They were coming together in a cohesive unit, anticipating each other's needs and laughing on breaks. Work was very, very good.

On her way to the elevator, she walked by another studio that should have been empty, but the lights were on. Mateo's voice drifted out through the partly open door, and she couldn't help herself. She peeked inside.

Mateo stood in front of his binder on the floor, watching himself in the mirror as he ran his lines. Jazzy watched him for a few moments, her heart full at the sight of him. She knew he was taking precious time away from home to get this right.

The next day, Jazzy and Mateo were coached on their Instagram and TikTok takeover, which Keith had been hyping on the *Bridges That Burn* feeds. They met with him in the morning while the ensemble rehearsed and he gave them a quick tutorial, sent them some promo graphics and some ideas of what to post. It was pretty simple in the end: film each other and the cast throughout the day and make it seem like they were best friends. They were instructed to post about the *Bridges That Burn* takeover on their personal accounts. Mateo had finally set up his own and had already amassed over one million followers. Jazzy thought her five hundred thousand were pretty good, but she'd built that up over years.

Mateo was definitely going to sell tickets.

"Hey, good morning, y'all, it's me, Mateo, and this is Jazzy. We're taking over *Bridges That Burn*'s Insta, and we are ready to show you how we put on a show!" Mateo's arm was slung over Jazzy's shoulder and they both smiled up into the camera on his phone in selfie mode.

"That's right, follow the *Bridges That Burn* account and watch our stories all day as we document what it's like to bring a Broadway show to life."

"See you soon!" they said in unison.

Smiling at her, Mateo sent Jazzy the video. They both posted it to their personal Instagrams, then spent the day having a blast and filming it as proof that they were friends. Some videos they sent to Keith to edit and put on TikTok, but mostly, it was just the two of them posting to the show's Instagram stories.

Jazzy had thought it would be a chore to document so much, but it ended up being incredibly fun. Mateo seemed to already have a knack for knowing exactly the kinds of things that would get engagement. He caught Simone in one of her struts across the stage and knew exactly what stickers to apply to the video. Carson and Blane performed their lift for him so he could make it a GIF.

Everyone in the room had given permission to be documented, so while Mateo filmed, Jazzy grabbed a fedora from Jason's pile of stuff. "Keep it, Jazzy. No man should be wearing a fedora!" Simone had called. Jason had thrown an apple slice at her.

With the offending hat on her head, she put on an intrepid reporter character, interviewing various cast and crew about their jobs.

Mateo couldn't stop laughing at her deep Very Serious Reporter voice.

By the end of the day, the scenes they'd rehearsed had gone well, the *Bridges That Burn* Instagram following had grown by thousands, and Jazzy and Mateo had done their job.

Perhaps a little too well.

After being dismissed from rehearsal, they were in front of the building again for their good night video. Mateo had his arms over her shoulders as she stood in front of him. He held the phone out as they said good night, and then, smiling hugely after such a successful day, he kissed her on the cheek, lingering just for a moment.

Jazzy closed her eyes and nestled back into his chest, then turned her head and looked at him. He put his forehead onto hers and they smiled.

And then they broke the internet. The hashtag theaterkid internet, anyway.

WE SHIP JAZZTEO

Either one of them could punch me in the face and I would thank them

Name a more iconic couple, I dare you

How do I get them to adopt me?

I hate how much I love them lol

Jazzy scrolled her mentions on Twitter that Friday evening at home, confronted again and again with a GIF of Mateo kissing her cheek and her closing her eyes like it was the best thing that had ever happened to her. The week had ended with her and Mateo being the talk of Broadway social media.

They had been "shipped", as the kids say. The Broadway fandom, and its many factions, wanted them to be in a relationship.

And that was going to sell tickets, so Jazzy decided to ignore it. Because she and Mateo had decided that they were just friends. And there would be no more kissing. No matter how many times Jazzy thought about it as she fell asleep.

A text came through.

Hey, shipmate, wanna come run lines with me tomorrow? I'll make brunch.

Jazzy chuckled, glad that Mateo found their "shipping" just as absurd as she did. And Sasha had laid down the gauntlet that afternoon at rehearsal. No more calling "line!" They were really for real off-book now.

The show had begun to take its final shape. Until previews and audiences reactions were gauged, of course.

Chocolate chip pancakes?

Okay, sweet tooth. See you at eleven.

§

Jazzy, completely satisfied, patted her belly. Mateo's pancakes were fluffy and golden and she'd eaten five. He seemed very flattered as he removed their dishes and began to clean up. "Where did you learn to cook like this?"

Mateo had his back to her at the sink. "Ten years of being here alone. Had to do something. We have a chef who's taught me a lot."

Jazzy felt the pancakes turn to lead in her belly. "Oh. Right."

"Oh, man. That was supposed to be a joke." He turned to her, his hands wet, and gave her that huge grin of his as he dried them on a dish towel.

"No, yeah, super funny. Good one." Jazzy's voice was sarcastic but her stomach lightened.

"Hey, if you can't laugh at how stupid life is, what can you laugh at? I mean, come on. My mom moved to this city, got herself through college, raised me alone, found out I had a talent, I was somehow seen by the right people at the right time in pop music history, I was huge and I was everywhere and I became a fuckin' millionaire, and then I was gone because I partied too hard while that same powerhouse of a mom got dementia at sixty? How is that not laughable?" He shrugged, his smile wide.

"You really are a human ball of sunshine, aren't you?"

Mateo threw the towel on the island and crossed over to her. "It's laugh or cry. And crying is good sometimes. But I'd rather laugh. Come on." He held out his hand and she hopped off the stool, the sparkles igniting at his touch. She tried to tamp them down as she got her binder from her bag.

Mateo picked his up from the counter. "Do you mind if we do this in my mom's room? I'd like her to hear it since . . . You know. She won't be able to see it."

"Of course."

They settled into the seating area in front of the windows and ran through all their scenes together, then the ones that he had without Amelia. Judith had been in and out, monitoring Marisol every once in a while.

He was so close, almost there. Jazzy was glad for it and perhaps— Okay fine, she definitely could have been a little more sympathetic in the beginning. He was onstage with her almost the whole show and that is a lot to memorize. He was doing great.

A couple of hours later, Jazzy closed her binder. Mateo was looking out of the window at the magnificent view of the city. She could just see Central Park to the east, the Hudson to the left, and the sun shone on everything they could see.

He seemed contemplative so Jazzy let him think. She gazed out of the window, too.

"Do you have any idea how nervous I was at the audition?"

Jazzy looked over to him, the light of the afternoon sun doing wonders for his already perfect features. "You were? You seemed so easygoing."

Mateo sniffed. "Most nerve-wracking thing I have ever done in my life. When my agent told me I was reading with you, I was full of anxiety. I don't know if you know this, but I have admired you for so long."

"Really?" Jazzy sat forward, disbelieving.

His mouth dropped open. "You didn't know that?"

"Mateo . . . " There was a warning in her voice as she thought about the kiss. The heat of his hand on her cheek.

"No, not like that." He bit his lip, his gaze intent upon hers.

Great, now she wanted to nibble his lip, too. This was not the direction she could let the conversation go.

He seemed to feel the same way when he cleared his throat. "To be very clear, I mean, your work. Though it is nice. It's nice to have a friend. A close friend."

Jazzy nodded.

He sat forward. "So something you should know, as my close friend, is that Mateo Williams, pop star, really just wanted to be on Broadway."

"What?" Jazzy drew out the word, letting a smile sneak across her lips.

"I was your age when you were in *After All*. I saw it. Three times. And I thought if you could do it, so could I. I wanted to pursue the stage. But then I got the record deal. And I thought, well, maybe someday. And then someday came." He waved his binder at her. "This is a dream come true."

This was all verging on a Feelings Territory Jazzy didn't want to navigate. Best to deflect. "Good thing I didn't veto you, then."

Mateo threw his head back and laughed. "Yes, thanks for that."

"You really wanted to be on Broadway? I mean, you sang some of the best pop songs of the early 2000's, and there were *many*."

Mateo looked at her sideways for a moment. "Don't believe me? Come on." He stood and strode over to his mother's bedside, tucking the covers lovingly under her chin. "*Mami*, do you want to watch a video?"

From her chair at the window, Jazzy watched as he slid one of the VHS tapes out of its battered cover and inserted it into an ancient VCR. He flipped on the TV. She wandered over and took a seat in the chair next to Marisol. Tentatively, she reached for Marisol's hand and enclosed it in her own. Her skin was impossibly soft, her bones like a bird's.

Mateo sat gingerly down on the other side of the bed, his expression gentle as he took in Jazzy's hand in his mother's. "You ready?" He pressed play on the remote.

Static filled the screen, then Jazzy could see a darkened room and heard the unmistakable murmuring of an audience. As the picture focused, she could see what looked like an elementary school gym. The audience sat on folding chairs in front of a tiny stage. She guessed someone had put a camcorder at the back of the audience. The numbers "8 20 99" were stamped across the bottom of the screen.

"1999. I was seven. Just you wait."

The lights came up and a bunch of tiny kids in ill-fitting suits on a rudimentary train set began the opening scene to *The Music Man.*

"Oh my god," Jazzy breathed. "You were Harold Hill, weren't you?"

"You're the only person besides the people in that room who have ever seen this."

Jazzy was transfixed as the little kids performed "Rock Island." Marisol's fingers moved in her hand and she made a little noise. Jazzy startled and looked over at Mateo.

He was smiling softly at his mom. "She loves this video."

"Oh. Of course." Jazzy watched the kids on the screen, unable to keep her eyes off of the tiny Mateo. It was the most precious thing she'd ever seen. The play was a third-grade play, that was for sure, but Mateo shined. He was already a superstar, convincing the town of River City, Iowa that oh yes, they got trouble.

Jazzy was transfixed. "Look at you. You were born for this. Mateo—" She looked right into his eyes. "You were *born* for this."

His lips parted for a moment until a smile began to spread across his face.

"Mateo?" Judith called from the doorway. "Could I speak with you for a moment?"

"Sure." Mateo stood, his eyes on Jazzy. "You'll be okay?"

"Are you kidding? I want a copy of this."

He was chuckling on his way out of the room.

The little girl playing Marian was adorable. She had long, blonde braids and reminded Jazzy a little bit of herself, with a big voice for someone so small. As she began to sing "Goodnight, My Someone," Marisol's fingers tightened around Jazzy's and she made the humming noise again.

Jazzy placed her other hand over Marisol's. "This is one of my favorites, too." Gazing at Marisol's delicate face, she began to softly sing about the love she was waiting for, the one she knew was out there.

Marisol's fingers tightened and released on her hand, so she finished the song, surprised to find tears in her eyes.

There was a shuffling behind her. Jazzy turned to see Mateo leaning against the doorframe, his eyes shining. His smile was so sad, Jazzy's heart broke into a million pieces.

She stood and placed Marisol's hand down on the bed and patted it once. Turning, she picked up her binder and walked toward Mateo. With her free hand, she squeezed his fingers, hoping to convey how much she cared for him.

He squeezed back.

Jazzy rose up on her toes and pressed her lips to his cheek. Without another word, she walked to the penthouse elevator, knowing Mateo was watching her go.

She wiped away the tear running down her cheek, surprised at the sadness spreading through her. "Sweet dreams be yours," she whispered to Marisol as the elevator doors closed.

# Sixteen

On Monday Jazzy was standing stage left in the studio, waiting to make her entrance, chewing on her thumbnail. Mateo, after finishing a conversation with Drew and with a big smile on his face, loped over to stand next to her. Secretly, he hooked his pinky into hers.

"Thank you."

She squeezed his pinky with her own and then they dropped their hands. "Sorry I ran out of there."

"Don't be. Judith said that was really nice of you. To sing to my mom."

Jazzy gazed up into his dark brown eyes, to the depths of pain and sorrow she knew he must feel, despite his insistence on the laughter. "Anytime."

"Let's do this people, Act One, Scene One, go!" Sasha called.

Before their cue, Jazzy glanced down and noticed something. Mateo was binderless. He hadn't done a single scene without at least consulting it beforehand. She gazed down at his empty hands then, alarmed, up into his face.

An amused twinkle in his eye greeted her.

The pianist played the intro music and rehearsal began.

Mateo was utterly, completely magnificent. Brilliant. He knew every line, every cross, every dance. He moved through the room no longer the man who felt like a college freshman in a cast full of seniors. He was confident and full of life and passion, giving her everything she had been missing the whole rehearsal process. True partnership. Their kiss seared into Jazzy's bones when Amelia finally admitted her love for Cole and the act ended to great, uproarious applause.

The cast descended on Mateo, rubbing his head, pulling him into a group hug, slapping his back. They celebrated for a few moments before the planned cast meeting before lunch. Sasha spoke up.

"Mateo, I think we can all agree, that was absolutely magnificent."

Parker squeezed him in close and Carson kissed him on the cheek. Mateo blushed.

"I'm sorry it took me so long," he said.

Sasha couldn't seem to contain the grin bursting across her face. "I am very relieved because I had a very different speech planned before this morning's run through. So instead of that . . . Reid?"

The exhausted but pleased cast took a seat on the floor and various set pieces, draping themselves around each other.

Reid stood in front of them, slightly uncomfortable with the attention as always. "Okay, everyone. As you know, previews begin in a mere two and a half weeks."

Jazzy grimaced at Mateo, sure that he would share her sentiment, but he just smiled easily and leaned back on his hands, his legs crossed out in front of him.

"On Thursday, we'll have our sitzprobe—"

"Our what?" Mateo looked extremely confused.

Everyone chuckled a bit, even Reid.

"The first sing through with the orchestra." Reid went on. "Our set reveal is on Friday. Now, most of it did make it from Seattle, so it won't be too much of a surprise for most of you when we head into tech. We will do the filmed reveal for social media though. That being said, ticket sales are going very well. Keep the buzz up, because we've got one. Keith, anything to add?"

Keith nodded from his seat behind the table. "Posters are up and the marquee is in place. Keep pushing on your personal social media. Carson and Blane have a takeover this Wednesday, Jason, you'll be next Monday once we get into the Schubert. We have a few others scheduled as well. We'll be filming your commercial before the first preview, once we get through tech. And Broadway.com will be coming to the set on Friday for an interview with our stars." He smiled over at Jazzy and Mateo, who had been told this by their agents. They nodded in unison.

Reid continued. "On that note, next Monday, we'll be in tech." The cast groaned collectively, even Mateo, who had never been through a hellish tech week before. Not since he was seven, at least. "Your costumes should be ready to go, so we'll do a parade first thing, then jump into it. Please prepare yourselves for some long and frustrating days."

"Yay, that's my favorite part," Jazzy whispered to Mateo. She had loved her costume fittings and seeing what the designers had in mind for Amelia. She couldn't wait to see the finished product and walk onstage for the approval of the production staff.

"The long and frustrating days?"

"Ha, no. Getting into costume. I always really *feel* the character then, you know?"

Mateo gazed at her affectionately then turned his attention back to Reid.

Reid went on. "And then— You can go to lunch in a second, Carson. I see you."

Carson stopped dramatically miming that he was starving. Blane rolled his eyes at his boyfriend's antics.

"We will also let you know about the cast album recording. That is still in flux until the show is frozen." Reid paused to clear his throat and consult his notes. "Finally, we will be doing a backer's showcase once we're in the theater, that Friday." He held up a hand to silence the surprised gasps. "I know that's soon, but we've had a long rehearsal process. They understand that they will be seeing what is, essentially, a rough cut."

"Hey, rude," Simone spoke up jovially.

Everyone laughed, including Reid.

"I just mean you don't have to worry about being completely perfect. And then we have one more week of tech and dress rehearsals after that until our first previews begin. Then, August twentieth! Opening night!"

Everyone cheered, but Mateo had an apprehensive look on his face.

"Hey, wait a minute." Jazzy tilted her head to the side when they were dismissed. "Wasn't August twentieth—"

"Yep. The day I played Harold Hill. It was fate." Mateo stood and then reached out his hand to help Jazzy up. He held her gaze as a moment passed between them, his hand warm in hers. This thing between them, whatever it was, was real and lasting. And she was so very proud to be his partner.

"How'd you do it? Today?" Jazzy said quietly after a moment.

Mateo waved to a couple of the ensemble members leaving for lunch before shrugging and looking down at his shoes. "Something clicked. And I spent the weekend really studying instead of just curling into an anxiety ball, staring at my binder like it was going to bite me."

"Oh?"

His eyes suddenly lit up and met hers. "*You* clicked, Jazzy. When you said I was born for this? It clicked."

"Me . . . Oh . . . "

"Come on, let's get lunch. I'm starving."

§

Mateo continued to be brilliant for the rest of the week. His enthusiasm and performance were infectious. Acting with him was easy. It was the easiest thing in the world now that he knew his stuff. His voice soared above them, clear and bright, and blended with Jazzy's perfectly. The whole cast seemed to jell around the two of them, a cohesive unit.

Jazzy found herself anticipating each rehearsal with excitement as she sat next to Patti and drank her coffee every morning. Simone had made good on her promise to buy Jazzy something pretty all those weeks ago, even though Jazzy never admitted to feeling anything for Mateo. The French press made delicious coffee, so she hadn't needed to go to H&H very often. She enjoyed the routine of grinding the beans and pouring the water. It was a lovely ritual to start her morning.

She did miss chatting with Kara. The cheerful barista hadn't been in the last time she went. And regular coffee was not an almond milk latte with just the right amount of foam.

On the morning they were moving into the theater, she hastily put away the French press and walked over to the coffee shop.

"Oh my god, hi!" Kara seemed to bubble over with excitement.

Jazzy smiled widely, enjoying the scents of fresh bagels and rich coffee. "Hey, you. Where have you been?"

"I spent the month at my parent's place after the semester ended, but I'm back now. I'm so glad to see you, I've been *fully* dying over it all." Kara moved over to the cappuccino machine, knowing Jazzy's order already.

Jazzy put her elbows on the counter. "Fully dying over what all?"

"You and Mateo? You held out on me! I didn't know you were going to star on Broadway with him." She pulled a lever down and the machine made a noise like a freight train.

"I didn't know it at the time," Jazzy called over the racket.

"Didn't know what?"

She'd know that voice out of thousands. Jazzy turned to find Mateo right behind her, smiling brightly at Kara.

"Hi," he said in Kara's direction. Then to Jazzy again, "Didn't know what?"

She wasn't prepared to see his smile and it caught her by surprise how badly she wanted to hold him close and

215

let his lips find hers again. But of course, she didn't do showmances, so it didn't matter and she needed to get a grip. She stammered, "Didn't, uh, didn't know that after we met here we'd be working together."

"Ah, yes. That was fate, too, huh?" Mateo looked right at her, seemingly unable to look away.

"Guess so." Jazzy couldn't tear her eyes from his either. This really had to stop. .

"Here's your latte." Kara made a big show of putting the drink down and looked at Jazzy with a satisfied smile on her face.

Jazzy let a smile sneak over her lips and picked up her cup. "Mateo, what do you want? It's on me. Kara makes a mean almond milk latte."

Kara glowed, clearly smitten with Mateo's presence and Jazzy's praise.

"I'll take a full-fat, large, iced, caramel-spice latte, please. Thanks, Jazz." He winked at Kara, who seemed to vibrate with pleasure as she began to make his drink.

He pulled a face at Jazzy, who was taking a delicious sip of her coffee. "Hot coffee in the summer should be outlawed."

"Incorrect. Iced coffee should be outlawed completely."

"Oh wow." Mateo drew out the word, nodding and pretending to be insulted. "Wow, wow, wow. I see how it is."

"Coffee is a hot drink and this is the hill I will die on." She stuck her chin out in defiance.

Mateo chuckled, his grin widening as he continued to look into her eyes. "You know, with the sun on your face, your eyes are the lightest blue I've ever seen them."

*No showmances no showmances no showmances . . .*

Again, she found herself without words. Was it the air in this coffeeshop or what? Dammit.

"Here you go! Jazzy, that's $14.65." Grinning hugely, Kara looked from Mateo to Jazzy and back to Mateo.

Jazzy could read Kara's expression as she handed over her card. She shipped them, too. The difference was, she'd witnessed their connection in person and had every right to.

"Come on, my car's outside." Mateo tipped his latte in Kara's direction. "Thank you, Kara. We are grateful for your talent in the caffeine arts."

Kara bounced up and down a bit, giggling. "You're welcome."

Jazzy slipped a five into the tip jar.

§

Jazzy, Simone, and Mateo led their castmates through the ornate lobby of the Schubert Theater on 44th Street, what would now be their home. In front of them, a camera crew was filming their reactions to being in the space for the first time.

The hundred-year-old theater even smelled historical. Jazzy felt like she could hear the cast of *A Chorus Line* singing "One". She could feel the presence of

Bernadette Peters in *Gypsy*, her legendary voice crying out for "Rose's Turn".

As they walked forward, she turned to Simone, who had a reverential look on her face as they entered the theater's house. Green upholstered seating spread out before them. Jazzy looked behind her as they walked toward the stage. Two levels of balconies rose up steeply, and she gazed at the ornate mask designs that had been restored to their original glory in the nineties. The boxes on either side of the house boasted the same ornate decorations, and before her, the red curtain was closed.

Fifteen hundred seats. One of the largest houses on Broadway. Could they really sell this place out?

The camera crew stopped at the foot of the stage, lenses pointing in the cast's direction.

Jazzy looked excitedly to Simone and then to Mateo and grabbed both of their hands. Mateo grinned. Simone squeezed her hand.

The curtain opened with a swoosh and Jazzy gasped.

The stage was lit with purple and amber lighting. As they already knew, the set was rather abstract. Not quite all the way upstage, industrial piping and wooden platforms built in a circle climbed two stories high at various levels and degrees. Ladders and staircases connected them all, and Jazzy could already feel her quads protesting when she realized how much climbing they would be doing.

On a stage left platform, there was the mayor's office with a large fancy desk and leather chair, basically the villain's lair. Stage right boasted Cole's small apartment, a shabby twin bed and crates for a nightstand and dresser—every bit the poor college grad's first apartment. At the center of the circular set in the middle was River's science lab. Jazzy could see a computer and Bunsen burner surrounded by flasks she knew were made of plastic.

A great rumbling began underneath the stage and the cast all gasped in astonishment as the circular set turned one hundred and eighty degrees. On this side, there was a town hall, a corporate office, and Amelia's apartment. In front of the turntable, on runners, a mossy riverbed rolled in at stage right. Styrofoam boulders were painted realistically and the whole cast gasped as the water feature was turned on. The river actually babbled! Total theater magic. Then, rolling in on stage left, was a small classroom. The great set turned again and the lighting changed. Jazzy could see in her mind's eye how amazing the choreography was going to look. They had been practicing without the piping and the platforms, but now, Jazzy could see the angry townspeople scene, all of them at various levels singing passionately about saving the river.

It was going to be incredible. Visually stunning and beautifully acted.

But seeing all the levels laid out in front of her, she squeezed Mateo's hand.

*Please don't forget where to go.*

He squeezed back. She was impressed and eager to get on the set and play. The changes made from the Seattle run seemed to suit the changes they'd been making in rehearsal.

"What do you think, everyone?" Reid called from the stage. Cheers went up from the cast. "Glad you like it. Let's get you into your dressing rooms, shall we?"

Backstage, Jazzy stared at the closed door in front of her, her hand on the tag bearing her name. She spoke as if she had entered a church. "This is really mine?"

"You're the star, aren't you?" Reid smiled and swung open the door of the Schubert's "star" dressing room.

She stepped into the room reverently. The first room was a receiving room, about ten by twelve feet, into which she would put a couch. And a bar cart. And anyone could come and hang out with her. She would leave it open, always, so her cast knew she knew she was part of the team. She smiled at the thought of how Simone would no doubt make herself at home.

Good.

She opened the door on the opposite wall, and gasped. This sweet little space was all her own. On the right was a bathroom door, and in front of her was the requisite countertop and a mirror with a line of lightbulbs around it. She could already see how she would make this her own with some paint and photos. She went to her costume rack and ran her hands over all of them before turning back to Reid.

"Thank you, Reid. I can't believe I get to be in this room. Bernadette has used this dressing room. Twice. Ann Reinking. Betty Buckley. I'm just . . . " Jazzy spun slowly on the spot, feeling the spirits of her heroes all around her. "I'm so incredibly grateful. Thank you."

Reid smiled, but was all business as usual. "You got it. Put on your first costume, okay? We're starting the parade soon."

Ten minutes later, the cast tripped across the stage in all of their various costumes as the designers took notes. Once they were done and approved, Jazzy and Mateo changed into their street clothes and made their way back to the stage. Jazzy went simple as usual—her trusty black sleeveless jumpsuit. Mateo wore a short-sleeved button down of deep forest green that caught the flecks of green in his eyes, which she definitely didn't notice or care about. Two stools awaited them onstage and after introductions, they balanced on them in front of the camera and the Broadway.com interviewer.

The set was lit up behind them, and they faced Peter Thomas Bradshaw who sat on a stool a few feet away. The slight man in thick black glasses nodded at the camera operator and began his questions. He started with queries about the show and their roles, which Mateo and Jazzy answered enthusiastically, then he dug into the personal.

"Mateo, this is your Broadway debut."

Mateo, his hands folded in his lap, glanced down humbly. "That's right."

"How exciting. It has to be said that you haven't been seen much in recent years, since your last album. What made you decide to do this?"

Jazzy bit her lip, anticipating his answer.

"I have always wanted to do theater. It's something that's been in my blood since I was seven years old. This year, in the winter, I was just feeling restless and . . . I don't know, I was ready to do something. Ready for a change. Things in my life had gotten— Well, I wanted a distraction, and I was ready to work again. So I called around and got a theatrical agent, and here we are."

"Not quite as difficult for you as for others to make it to the Broadway stage." Peter wasn't holding back, unaffected by Mateo's smile. Jazzy thought he might be one of the only people on earth who could brag about that.

Mateo's eyebrows lifted up. "That's true. And let me tell you, I did not make my castmates lives very easy for a while. I haven't been in a musical since the late nineteen hundreds, you know."

Jazzy almost snorted but caught herself, while Peter barked out a laugh.

"It's been incredible. This cast welcomed me with open arms, and I am so grateful for their kindness and patience. They shove with love, and it means so much to me."

"Shove with love?"

"They'll put me where I'm supposed to be, whether or not I need to be shoved there."

Peter chuckled. "And what has it been like working with Jazzy?"

"Oh." Mateo looked at Jazzy who smiled up into his face. His eyes didn't leave hers for the answer. "It's been a dream come true, to be honest. She's just the most professional, talented human being I've ever known, and I'm very lucky to have her by my side." He turned back to Peter. "We all are."

Peter turned to Jazzy.

Jazzy looked down at her hands. "Thank you, Mateo. That means a lot."

"And what about you, Jazzy? It seemed fated for you to be in this show with *Something Blue* closing so quickly and Annie stepping out of this role. How did you feel when Mateo was cast?"

"Well . . . " Jazzy glanced at Mateo. He just smiled at her and she turned back to Peter. "I was a little apprehensive, to be totally honest. He was great in the audition, but I was worried about his inexperience. I'm just gonna say it . . . Before I knew him, it felt like stunt casting. But then we got in the room. And once he learned his *lines*—"

Mateo laughed and put his palms up facing Peter. "I have been read!"

Jazzy chuckled and met Peter's eyes. "Peter, he is so impressive. I am telling you, this man is a star. He was absolutely born to be on this stage and I am so excited for the public and all of his fans from before to get to see him in this role. He's surprised me at every turn. He is magnificent."

"Thanks, Jazz." Mateo's voice was soft and low when he turned to look at her.

They held each other's gaze until Peter cleared his throat. "What are you most excited for people to see?"

The interview went on for a few more minutes, and then Jazzy and Mateo went back to their dressing rooms to gather their stuff and go home for the weekend. After dinner with Simone that evening, Jazzy planned to rest and relax all weekend before tech week.

"Jazz?"

"Yeah?" She closed her dressing room door behind her and saw Mateo in the doorway of the outer room.

"Thanks for saying those things."

"It was the truth. You're magnificent."

"Thank you." The sparkles inside her began to twinkle as her gaze traveled to his lips.

"Jazzy, let's go! I'm starving!" Simone called down the long hallway.

The spell was broken and Jazzy hurried away, chanting *you don't do showmances* in her head. "Have a good weekend, Mateo," she tossed over her shoulder.

"You, too."

A glance back showed that he was still looking at her, a soft smile on his lips.

# Seventeen ♫

The humidity of the New York summer settled around Jazzy and Simone as they sat at an outdoor table at The Mermaid Inn. The café lights above them already glowed brightly and Amsterdam Avenue was abuzz with people enjoying the evening. The patrons around Jazzy and Simone were all in their summer casual best, including Simone, who wore a pink jumpsuit with white stripes.

Jazzy's black cotton sundress stuck to her back. "You sure you don't want to eat inside? It's August."

"Jazzy, remember winter?" Simone raised her wine glass to her lips, a frosty rosé sloshing in the glass. "Winter is bad. Soak up the summer while you can."

Jazzy picked up her own glass. "That's right. That's right." She sipped. "You know, you always remind me to be grateful and in the moment. I really admire that about you."

Simone's eyebrows darted toward her hairline. "Wow. Thank you."

"You're magnificent. Mateo is magnificent. Everyone is magnificent." Jazzy knew she sounded a little drunk.

"You've only had half a glass of wine, sweets." Simone motioned for a waiter and asked for a breadbasket as they waited for their entrees.

"Do you ever wonder if you deserve what you've gotten?" Jazzy said through a mouthful of crusty white bread a few moments later.

"I've worked for everything I've gotten, twice as hard as anyone. So, no." Simone smiled.

"Of course. Of course you have. Jesus, I can be such an asshole." Jazzy sat back and tried to apologize to Simone with her eyes.

Simone sat forward and said, in a no-nonsense tone, "There's luck, Jazzy. There's being born white and blonde and with parents who support you and have the money to move you to a city far away to pursue your dreams. That's lucky. There's being born so talented everyone is dying for you to be the star of their show.

That's lucky, too. But Jazz, you work hard to cultivate that talent. You work when you're off the clock, you work in your sleep, probably. Why do you think I've been making you have fun all summer? Because you work too hard. Shawn was right about that."

She paused to take a sip of wine. Peering at Jazzy with affection, she said, "It's not the oppression Olympics. That's a game that nobody wins. We've all had ups and downs. Some of us are born on third base and some of us are born at the hot dog cart outside of the stadium. I'm not going to blame you for being born halfway to home. As long as you try and be a good person, and do the right thing, and acknowledge that luck and privilege play a role, which I think you do, Jazzy, you deserve everything."

A surge of love ran through Jazzy for Simone's generosity of spirit. "So do you." She lifted her glass and Simone clinked it before they both drank. The wine went straight to Jazzy's head. "You are a leader. I'd vote for you. Why aren't you running the world? And god, Simone, your River is incredible. I know that people talk about my duet with Mateo as The Song, but you're the one who's going to bring the house down. And if you don't win the Tony, I am going to yell at the Administration Committee myself."

Simone tilted her head back and laughed delightedly. "That's right you are!" She drained the rest of her glass. "It really is a dream come true for me."

"You should be so proud. I mean, I'm proud enough for both of us, but I hope you are, too."

"Thank you. I am." She regarded Jazzy with a twinkle in her eye. "Was this about Mateo?"

Jazzy hesitated, and then nodded. "I was just thinking. He kind of swanned into the principle role in a Broadway show, and I resented him for that, I think. At the beginning. But I kind of did the same thing."

Simone rolled her eyes. "Oh stop it. That has nothing to do with anything. The problem is you're in love with each other and you won't admit it."

"Simone . . . " Jazzy groaned and slapped her hands over her eyes. "Stop!"

"I will not. The way he looks at you, girl. Come on. And I see you now, looking at him. He was joking around with Jason the other day, doing this goofy little dance? And the look on your face. My god. You're both transparent." The server approached with their entrees, tuna for Simone and salmon for Jazzy. They both thanked him and he smiled before walking away.

Jazzy pointed her fork at Simone. "And we are not."

"You are. You'll figure it out. I have faith." Simone tucked into her tuna, taking a huge, satisfied bite.

"Hmph."

Simone just waved her fork. "We're going dancing tomorrow."

"What?"

"You and me, and Blane and Carson and the rest of the cast. We're all going dancing. It's the last night we'll have until we start tech, then previews, then the run. And if I know you, you're not going to party at all once the show starts. So tomorrow, we party."

"I don't—"

"It's non-negotiable." Simone took another large bite and grinned, closed-mouthed.

Jazzy sighed through a smile. She knew that if she tried to stay home, Simone would show up at her door with a party dress, demanding she leave anyway. "All right. But I'm not getting drunk."

Simone shrugged with a little laugh. "Says you."

§

"I'm not *drunk*, Simone, I am *happy*."

Next to her, Simone laughed out loud, in her own drunken way. Both of them had maybe had one too many.

"You were flirting with that guy and Jason looked like he wanted to *murder* him." Jazzy whispered, stepping up onto the curb, which she thought was much too high.

"Thass'good. Jason should be jealous."

Jazzy giggled. "He was, truss'me. Murderous. Like Sweeney Todd levels. God, that's good." She laughed again, nearly tripping on a crack in the sidewalk. "I'm funny. Geddit?"

Simone held her up somehow. "I get it, I get it. You're very funny, Sondheim. Look, iss'your building!"

"Yaaaaay, home. I love home." Jazzy clapped her hands and then pushed open the door and waved to Nick, the security guard.

"Ms. Summers, are you good to get upstairs?" he said.

"I am," she said happily. "Thass'Nick. He's very nice to me. Nick! This's Simone."

Nick stood up from his chair, as if to help get the stumbling Jazzy to the elevator but Simone waved him off happily. "I've got her, don't worry. We're juss'fine."

Simone tossed Jazzy's clutch on the floor when they finally managed to get the apartment door open. "Patti! Come to Auntie Simone!"

Patti skittered under the couch as Jazzy threw her heels on the floor and stripped off her tight purple dress.

Simone snorted and crashed back onto the couch.

"What? I'm *hot*." She tried to pull on a pair of shorts but tipped over onto the bed.

Simone's laughter dissolved into gasps and she covered her face with a pillow. After a moment, she pulled it away long enough to say, "If Mateo could see you now."

"Shhhh. No Mateo. Nothing Mateo. He is just a friend and I love him." Jazzy slapped a hand over her mouth.

Simone shot up straight. "You *what*."

"Nothing!"

"The truth shall set you *free*. I knew getting you drunk was the right choice." Simone tossed the pillow aside and wobbled over to the bed. She fell down beside Jazzy. "All the truth comes out when you've had three vodka sodas. Have I mentioned what a lightweight you are? 'Cause I had five and we're the same drunk."

Jazzy wasn't looking at Simone. She wasn't hearing her either. She was staring at the ceiling, which was starting to spin, the words *I love him* tumbling around in her brain.

After a while Simone got up and stumbled over to the little kitchen, filled a glass of water, and brought it over.

Jazzy sat up and drank the whole thing before turning to Simone, while trying to understand herself. "Do I love him?"

"I can't tell you what you feel."

"Yuh huh, you've been doing that since day one." Jazzy chuckled and managed to finally wriggle into the shorts. She began twisting around to wrestle with her bra.

Simone laughed, too. "Okay, I can. Here'sh what I know. I know that when someone is so endlessly frustrated by another person that they can't shut up about it, when they talk about that person for hourshon end, when that person is the only one in the thoughts . . . their thoughts . . . "

Jazzy slumped back down on the bed, giving up on the bra. She flung her arms over her face.

Simone kept going. "I know that when someone describes a kiss as a *super nova*, and then that same someone denies denies denies . . . and then that someone seems to let their guard down around the other person, that someone lets him in a little bit, and the conversation changes to how much they admire that other person—"

"I'm getting confused," Jazzy moaned.

"Shh, lemme finish. I know when the look on two beautiful faces looks like yours and Mateo's when you're together, I know that's love."

Jazzy could feel Simone staring at her. She peeked out from under her arm. "Oh no."

Simone tilted her head to one side.

Jazzy sat up. "Maybe I love him. Oh my god. He's so . . . Oh hell. I do. I love him. Do I love him? Am I in love? I am. I am in love with Mateo. Simone, why didn't you *tell* me?"

Simone just laughed and laughed, shaking her head. After a moment, she swayed over to the kitchen where she filled a glass with water.

While Simone was distracted, Jazzy slipped off the bed and onto the floor where she located her sparkly clutch. She pulled her phone out of it, typed, and pressed send. No hesitation, no trademark Jazzy Summers caution. The phone made a satisfying *swoosh* noise.

"Jazzy, what did you do?"

She looked down at the phone, eyes widening. "I think I just told Mateo I love him?"

"Why would you do that."

"Because I want to be brave. Like you were flirting with that guy tonight. Knowing Jason was watching. I want to have feelings and say them." Jazzy stood up, feeling lighter but still slurring. "And I think I could fall in love with Mateo."

"Jasmine Maleficent Summers—"

"Not my name." Jazzy snickered.

"I am deeply proud of you. And you can't take it back now. I hope you don't regret it in the morning."

"I won't."

§

*Oh god oh god oh god.*

Hey I lovey ou

No response. Jazzy stared at the blue bubble and her drunken typos. She couldn't take them back, but she could blame them on the alcohol. The late morning sun streamed through the window, the coffee was percolating, and Patti purred next to her. It should have been a nice, relaxing morning to enjoy the day before tech began. But all Jazzy could feel was a knot in her stomach as she stared at her text chain with Mateo.

As she was staring, the three little dots popped up. Mateo was typing. Jazzy held her breath and resisted the urge to hide under the covers for the rest of the day. Or forever.

You love me, huh?

He followed that up with a beer emoji and a laughing face.

Okay. Okay good. He got that it was a drunk text. But oh *god*. She was never going to live this one down.

And the problem was, in the light of day, with a slight headache but a clearer head, Jazzy didn't want to take the words back. Simone was right. She had been in total denial. Mateo had wriggled his way into her heart and there was no getting rid of her feelings now.

But what if it was just the showmance of it all? Pretending to fall in love with someone every day could totally trick her brain into thinking she actually loved Mateo.

That was probably it. Her drunk brain was just merging her feelings and unable to tell the difference between acting and reality. That's all.

That's *all*.

Jazzy spent the day cleaning her apartment, doing a steam on her throat—she'd made sure to keep the yelling to a minimum at the club—and swinging a toy around for Patti. She tried to forget about the text to Mateo and didn't answer his. Every time she thought about it, it felt like someone was pinching her between the brows.

Monday came much too quickly and Jazzy found herself in her dressing room going over her first act notes. She didn't want to forget anything during tech rehearsals. They were hard enough without unprepared actors. Over the weekend, a crew had brought all of her things, most of which had still been packed from *Something Blue*, into her dressing room, so she was very comfortable. She had both rooms painted a pale, calming blue and brought in several lamps. In the receiving room, where she would greet guests and do interviews, were the white couch and a small dresser, which doubled as a bar. A couple of clear acrylic chairs sat on either side of it, and in the corner, a minifridge was stocked with water and snacks. An electric kettle sat on top beside a box of tea and her favorite mug.

On the walls, she'd hung posters of the all the shows that had run at the Schubert, to remind herself that she was part of a legacy, and to do her predecessors proud.

"Cast to the stage in five minutes. Five minutes, cast to the stage."

A knock sounded on the doorframe as the loudspeaker crackled above her head.

She felt herself shiver at the sight of Mateo in the doorway. *Basket case.*

"Hey, Jazz."

"Hey." Jazzy's hands were suddenly clammy. *I don't love you I don't love you I don't love you.*

Mateo, his expression tender, came in and sat down next to her on the couch.

Her heart beating rapidly, Jazzy closed her binder.

His deep brown eyes were twinkling. "About th—"

"I should really get ready to go." Jazzy stood quickly and slammed the binder on the dresser. "I have to pee before we go out there. You should, too. It could be a while before we get a break. You know, they have so much to do with the lighting grid, and the set moves around so much, that's going to take a lot of practice. Gonna be a long day, ha ha, you know? Anyway, see you out there!"

She babbled all the way to her private bathroom where she shut the door and leaned against it, breathing hard.

*Great job, Jazz. Not at all transparent.* She tipped her face up to the ceiling, wondering when she'd become so chaotic.

All day long, as they moved around the stage, sang through some songs and read through some scenes, she avoided Mateo. He kept approaching her on breaks, but she would busy herself with her phone or another conversation, or run to the bathroom again. If she could ignore him today, hopefully he'd forget about it by tomorrow, and then by Friday, when they would do the backer's performance, perhaps they would be back to their normal behavior.

Their hot-and-cold-will-they-won't-they normal behavior.

"Ugh!" Jazzy closed and locked her apartment door after the long, trying day. Not only had dealing with Mateo been frustrating, it was *tech week*. There really was no way to describe how difficult it could be to make a whole Broadway show move seamlessly. Every element had to come together: lights, sound, the whole moving set, everything.

She slipped off her shoes, exhausted, and made her meal. As she dried the dishes an hour later, her phone rang. Suspicious, she took it out of her bag. She'd talked to her parents yesterday, and they were practically the only ones to actually call her.

Oh.

Of course.

Mateo.

She silenced the phone and went back to the kitchen to feed Patti.

It lit up again. "Oh my god, Patti. What do I do? I can't just talk to him like normal. What is he even calling for? No one under the age of thirty-five *calls*."

The phone went dark. Two seconds later, it lit up again.

"Oh good lord. One stupid drunken text and he has to have a *summit* about it." Jazzy knew she was being unreasonable, but she didn't like Feelings Territory and was eager to leave. She watched the phone blaze his name across the screen, then go dark again. "Okay, if he calls one more time I'll answer it. Right? I mean, if it's that important?"

Patti flicked her tail, curled into a ball on the couch, and closed her eyes.

"Not helpful," Jazzy told her.

Mateo called again. With a shaking hand, she answered. "Mateo, hey, sorry I missed you." She winced at her lie and tried for cool and casual. "What's up?"

237

"Jazzy." Mateo's voice was thick and low, unlike anything she'd ever heard.

She stood up straighter, ready to do anything to make him not sound like that anymore. "What is it?"

"My mom died."

# Eighteen ♫

Jazzy was glad to hear that Mateo had been with Marisol on Monday evening when she passed away. He had made it just in time. Her funeral, which had long been planned, was held on Wednesday. The cast was given the morning off in order to support Mateo, and the rest of the week was reconfigured to give him time to grieve.

Wednesday dawned sunny and warm. The Upper West Side funeral home was fancy, but this reception room was the smallest, plainest one.

Simone and Jason were already in the second row of chairs when Jazzy arrived, with Blane and Carson just behind her. She nervously smoothed her hands over her black shift as she approached Mateo, whose face was blank. He stood at the back of the room facing the casket, but his eyes seemed to be looking somewhere else entirely. She put her hand on his arm gently. When he pulled her into a hug, she tried to squeeze all of the comfort she wanted to give him into it.

"Jazzy," he said. "Thank you for coming."

"I am so sorry, Mateo. I'm here for whatever you need."

"Thank you." He pulled out of the hug, his eyes full of sadness. "I needed that."

Blane and Carson stepped forward to give their condolences, followed by the rest of the cast. Jazzy took a seat next to Simone, who reached for her hand.

"How is he?" she said.

"I don't know," Jazzy said truthfully. Her eyes were beginning to sting with tears.

In the next twenty minutes, the small room filled up, though when everyone sat down in the stiff-backed chairs, it seemed that the company of *Bridges That Burn* made up most of the audience. After some words from the funeral director, Mateo approached the podium standing next to the closed casket. He placed his palm on it then turned, cleared his throat, and began to speak.

"Contrary to her culture, my mother wasn't a religious woman. Puerto Ricans, we're very Catholic, you

240

know? But as she told me all the time when I was a kid, no god gave her a husband, no god gave her a child. She had to do that part herself. So what was the point in worshipping something that didn't give her the thing she wanted most? That's what she always told me.

"But she didn't need religion to be one of the best people who ever lived. There was nothing she wouldn't do for me, or for the people in the Inwood community. Before my record deal, she arranged food drives, watched kids so parents could have some time off. Our apartment was practically a day care on the weekends. It was like having siblings. She remembered everyone's birthday and arranged block parties every summer. And when my record took off, there was no one there for me at the end of the day but her. She was a powerhouse, looking out for me every step of the way.

"It was devastating to get the news that she wouldn't be around for as long as I wanted her to be. Which was forever. But we made the most of the time we had together." Mateo looked down at his hands folded on the podium. He had no notes. He was speaking from the heart.

Jazzy sniffled and dabbed her eyes with a tissue. She wished she could have known Marisol as that powerhouse.

Mateo told about the special things they had done together in the penthouse: sharing cooking lessons, watching old videos, sunning themselves on the roof deck. He did not speak of her decline, only of the good memories and how lucky he was. Then he invited Judith and Julissa, her long-time nurses, to read two beautiful poems about a life well lived. The funeral director then said a few words.

Just like that, it was over.

Mateo stood next to the portrait of Marisol as folks gave him their condolences on their way out.

The cast and production team paid their respects and left. Sasha squeezed Jazzy's arm on her way out and said, "Stay with him if he needs you."

A few friends from his old neighborhood hugged him tightly; some promised to send him casseroles. Judith and Julissa both said tearful goodbyes. There was no one there from his pop star days. He had no other family.

Mateo was alone.

Jazzy took his hand, not sure of what to say.

"I'm not . . . " He cleared his throat. "I have to witness the cremation. Do you think you could meet me at the house later?"

Jazzy nodded. "Of course."

"Thanks. I just have to . . . " He nodded at the funeral director in the corner of the lobby.

As he walked into the office with the stately older man and the door closed behind them, she turned to the easel on which a photo of Marisol was rested. The woman glowed out of the photograph, full of life. It was hard to believe this was the same tiny woman in the hospital bed.

Two hours later, Jazzy and Mateo entered the vast penthouse, which already felt emptier. Voices from down the hall near his mother's room drifted toward them. Alarmed, Jazzy took in Mateo's neutral expression.

"The freight elevator is on the other end of the place, watch the floors." A burly man with a heavy New York accent appeared in the great room, guiding the hospital bed. Another man was at the other end. When he saw Mateo he said, "Oh, sorry, kid. The front desk said you wanted this gone as soon as possible."

Mateo waved his hand indifferently.

The burly guy said, "We're, uh, sorry for your loss."

"Thank you." Mateo watched the bed as they wheeled it down the other hallway.

Jazzy heard the freight elevator doors open and close.

Mateo stood in the middle of the great room, looking lost.

"Are you hungry?" she said softly.

He shrugged.

Jazzy gently took his arm. She led him over to the kitchen and sat him down on one of the stools. He complied with no resistance. "I am not a cook. But I am a whiz with this." She held up her phone, open to a delivery app.

The corner of his mouth turned up just a little.

"Do you feel like anything or will it all taste like sand?"

His mouth turned up a little more. "Sand, definitely. So whatever you want. I'll pay you back."

"You absolutely will not." Jazzy sat down at the island and began to scroll, deciding she should over-order something he could easily heat up later. Thai food. As she was choosing dishes, she heard Mateo get up and wander down the hallway. She followed him after she'd placed the order.

He stood in the middle of his mother's room, empty without the bed, his hands in his pockets, his tie askew.

Jazzy rested her head against the door frame. Her heart was in pieces for him.

His gaze met hers, sad and soft and a little relieved. "You know, you anticipate the worst thing ever happening to you. And you don't know how on earth you'll deal with it when it does. I feel guilty but . . . I'm almost a little relieved that it's here, so I don't have to worry every day of my life that I'm going to get that call."

Jazzy nodded, having had no experience with grief, not in any real sense. She'd lost her grandparents as a child, but her parents were still thriving in Indianapolis. She couldn't imagine what Mateo was feeling. All she could do was be there for him.

"I don't know what to do. So much of my time was spent in this room." He heaved an enormous sigh and rubbed the back of his neck. "What do I do?"

She went to him and held out her hand. He took it. They walked to the window and gazed out for a few moments. The summer sun was turning the city gold below them. "Well, eight shows a week is quite exhausting. You'll have that," Jazzy finally said after casting about for anything to say that might help.

Mateo chuckled. "I'm very glad I have that." He turned to her. "Glad I have you."

"You do."

They gazed into each other's eyes. That moment felt more intimate, more warm, than anything Jazzy had felt with anyone before.

"You know," Mateo said, as he looked out to the city again, "she didn't have many friends in the end. There were the few at the funeral, but everyone else wanted something from her, or were jealous, or just abandoned her. It was sad. But we always had each other. She was my rock. Even when she wasn't really here anymore."

"I'm so sorry, Mateo." Jazzy felt wholly inadequate.

"Life feels weird." He thunked his forehead against the window.

"I bet." God, she was not very good at this.

Mateo was quiet, his head still against the window.

Jazzy threaded her arm through his and gently pulled him close. "Let's get through today. Today? Bad day. But it will be over soon. You'll wake up tomorrow and things will be . . . "

He sagged against her as if he needed her to prop him up. "Will be . . . ?" He sounded skeptical.

"Weird in a different way. But a new day."

He huffed out through his nose, but smiled. Not his big, bright, Mateo smile, but something akin to it.

Over the Thai food and a few beers, he told stories from when he was a child, like the time Marisol stormed into his school, outraged that his teacher had admonished him, saying he couldn't paint a certain way. "Art is art!" Mateo imitated in a high-pitched voice. "You cannot tell *my* son how to do art!"

Jazzy laughed along as he remembered the smallest details about Marisol. After a while he asked her about her own suburban childhood. She recounted days of theater camp, her first few shows, her parents' insistence on the move to New York. He listened and laughed and she was glad to be there for him, though his sadness lingered behind every smile.

While she cleaned up the kitchen, he wandered down the hall again. She put the last container in the fridge, and looked toward Marisol's room.

Mateo slowly closed the door and put his palm against it.

The beeping machines were silent.

He nearly collapsed against the door. "I'm exhausted."

"Of course you are. I'll . . . I'll get going." She turned to go collect her bag.

"No, please don't."

Her heart sped up.

He walked toward her, his fatigue evident in every step. There was a plea in his voice. "I mean, go if you want to, obviously. But I don't want to be alone. If that's okay. You could stay. I have the room." He sheepishly gestured to the ostentatious living area.

Jazzy ignored the thrumming of her heart. Of course she would stay. She would do anything he needed today. "Let me just text my neighbor to feed Patti."

His smile was like a firework, one that fizzled quickly, granted, but it was there.

Half an hour later, Mateo looked her over. "Comfy?"

"I'm keeping these." Jazzy lovingly stroked the sweatpants Mateo had given her. They were too big, but were the softest fabric she'd ever felt.

He chuffed out a small laugh. "They're all yours. Find everything okay?"

She had. Mateo had led her to a swanky guest room with its own bathroom, and given her a new toothbrush. She'd luxuriated in the large glass shower. The soaps were all the most expensive stuff she'd ever used and she felt incredibly pampered.

"Do you want to watch something? It's still kind of early."

"Sure." Jazzy followed him into his room, glad to be able to provide some comfort.

His gigantic room had a king-sized bed in the center of one wall, with about a thousand pillows on it. The windows on another wall showed the city all lit up. The view was breathtaking. Across from the bed was a giant flat-screen.

He flopped on the bed, obviously exhausted, and patted the spot next to him. "Comfort TV. 'Great British Bake-Off?"

"Oh, absolutely." She crawled across the vast bed and plopped down next to him. They had watched the bakers get through the first challenge when Jazzy heard a sniffle.

She looked over and saw tears streaming down Mateo's face. Quickly, she reached for the remote and turned off the TV. The room was dark with only the city and the moon lighting it up. She put her arms around him, stroked his head, and let him cry. Which he did, for a good long while.

After quite some time, Mateo sniffled and sat up. He reached for the box of tissues on the bedside table. He wiped his face and then gazed upwards at the ceiling.

Jazzy felt helpless. She placed a hand on his arm.

He looked over to her and smiled shakily. He scooted back against the headboard, opening his arms.

Snuggling into him, Jazzy was grateful that he didn't seem to need her to talk. She didn't know what to say.

"I knew it was coming. But I'm just so— I'm devastated."

"Of course you are." She felt his rapid heartbeat beneath her cheek.

He stroked his hand down her back, gently. "When I met you . . . I was alone. I thought I was going to be alone when this happened. I've been alone for so long.

And now . . . I'm so glad you're here. I'm so glad I have you and Simone and Blane and . . . "

"Show family," Jazzy mumbled into his chest. "We're a show family."

Mateo squeezed her closer.

"I was lonely, too." Jazzy felt brave not having to look at his face.

"You were?"

"Extremely. Y'know, because I'm a stuck-up workaholic."

Mateo chuckled, and his arms tightened around her. "You are? I never noticed."

"But I was lonely. And I'm really glad I can be the one for you to lean on." She looked up into his eyes, which were a little puffy.

He was smiling gently. "I'm glad you're here, too." He placed a hand on her cheek, stroking it gently.

Jazzy settled back into his chest. "Tell me more about Marisol. If you want to."

His arm squeezed a little tighter around her. "Oh man. Let me tell you about this neighborhood board meeting from when I was eight." Mateo relaxed against the headboard and she settled in for a story, feeling weary but content.

§

Jazzy opened her eyes to sunlight streaming into the bedroom.

249

Sometime during Mateo's stories, he had slid down and under the covers, inviting her in. Without even thinking, she'd joined him and he gathered her against his chest like she were a life preserver. Now she woke up in that exact position, safe in his arms.

He was snoring softly against her neck.

Gently, she lifted his arm from around her and slid out from under the covers. She hadn't been given the day off and she did need to get to the theater.

Bending over, she pressed her lips to his forehead, while visions of the little Mateo that Marisol would have done anything to protect danced across her mind. His little hat when he played Harold Hill. The sweet pop icon and the demanding diva. The coffee shop flirt. The forgetful, aggravating co-star. And yes, the man who kissed her so thoroughly she saw stars. All versions of Mateo gathered in her heart and she promised to hold them there, to keep them safe.

"Sleep well, my someone."

# Nineteen ♫

Thursday's rehearsal without Mateo didn't have any light in it. Jazzy was sleepy, and though Julian was fantastic, their chemistry was not the same. But the four days of tech had done wonders for the show itself. When the set rotated on the turntable now, everyone knew where and how to stand or move. Everything was coming together.

Jazzy tried to find the thrill in it, but Mateo's devastated face kept surfacing in her thoughts. He hadn't answered any of her texts since she'd left his bed.

She entered the theater on Friday morning, nerves jangling a bit. She had to admit that was fifty percent because Mateo wasn't there. The backers would be the first to see any of their work outside of the production team and she wanted to do a good job. If any of them didn't like what they saw, they could pull out, and the show would fail, and she would be out of a job. Again.

Before letting herself fall down that rabbit hole, she stared at herself in the mirror. "That is not going to happen. What you have to present is sensational."

The speaker crackled above her and Reid's voice rang out. "Company meeting on the stage in three minutes. Three minutes to the stage, please."

She immediately left her dressing room and made her way to the stage, where she found a very welcome sight. Mateo, tall and beautiful and solid, was talking with Sasha. She stopped short, all at once surprised and elated to see him.

He seemed to sense her presence. When he turned to look at her, she felt an unmistakable flutter in her heart.

And then his face lit up with a wide grin.

The fluttering in her heart intensified, the sparkles beginning to shimmer. She beamed back and gave a little wave.

Jazzy noticed Sasha glance curiously at her as the rest of the cast trickled onto the stage.

Simone stepped onstage and looked from Mateo to Jazzy. Her lips narrowed into a knowing smile and she nudged Jazzy. "You're looking at him like you want to lick his neck."

Jazzy snapped her gaze away from Mateo, and felt herself blushing tip to toe. "I am *not.*"

"What happened after the funeral?" Simone was obviously not going to let this go.

"Nothing happened, we just went to his place and talked," Jazzy muttered, while scraping her shoe against the stage floor. "His mom just died. He was sad and needed a friend."

Simone looked at her for a long moment, her saucy expression fading. "I'm glad he had you. And when he's ready, you should tell him—"

"Thank you all for being so prompt," Sasha said. She motioned for them to all gather in a circle. "As you can see, Mateo is back and he would like to say a few words."

Everyone applauded and turned their attention to him.

"Thanks for coming, everyone." He seemed a little apprehensive as he stood with his hands clasped. "I wanted to tell you how much I appreciate all of your support the last few days. And weeks. It meant so much to me that you were there for my mother's . . . for me. On Wednesday. And the flowers were beautiful."

"Blane and Carson arranged that." Parker's voice was low. "It's the least we could do."

"Thanks, guys." He looked around the circle, took a deep breath, and went on. "I wanted you all to know that I appreciate you, and also wanted to acknowledge that

I'm back already. I know it might seem weird. But I can't stay in that apartment by myself. It's too—" He sighed, and Jazzy felt all of them shift nearer to him. "Anyway, here I've found some real support, and true friendship."

He caught her eye, and she noted the word. Friendship.

"Basically, I need you. And Julian, thank you so much for stepping in for me this week."

Julian nodded at him. "Anytime, brother."

"But I didn't want to let any of you down by not being here. Not after all you've done for me. To get me here. Earlier this morning, Sasha and I met to go over everything that I've missed, so I will be prepared for tonight. I am so ready to put our beautiful show in front of people. Let's do this."

The cast seemed to move as one toward Mateo, gathering him in a gigantic group hug.

Over the top of Carson's head, Mateo looked at Jazzy, his gaze soft. A longing to feel him next to her again, warm and comforting, filled her to the brim.

"All right people," Sasha called.

The cast separated from the hug but stayed close to one another. Mateo was between Simone and Jason, who had their arms around him.

"Mateo, we are so glad you're here," Sasha said. "And today I want to do a full run through, no stopping and starting. Are you ready?"

"Hell yeah," he said with conviction.

Cheering filled the stage. Fifteen minutes later, Act One began.

Jazzy presumed that the stage would have thrown Mateo off his game, but it didn't. It seemed that he only needed to really drill something into his head once, and once it was finally there, nothing could stop him—not the rotating stage, not the vastness of the new space, not a forgotten prop.

He was magnificent.

Together, they were unstoppable, their voices mingling seamlessly, their love story searing and delicate. The run-through went beautifully with only a few hiccups that were easily fixed before the showcase.

That evening, Jazzy stood in the wings where she could hear the backers audience filling out the front rows. The curtain was open to the stage and she felt a fluttering in her belly and a presence behind her. Without turning, she said, "Hi, Mateo."

He stepped next to her, grinning, handsome in his first costume, gray pants and a blue shirt. "I can't believe we're about to do this for an audience."

"I know. How do you feel?" She looked up at him, her gaze locking into his. She hoped he could tell she wasn't just asking about performing.

He turned to her and gently took her hand, his thumb stroking her knuckles. His eyes sparkled at her and his face grew serious. "With you, I feel like I can do anything."

"You can," she whispered. Jazzy's heart pounded and she stepped closer to him, their fireworks kiss dancing in her mind. He stepped forward too, their eyes locked . . . and the orchestra started the overture. She came back to herself, realizing that anyone could be standing in the wings. And were. Behind Mateo, she saw Simone staring at her knowingly, her eyes wide.

Jazzy escaped by stepping onstage at her cue.

§

"Let's talk about you, what have you been up to?"

"Jazzy, we've been together for twelve hours a day all week, you know exactly what I've been up to." Simone busied herself pouring soda water into Jazzy's vintage cocktail glasses. She handed Jazzy one, while giving her a probing glance. "I want to discuss the I saw exchanged before the overture."

Ignoring the question, Jazzy took a sip of the cocktail and nearly sputtered. Strong. "How's Jason?"

"Fine. Probably not for me anymore. But a good balm after Mathieu. And right now? Not important." Simone plopped onto the couch next to Jazzy, both now in street clothes after the successful backer's showcase. She stared at Jazzy, her whole face a question mark.

"That makes sense. Felt really good to do the show tonight. Didn't it? The backers seemed to like it." Jazzy took another tentative sip of the strong drink, trying to ignore the intensity of Simone's stare.

Simone's expression was full of disdain laced with mirth.

"I don't want to talk about it here." She gestured to the open dressing room door before plucking at a thread on the pink throw pillow between them.

Simone merely kept looking at Jazzy, reached up without taking her eyes off of her face, and flung the door closed behind her.

Jazzy laughed despite herself.

Simone continued in a low voice. "There is serious juju going on between you two. You told him you love him—"

"Which he ignored. Thank god." She rolled her eyes at Past Drunk Jazzy.

"—and then something happened. I can feel it. What happened?" Simone straightened her faux-leather skirt down her thighs and crossed her long legs.

"Nothing."

"Jazzy."

Her chest tightened until she needed some release. Finally, she gave in. "No really, nothing. After the funeral, he was sad and alone, so we went back to his house and talked about a lot of things.

"I stayed over. That's all. You didn't think he was going to—" She whispered the next word. "—*fuck* the night of his mother's funeral, did you?"

"Okay, you whispering 'fuck' is the Jazzy-est thing you have ever done." She huffed out a laugh. "But no, of course not. It's just, you were hot and cold, on and off, right? And now, there's something there, something has changed between you. He asked you to stay with him on the worst night of his life. That *means* something."

Jazzy ran her finger under the cuff of her shorts. "It means he needed a friend."

"Mm." Simone was clearly skeptical.

Jazzy looked up at her, feeling fiery. "He did. He doesn't have anyone at all. No one. Not a single person from back in the day, no family, no real friends. And I want to be that for him, if I can."

"And that's it. Friends."

Jazzy crossed her arms stubbornly, having abandoned her cocktail on the coffee table. "Yes."

"Weird how you haven't said 'I don't do showmances' yet. Are you feeling okay?" Simone reached over and placed her palm on Jazzy's forehead.

"Har dee har." She rolled her eyes, but she was smiling. "I don't. That's a given. So even if Mateo had feelings for me, which he has never indicated or admitted or said out loud, it wouldn't matter. Because I don't do—"

"Ugh, don't say it." Simone held her hand up. "But he did ask you out. Right?"

Jazzy rolled her eyes. "That was before he really knew me. And then he *did* let me know what he really thought of me, you remember. He out loud told me to my *face* that I was stuck up."

"And the kiss?"

Jazzy was silent for a moment, staring daggers at Simone. "A gin-fueled one-off."

A fierce showdown ensued until Simone sighed and gave in. "All right, suit yourself. But all of us can see it, and we're taking bets."

"Sim*one*!" Jazzy would have hit her with the pillow if she didn't fear spilling the drink all over the pretty couch.

Simone just chuckled and took another sip.

Jazzy regarded her own cocktail glass. "I really should stop drinking now. Previews start next week."

Simone reached over and put the glass back in her hand. "One drink won't kill you."

"If I can't sing on Monday, it's your fault." Her tone was accusatory but she took a healthy swig nonetheless.

Simone's gaze went to the dresser. "Why do you have a bar in here anyway, if you don't drink during a show's run?"

Jazzy shrugged and looked down into her glass. "In case people want to hang out."

Simone sat forward, her eyes searching. "You need a friend, too."

"That's why I have you." She grinned, clinked Simone's glass with hers, and took another generous gulp of her cocktail.

A knock on the door set her heart pounding. *Mateo?*

"Girls, are you drinking without us?" Carson breezed inside.

And without any warning, the little room was full. Fifteen minutes later, Jazzy gazed around. Simone sat with her legs swung up in Jason's lap, Parker was in a chair with Carson sitting on the floor in front of her. Blane was mixing drinks for everyone, and the rest of the cast got cozy in the cramped quarters, spilling out into the hallway.

Her heart swelled and she looked at Simone, who raised her glass in her direction. *This* is why she had the bar.

Mateo, however, was conspicuously absent. Blane said he'd practically run out of the stage door. Jazzy thought that was weird, but grief does weird things. He probably needed to be alone. She would let him be and check in later.

§

Missed saying goodbye, wanted to check in. How are you?

A bit formal, but it got the message across. Almost immediately, he responded.

Just needed to be alone, thanks.

Oh. Well, fine. That's fine, his mom just died. She turned her attention to the ads above the subway doors. She wasn't going to read anything into the six cold words. He was grieving and had needed her the night of the funeral. If he didn't need her anymore—

260

But then what was that moment before the show?

*With you, I feel like I can do anything.*

At home later, she flopped on her bed next to Patti, who lifted her head and glared at Jazzy for disturbing her. "Sorry. But we're doing it again. The hot and cold thing. What am I supposed to do, Patti?"

The cat snuggled down again.

"I know. I should let it go. Be his friend, do the show, enjoy it." She opened her phone, intending to answer his text, but then thought better of it. She instead navigated to Instagram where there were countless photos of her and Mateo together, in a tag called "jazzteo". She didn't love the mashup nickname, but it worked.

The theater kids had been working overtime. They had pulled photos from every social media feed of every member of the cast, had used Jazzy and Mateo's takeover of the show's page over and over, creating collages and videos and edits.

It really did look like they were a couple.

Frustrated, she tossed the phone aside and decided to get started on meal prep for the week ahead. The last few days of tech would be grueling for sure, and she wanted to be prepared. A little thrill ran through her at the thought of their first real audience the next Friday. The invited dress the night before would be industry folks, but a real audience on Friday was going to be wonderful. And then, once previews were over, they would be recording the original cast album, finally.

Jazzy had plenty to look forward to and wasn't going to worry about Mateo.

Except that she did. And she texted again. Twice.

> If you need a friend, I'm around.

And then something a little more innocuous.

> Do you want to meal prep together sometime? I have lots of tips on how to manage 8 shows a week . . .

No response.

Every time her phone dinged with a GIF from Carson or a snarky text from Simone, she jumped, but Mateo had gone dark. Understandably so. He was probably processing last week on his own time, in his empty house.

Jazzy's heart broke at the thought of him all alone in there. It was Sunday night and she had just poured a cup of tea and was about to watch one of her old favorite movies to put herself to sleep. The week stretched ahead, every hour filled with *Bridges That Burn*—not just final tech and dress rehearsals, but press interviews, the commercial shoot, and a podcast recording.

Her buzzer went off, startling her. She put the tea on the coffee table and walked over to the intercom. "Hello?"

"Ms. Summers, a Mateo Williams is here to see you?"

Jazzy's eyes widened and goosebumps appeared on her arms. "Oh! Send him up, please. Thanks, Nick."

She unlocked the door and set about making sure nothing embarrassing was lying around. She glanced down at the silk pajama set she was wearing. Too late to change it now.

Soft knocks sounded on the door that was ajar.

She went to it and opened it all the way, her body filled with longing and her heart filled with hope.

Mateo stood there in a gray t-shirt and jeans, his expression ravaged. She had never seen him this way. Desperation seemed to emanate off of him as he wordlessly stepped across the threshold. She closed and locked the door.

Night had descended upon the apartment, save for the candle burning on the coffee table, next to the now-forgotten tea.

"Mateo?" She stepped closer to him, and he moved toward her at the same time.

His eyes met hers, full of desire behind the pain, and he reached out his hands, drawing them softly down her arms.

She shivered.

"Jazzy . . . " He seemed to see her for the first time, in her silky night shorts and tank top. His eyes blazed into hers, wanting, desperate. His voice was rasping, thick with emotion. "Jazzy . . . please . . . Make me feel anything else."

Without hesitating, she closed the gap between them.

# Twenty ♫

Mateo's arms circled her waist slowly, as if asking permission. Not quite believing this was happening, she wrapped her arms around his neck, drawing him closer. She felt his energy, his warm Mateo-ness, in his embrace. Body against body, his hand cupping her cheek, he looked into her eyes. The desire in his was now coupled with a plea. Fervently, Jazzy nodded.

She'd known she wanted him but hadn't realized how overwhelmingly so.

The air between them pulsated until finally, something broke apart in the universe and his lips captured hers. His kiss was frantic, desperate, like he wanted to forget everything else existed. She nearly did. Everything fell away. Only Mateo, finally Mateo, was real to her.

When his lips parted, she slid her tongue into his mouth. He moaned aloud, and pulled her closer still. All thoughts of showmances left her head. She was consumed by his scent, that familiar citrus and spice, as his hands roamed her back. She was so completely aware of him, the perfection of his lips, the way his smile lit up her world.

He found the gap between her silky tank and shorts and brushed the skin of her back with his fingers gently.

Then suddenly he pulled away. He gazed at her for a moment breathing hard, his eyes clear, before pressing his forehead to hers.

She felt his hot breath on her face, the beating of his heart beneath the solid muscle of his chest. His sweet, broken heart. "Mateo—"

He pulled back again, his breath ragged, his eyes hungry now.

"Yes." Her voice was a frantic whisper.

"Yes," he said and his mouth was on hers again. He took his time, lingering, brushing his lips against hers, nipping and playing, before slowly, slowly parting them.

When he broke their kiss again, his eyes were full of wonder. He searched her face for a few moments, his mouth curving into a smile. "Is this really happening?"

"I really, *really* hope so." She rose up on her tiptoes and brushed her lips against his jaw. With a slight moan, he angled his head to kiss her again and captured her bottom lip lightly between his teeth. Gasping, she let her hands slide down his chest and found the bottom of his t-shirt. Impatiently, she tugged at it and gave off a frustrated groan.

He chuckled at her, took a small step back, and pulled off his shirt.

For a moment, Jazzy was consumed by the sight of him, golden in the candlelight. Meeting his eyes, she stepped forward, feeling ready and vulnerable and nearly desperate. He pulled her close and she ran her hands along the taut muscles of his back, not quite believing that this thing she'd been wanting was finally happening. Mateo was *here*, now, real. His lips set fire to her neck. The starlight inside of her swirled. She wanted to feel his lips against hers, against her skin, again and again. It felt as though she would never be sated.

He pulled back again and she reeled a bit. "Woah." She couldn't help a small laugh escaping.

He let out a small chuckle. Tenderly, he tucked a strand of hair behind her ear. "I agree." He let his hand slide down her arm and glanced over at her bed.

Jazzy bit her lip, hoping it was sexy and not the oh-boy-I-hope-we're-good-at-this nervousness she was feeling. Still a bit dizzy, she let him guide her to her bed.

Gently, he kissed her again and lowered her onto the soft down comforter. But then his warmth was gone and she opened her eyes.

He stood beside the bed, his lips parted, gazing at her in a way that made her feel like a goddess. So slowly, torture-slowly, he stroked his hand down her thigh. Her heart began to gallop and she felt herself flush with a desire so deep that she didn't care what happened in the morning. She needed him. Now. She reached for his hand and tugged him down.

He lay down, half on top of her, and the weight of him felt like the warmest blanket, like security.

"I can't believe I'm here." His voice was raspy with desire.

She didn't answer, just pressed her body against him and sought his lips again. Kissed him so he could forget.

Gently, he stroked her waist, over the silkiness of her top, slowly moving his hand upward until he brushed against her breast.

She moaned, arching up to him. They had been so intimate—dancing together, stripping themselves bare onstage—that Jazzy wasn't surprised to find that this too felt natural. That Mateo touching her, knowing her, every part of her, was exactly how it was supposed to be.

When she looked at his beautiful face again, his expression was thunderstruck or enamored or both. Jazzy didn't regret the drunk text to him one bit. Not in that moment.

Their eyes met, and at the same time, wide grins burst across their faces. Jazzy curved her hand around his nape and brought him closer. For a deliciously long while, she lost herself in his touch, the smile she felt when he kissed her.

Jazzy let her hands roam his chest and stomach until she found his belt buckle. She pulled away from him and arched an eyebrow.

Mateo put his hand on hers and arched an eyebrow back. "Are you sure?"

She nodded, wanting to feel all of him, wanting to make him feel everything that was good in this world and nothing that was bad.

He practically jumped off of the bed. When she laughed at him, he gave her his Mateo grin. Her heart leapt in her chest as he unfastened his belt and kicked off his jeans. She gasped. The V of Mateo's hips disappeared into his boxer briefs, which hugged the muscles of his upper thighs. His dancer's frame, lean and strong, was on full display. She couldn't help gaping a little. She'd felt all of this through his clothes, but never imagined he would be quite so sexy.

His expression turned into longing as he gazed at her.

"Get back over here," she demanded.

He came back to lie half over her, familiar and comforting, as he roamed his lips over every bit of her exposed skin. Her shoulder, her neck, her cheeks, all received his adoration. He stroked one hand down her thigh again.

She sighed with pleasure. "Mateo . . . "

"Yes?" He pulled back, but his thumb continued drawing circles on her hip.

"I think I have far too many clothes on."

That smile right there, that was the goal. Oh, she would do anything to see that smile, to cause it to happen.

He raised himself up and positioned himself between her legs, pulling her with him. She raised her arms over her head.

He reached down, his gaze tender, and pulled the silky tank top over her head. At the sight of her, he let out a moan that reached into her chest and wrapped around her heart. Lying back down again, she felt wanted and adored, needed in a way she'd never felt before.

Mateo cherished every inch of her, tracing her nipples with his tongue then trailing up to her ear where he nipped her ear lobe. For the first time, she felt broken open, seen.

"I have never wanted anyone like this. Never," he whispered as he trailed his hand down her belly, his teeth against the vulnerable curve of her neck.

Her heart felt as though it might burst. Her body felt like it was on fire. She could feel his erection between her thighs and she traced her hands along his back, his broad shoulders, then down his chest. She broke their kiss gently and looked into his eyes, feeling vulnerable but unafraid. "I want you, Mateo. Please."

He picked up her hand and kissed the inside of her wrists, then found her lips again. She sighed beneath him, desire flooding her until she could barely take it anymore. It was no surprise to her that Mateo was worshipping her, taking his time. But she wanted him, all of him, and she was nothing if not single-minded.

She bucked her hips up to him, silently letting him know what she wanted.

He chuckled, low and sexy, and looked her in the eye. "First I'm going to worship you."

And he did. Oh, he did. He sat on his knees between her legs and swept his hand over the plane of her belly, then pulled at her shorts until they were tossed carelessly on the floor. His boxers soon followed and he resumed his position. Every part of her ached for him. Her body, her heart, her mind. She wanted him to know her, all of her, and from the nakedly adoring look on his face, she knew he felt the same.

His breath grew heavier as he stroked his hands down her waist and onto her thighs. His golden skin gleamed in the candlelight. He looked up into her eyes.

"I'm all yours, Mateo."

That seemed to be all the permission he needed. He snatched the breath from her lungs, covering her body with his lips, his tongue, his hands. She was lost in him, this man who felt so alone, this man who was becoming an important part of her life so unexpectedly. Every caress, every touch, told her that he worshipped her. That he was hers.

One of his hands clung to hers, held onto her for dear life.

The touch of his lips lingered, scorched onto her skin. Onto her heart.

When he slid his fingers down her inner thigh and found the center of her, she moaned aloud and gasped. She wanted to feel him, taste him.

She wanted to make him feel as though everything were all right.

Curling into him as he built the pleasure between her thighs, she sighed into his neck and trailed her tongue up to his ear. She tasted the salt on his skin and wanted to devour him. She was savoring every moment of his skin on hers, knowing it could be the only time she would ever feel like this. Breathing into his ear, she gasped, "The top drawer. Please, Mateo."

He gazed at her, a moment frozen in time. She lingered under his adoration and hoped he could feel hers in turn. A slow, sexy smile slid across his face.

"You're like rain, Jazzy. You've washed away everything I didn't want to be." And then he covered her completely, his skin on fire where it touched hers. She was safe, present, not thinking of the next thing, or rehearsal, or anything but him. Only him. His kiss was perfect, tender but insistent. She felt needed, not for her talent, not for her work ethic. For herself. He wanted her just as she was—stubborn and impatient and all.

271

He broke the kiss again and for another second, he held her. He brushed his nose along her cheek and then gazed into her eyes. "I've wanted this for so long, Jazz."

"Me, too."

It was cold when he left her side, but then she inhaled deeply as he straightened to put on the condom he'd found in her nightstand. This Mateo was a god, golden and beautiful and in her bed. She never wanted to let him go.

He looked over to her and breathed out, a smile forming on his lips. As he moved back to her, she stretched languidly and enjoyed his wide-eyed reaction.

"You are absolutely perfect, Jazzy Summers."

"I could say the same for you, Mateo Williams."

Her heart sped up as she opened up to him and he moved between her thighs, his dark eyes glinting with desire.

Closer. She wanted him closer. This was not enough, the way he was gazing down at her, his hand sliding over her waist. Her impatience caught up with her. She caught his hand and tugged him down.

Mateo's expression turned serious. She felt him press against her as he met her eyes. Her stomach flipped, her heart pounded, and oh, she wanted him. "Please."

Mateo looked at her like she was a piece of art before he caught her lips up in a languid kiss. His forearms resting on the bed, he caught both of her hands in his and laced their fingers together. She felt them intertwine, her heart beating with his, as finally, finally, he held her gaze and slowly, so slowly, he filled her completely.

For a moment, Jazzy couldn't breathe, couldn't believe how perfectly he fit inside her. His face slackened with a mixture of joy and pleasure. Wanting more, wanting all of him, she wrapped her legs around him and he melted into her. For a few delicious minutes, she was overwhelmed with Mateo, the slickness of his skin, his moans in her ear. The heart that beat in time with her own.

She couldn't believe it could feel this incredible. Ten years of sometimes adequate sex had not prepared her for the fireworks now popping through her chest. Mateo lingered his lips over her shoulder, the curve of her neck. His teeth lightly lashed across her clavicle, her skin tingling in its wake. Everything was new, sparkling, his breath, his low growl when she pulled him deeper inside of her. She savored every time he said her name. It was her he wanted. Needed.

And she reciprocated all of it. There was no going back now.

"Look at me, Jazzy." He pulled back slightly and she opened her eyes. He moved inside of her and everything took on a dreamy quality. He picked up her hand from where it rested on his chest and kissed every one of her fingers, feeling and seeing all of her.

In his eyes, she saw universes.

She pulled him close again and they moved together. Their rhythm was perfection, as she'd guessed it would be. Inside of her, her pleasure built until finally her body was quaking with an intense orgasm.

Mateo moaned into her ear, cried out her name as he climaxed right after her.

They gasped together for a moment, foreheads touching. Jazzy stroked his neck, beyond words, still thrumming with pleasure. His lips sought hers again and he kissed her gently.

Mateo broke the kiss and pulled back an inch, his gaze soft now, adoring.

"Wow." He brushed his nose against hers.

"Very wow." She let her legs slacken from their knot around him.

"You're incredible."

Still unable to form words—no surprise—she lingered again in their kiss, treasuring his lips on hers.

A few minutes later, he rolled to his side and pulled her back against his chest. His arm was snug around her.

She'd never felt so content.

Mateo stroked her shoulder with his thumb and whispered, "Thank you for making me feel."

"Thank you for making *me* feel." She turned a bit toward him and saw softness in his gaze. Almost wonderment.

He met her lips lightly. Jazzy rolled to face him and they separated, lying back against the pillows, gazing at each other. She stroked his strong jawline, and watched his breathing grow heavier. Watched the feelings they'd just displayed be replaced with the same pain he'd shown up at her door with.

She felt a sting in her heart, sad to see that their passion hadn't taken his pain away for a bit longer. "I'm glad you could forget. For a little while."

Mateo laced his fingers through hers, which were still stroking his cheek. He closed his eyes and kissed her palm.

After a few moments, he whispered, "What do you think happens?"

Jazzy shifted closer to him. "What do you mean?"

"When we die."

"Oh." Jazzy felt her heart breaking for him. She decided to tell him what she'd always believed. "My dad is a big fan of Carl Sagan. He's an astronomy professor. I didn't grow up with religion, but I grew up looking at Sagan's 'star stuff' quote on our kitchen wall. Do you know it?"

Mateo shook his head.

"'The cosmos is within us. We are made of star-stuff. We are a way for the universe to know itself.'"

His lips upturned in a soft smile.

"And I think Sagan was right. We are all made of the same stuff. We are here." She pointed to her heart. "And here." She laid her palm on his chest.

He put his hand over hers.

"We're all connected. I think that when we die, we're everywhere."

Mateo closed his eyes and breathed deeply.

Jazzy continued. "When I was nine, my grandmother passed away. She'd loved this sparrow that visited her bird feeder, right? She'd named it Freddie, and would often say 'Oh, I think Freddie will pay a visit today.' And he would, most of the time. So when she passed, every time I saw a sparrow, I would think it was her saying hello. Even though sparrows are so common. And maybe I only see them because I'm thinking of them. But maybe . . . Maybe it's her. Maybe her star dust got caught up in a sparrow's and she says hello to me. That's what I like to think anyway. We are everywhere."

He squeezed her fingers. "Star dust."

"Star dust."

After a short silence, he took a shaky breath. "I can't believe she isn't here to see me in the show."

"I know, love. I know."

Without any more words, he pulled her close. He breathed deeply for a while.

Jazzy stayed awake until she felt his breath grow steady and even. She drifted off then too, tangled up in him.

Through dreams of sparrows and Mateo's hands on her skin, Jazzy heard noises that didn't sound like Patti. She opened her eyes and saw him tugging on his jeans.

"Hey—"

"I'm so sorry, Jazzy." He looked strangely guilty. "I shouldn't have come here last night. I can't believe I did—"

Sleep hadn't yet left Jazzy's brain. "Wait, what?

Mateo—"

"Please forgive me for this. I took advantage of your friendship and . . . I think it's obvious that we're attracted to one another." After pulling his t-shirt down, he knelt at the side of her bed. "I swear. I didn't know that was going to happen. And it was . . . Damn, Jazzy, it was incredible. But we don't ever have to talk about it again. I'm so sorry."

Jazzy propped herself up on one elbow, as she struggled to understand. She shook her head, and the cobwebs cleared a bit. "Wait! Yeah, it was incredible. Why are you apologizing?"

"Because I promised you. I promised I would respect your wishes."

"Okay, well, last night my wishes were to be well and truly—" Jazzy couldn't bring herself to say the f-word, but with wide eyes glanced to the side of the bed where Mateo had done just that. "—by you."

He paused tying his Chucks and looked at her with an affectionate but sad smile. "I'm glad to hear that. But I promise it won't happen again."

"Hey, hold on! I didn't do anything I didn't *want* to do." Her voice broke at the last word. She'd thought last night was the start of something. More importantly, she'd believed it was the end of their frustrating hot-and-cold game.

She was apparently very wrong.

He reached over and softly brushed her hair behind her ear. "I know. But I feel like I manipulated you. Playing the

. . . the dead mom card."

"You didn't. Mateo, you didn't." She sat up on her knees and grasped his hands into hers. "I thought it was pretty obvious that I wanted last night just as badly as you did."

He cupped her cheek gently. "I'm really happy you feel that way. But we're about to run previews, we're about to record the album, we're about to open. This is— It's a bad idea. I don't think I'm in the right headspace to . . . "

Jazzy nodded. *Of course.* His grief had made him stop thinking clearly. And she didn't want to press if *he* didn't want this . . . whatever *this* was.

She bit her lip, hoping the hurt about to come would be bearable. "You're right."

She wanted to say more. She wanted to tell him that it had been the best sex of her life, not just because he was incredible at it, but because they were so connected. They couldn't seem to stay apart and she no longer wanted to. But he was deeply grieving. And if he wanted to concentrate on previews beginning and all of the work they were about to have thrown at them, well, she could respect his wishes. She could give him that.

He looked at her bedside clock and sighed. "I'm gonna run home and shower. See you in an hour?"

Jazzy forced a small smile across her face. "Hey, you rhymed."

Mateo chuckled, bent down, and kissed her forehead. "See you soon." He paused with one hand on the doorknob, and said, without turning around, "That uh . . . that text you sent. When you were drunk. You didn't mean that, did you?"

Her heart seemed to stutter as she considered how to answer. Maybe this question was the real reason he'd come over last night. In a wave of feeling so clear and real, she knew there was no turning back now.

Because, yes, she was absolutely in love with Mateo.

But she wasn't going to tell him that, not when his mother had just died and he was all mixed up emotionally. She also didn't want to lie to him, so she did the only thing that felt right. She snickered and said, "Just a drunken text."

His expression was a little sad when he turned and met her eyes and she felt caught. Seen.

He nodded once. "Okay. See you soon." He was gone with the closing of the door, both literal and metaphorical.

Jazzy felt like she'd been punched in the gut. Last night had been one of the deepest and most meaningful events of her life. She didn't regret it. She'd never regret it. But she had to let it go. For his sake. If he was sure they should just stay friends.

Patti slinked out from where she'd been under the couch all night and walked over to her empty food bowl. If she'd had eyebrows, one would be raised.

Jazzy rolled her eyes at the cat, and threw the covers off. She padded over to the kitchen and fed Patti, who purred happily.

"I don't *do* showmances," she muttered and heaved an enormous sigh. Alone again. Only this time, it felt much worse.

# Twenty-One ♫

"Oh look, there she is now!" Jazzy heard Kara say as she stepped through the door into H&H Bagels.

Mateo slowly turned around and gave her what she thought amounted to about one-third of a signature Mateo smile.

She smiled back tentatively.

"I was gonna get your coffee for you, if you hadn't already been in," he said.

Kara was watching them, holding her chin in her hands, and her purple nails drumming against each cheek. "So both of your usuals, then?" she said.

Mateo's expression was unreadable. "Sure."

The past three days had been so incredibly awkward. *This* was awkward. Jazzy could, of course, be professional with the best of them, *better* than the best of them. But with Mateo, it was different. She had to pull from the deepest recesses of her Stanislavski class to pretend she didn't have feelings for the wonderful man in front of her. The one who had melded with her so completely, who occupied so many of her thoughts.

The one who was currently chuckling quietly.

"What's so funny?"

Mateo shrugged. "We're so awkward now."

"No we're not." Complete denial would work, wouldn't it?

"Jazzy." He rolled his eyes.

Kara set their drinks on the counter. "One hot, one cold. Opposites attract." The barista grinned and stretched her hands out wide before nestling them together.

Mateo's eyes grew wide.

Jazzy got the reference. This hot-and-cold thing had to end.

Mateo handed her the hot coffee and he took the cold, then angled his head to the corner by the condiment counter. "Thank you, Kara," he said as they walked away.

Jazzy glanced around, not sure if this very public café was the best place to talk privately. But there was only one guy in a ball cap within hearing distance. "What's up?"

"I wanted to introduce myself. I'm Mateo Williams, I'll be co-starring with you in the upcoming musical, *Bridges That Burn*."

Thrown for only a moment, she had to grin. This could work. "Ah, nice to meet you, Mr. Williams. I'm Jazzy Summers. I'll be playing Amelia."

Mateo held out his hand. Jazzy reached out and took it. His was warm and soft and comforting, and he squeezed. "I'm looking forward to starting over." He made an exaggerated *oh silly me* face. "I mean, starting. And becoming friends."

"Me, too. It's a pleasure to be working with you." The awkwardness drained away and she felt better. She would still have to deny everything she felt for him, but this? This she could handle.

Mateo pumped her hand up and down twice. After they'd dressed their coffees, he followed her out of the shop. As usual his car was waiting at the curb. "Wanna ride?"

Jazzy, who'd usually declined because she liked the subway ride to collect her thoughts, climbed in after him. "Final dress today. Are you ready?"

Mateo inhaled deeply and exhaled audibly. "Yes. I am ready for today, and I am ready for a real audience tomorrow. You promise that invited dress audiences are very forgiving?"

"In my experience, yes."

He considered that for a moment. "Let's go, right?"
"Let's go."

§

# OMGCELEB TIDBITS: Jazzy Summers and Mateo Williams Set to Begin Previews . . . and a life together?

You heard it here first, kittens! This blogger personally witnessed some serious heat between one Broadway veteran and one about to make his debut. We've written about them before: are they fighting? Will they/won't they? Jazzteo stans: you have reason for hope. That's not a chemistry you can fake onstage.

One day after the truce was made, Keith read aloud yet another gossip item. He looked up from his computer and folded his hands together, placing them with deliberate calm onto his desk.

After several beats, Mateo offered, "At least we weren't fighting this time?"

But Keith smiled. "Oh you are not in trouble. In fact, I encourage Jazzteo completely."

Jazzy turned to Mateo, brows knitted together in confusion. He returned her puzzled look.

"I just heard from the front office. Ticket sales are through the roof. Tonight's preview is sold out. Jazzteo is the hottest thing on Broadway right now, and since Ethan Carter is rumored to be coming back, that is saying something."

Mateo grinned widely.

Jazzy chewed her lower lip. "So you want us to—"

"No, no. You don't have to do anything fake or pretend or anything like that. I never encourage a showmance, either. Authenticity is what sells the two of you. The invited dress rehearsal went brilliantly. I've been hearing from people all day. Sooo . . . In public, get caught once in a while hanging out? I highly encourage that."

"Oh, okay." Jazzy felt a ping of satisfaction.

"We can do that." Mateo was grinning ear to ear.

"Oh, and don't Google yourselves, or look at your Twitter mentions." Keith grimaced at them. "Or Instagram."

Mateo exchanged another puzzled look with Jazzy. "Why not?"

"The internet is *weird* when they want two people to be together." Keith ushered them out of his office, laughing along with them. "Now get back to the theater, and break legs tonight!"

§

**MATEO WILLIAMS (COLE)** This is Mateo's Broadway debut. His debut album, First Kiss, went triple platinum in 2008, garnering a Best New Artist Grammy nomination, after which he toured the world performing. TV/Film: DUDE, IT'S COOL (Himself), NOBODY'S SECRETS (Himself), "Total Request Live", "Law & Order: SVU", MTV's "Cribs" "Thank you to my fellow castmates for welcoming me with open arms. And mom, thank you for all of it." @mateowilliams

Mateo looked up from the *Playbill* he cradled in his hands almost reverently. "I have a Broadway bio."

Jazzy met his gaze in her dressing room mirror. "Yes you do. Pretty exciting, huh?"

"I kinda wish I hadn't listed my pop star credits. But whatever. If they could see me now." He grimaced a little bit, but his eyes were bright.

"Eh, people will want to know where they know you from. 'Wait, is that the guy with the insane house on *Cribs*? Or was he on *TRL* every day for a freakin' year?'"

Mateo squinted at her. "Okay, okay." He crossed the room and leaned on the counter, caging her with his arms. The heat of him behind her made Jazzy's heart burst into that starlight again.

"We can't all be Jazzy fucking Summers." His breath on her neck was hot. He must have seen her eyes burning with desire, her hands clamped on the counter, because he seemed to realize what he was doing. Eyes wide, he backed away quickly. "Sorry, sorry."

"You don't know your own powers, do you?" Jazzy placed a hand over her heart, begging it to slow down.

Mateo looked like he wanted to say something, but the door behind him flew open.

"Happy previews, queens!" Carson waltzed into the room, followed closely by Simone and Blane. "We're gonna have a little sip." He crossed to Jazzy's bar and plucked out five disposable shot glasses.

Jazzy frowned.

Simone caught it. "Uh uh, lady, listen. We're all doing a teeny tiny shot for luck, okay? Loosen us up to get this out of the way. It's the first preview."

Jazzy pursed her lips, trying to hide her smile.

"Unless you really don't want to for vocal reasons." Blane, always the caretaker, was helping Carson fill up the little shot glasses.

"But if it's not . . . " Carson handed her one. "Come on, fam." Simone had one arm threaded through Mateo's, who leaned into Carson's around his waist, who was leaning into Blane in that long-term relationship way, when you just know that person is there for you.

It was hardly anything, half a shot at most. Jazzy accepted the tiny cup and grinned. "A toast."

Everyone cheered and raised a glass.

Jazzy took in the sight of these beautiful new friends. Not just show friends. Forever friends. "To all of you. For breaking my habit of being too single-minded. For bringing me into your world when I needed it most. I didn't know what I was missing, and I'm so glad I found you. Blane, you're the steady hand that guides us all. Carson, you're the life of the party. Simone, you're the best listener around. And Mateo . . . "

She gazed into his eyes, feeling sparks everywhere. "You are a superstar. Break a leg tonight. We are all here to catch you, but you won't need it. You're a magnificent Cole."

"Cheers!" The shots went down easy.

The loudspeaker crackled. "Five minutes to places, cast. Five minutes to places."

"Thank you, five," echoed around the room, even from Mateo, who'd picked up the habit of making sure the stage manager heard you. Even if he was on a loudspeaker.

Five minutes later, Jazzy squeezed Mateo's hand backstage. "Ready?"

"One hundred and one percent." Mateo turned and looked at her as the overture started. "Thank you, Jazz. For everything."

"Thank *you*."

Together, they stepped into the spotlight.

For a first preview, the audience response was warm and receptive. This was not a typical Broadway musical with a huge cast of dancers and gigantic numbers. It was more intimate than that, more raw, and the audience seemed to be along for the journey. When Cole finally crossed the stage to Amelia and kissed her, they went wild.

Jazzy couldn't help the starburst inside of her as the lights faded out, and intermission started.

Mateo lifted her by the waist and spun her around on the stage once the curtain went down. He kept his hands there as she cupped his cheeks, excited and proud beyond belief.

"You did it, you're amazing."

His whole expression was euphoric. "I have never been this proud of anything I've done."

"I'm so proud of you, too." A beat passed as he gazed into her eyes.

"Come on, let's go downstairs and celebrate." Mateo tugged her toward stage right.

She laughed as he hurried her along. "We have a whole act left, Mateo."

"And I didn't forget anything in the first one, Jazzy. Amazing!"

They spent intermission with the rest of the cast, the buzz of a good show and a great audience putting all of them in excellent moods. The second act went off with only a couple of technical glitches, and a few forgotten lines, but not by Mateo. He was never going to let Carson live that down.

While they would hold rehearsals for things they needed to work on while the rest of the previews ran and changes were made, all in all, the show was a hit. *Bridges That Burn* was shortly becoming the hottest ticket on Broadway. The weekend's previews were already successful, and with one more week of rehearsing and performing, opening night was sure to be a smash.

On Sunday night after the first four performances, Jazzy wanted to commiserate with Mateo before the long week ahead. She floated down the hallway, feeling extremely satisfied, but stopped just short of Mateo's dressing room when she heard voices.

"I'm telling you man, nothing is going on. I don't like her like that, okay?"

Jazzy paused, not wanting to eavesdrop, but also a human being who was almost certainly being talked about behind an almost closed door. So she did what anyone would. She listened.

"I don't know, you seem really cozy lately. And what's the deal with the coffeeshop gossip blog thing?"

"Jason, why are you digging for gossip." Mateo sounded exasperated.

"Listen, Simone and I quit hooking up because she wanted to focus on the role and opening and previews and stuff. So. I was just wondering if there was really anything between you and Summers."

"Number one, you don't need my permission. She's just a friend. A good friend. And number two, she and Simone are very close, so isn't that who you should be talking to?"

"Right. Yeah. True. Okay. So it's okay if —"

"Yeah, whatever. I don't care what she does with her personal life." Mateo appeared in the crack in the doorway, his black show bag in his hand, his white t-shirt tight around his biceps.

Jazzy bit her lip and slipped into Simone's empty dressing room next door. She could just hear the rest of the conversation over the pounding of her heart. She stayed just inside the door, not wanting to miss anything.

"She's just a friend."

She tasted blood and quickly let go of her lip. She closed her eyes to the hurt that suddenly coursed through her.

She heard Mateo walk by, closely followed by Jason. She already knew Mateo wanted only her friendship, but hearing it loudly confirmed left a scorch mark across her heart. So it really had been a mistake to him.

He really had only been caught up in his feelings for that one night, so ruled by his grief and the attraction between them. And she really had been glad to make him feel something else.

But obviously, despite the daydreams that she'd tried to brush aside, it was going to stay a one-time thing.

Okay.

She straightened her shoulders and bit back the tears that threatened to fall.

Jazzy Summers doesn't do showmances anyway.

# Twenty-Two ♪

Sasha stood before the cast on the stage of the Schubert, surveying them like a proud mama hen. "Good work, all of you. I'm very proud of these changes and I think tightening up the second act was the right call. While we're not going to freeze the show until after the Sunday matinee, I think we've got it."

The final weekend of previews were to begin in a few hours, and they'd been rehearsing everyday as well. Exhausted but happy, the cast cheered.

Jazzy stood next to Simone and far away from Mateo. The week had been a whirlwind of performing every night, rehearsing things that needed it, and recording the cast album during the day, all before they opened next week. And they also had to fit in food and sleep. He didn't seem to suspect or even have time to realize that she was ignoring him. Though she totally was.

As hurt as she was that Mateo would deny everything to Jason, it *was* what she wanted anyway. Hadn't he said he'd respect her wishes all those months ago? And repeatedly since? When he'd asked her out after her Lowenstein's show, she'd been tempted. But after telling him no, he did say that he would respect that.

So really, his avoiding the messiness of being with her was a blessing.

Really.

Sasha dismissed them and Jazzy heard some of her castmates deciding on dinner plans before call. She had dinner waiting in her mini-fridge and was planning on some much-needed alone time before changing for Act One again.

But of course, Simone followed her to her dressing room.

She paused, catching Simone's eyes in her mirror.

"I demand to know what is happening." Simone pursed her lips and put one hand on her hip.

Jazzy knew there was no getting around telling Simone everything. Besides, this is what friendship was for. Working through the hard stuff. She sighed, and slumped in her makeup chair. Simone perched on the counter, shoving aside some of the makeup.

Jazzy glared.

Simone just smiled. "I don't know if you heard, but I *demand*—"

"I heard you, I heard you." Jazzy buried her face in her hands. "I just don't even know what to say. It's all stupid."

"Spill it."

"We slept together." Her voice was muffled through her hands.

Simone dramatically slid off the counter onto the floor. "You and Mateo?"

"Yes."

"You fucked him."

"*God*, Simone. Yes, okay?" Jazzy looked in the mirror. Her face was beet red, but she still thrilled at the memory of Mateo's body pressed against hers.

Simone peered into her reflected face. "And oh my god! It was the best sex you've ever had. Holy shit, tell me *everything*. When? How? How big is it?"

"Sim*one*." Jazzy finally met Simone's eyes. She took a deep breath. "Okay. It was a couple of nights after his mom's funeral. I had stayed with him after the service, remember? Then he came back and we did the showcase, and everything seemed fine. But all weekend he ignored my texts. Until . . . until Sunday night when he just showed up at my place—"

Simone stopped her, took Jazzy's hand, and led her to the couch, after making sure the outer door was closed. "This is a couch conversation. Go on."

Jazzy smiled. "He said 'Make me feel anything else,' and I guess I just . . . kind of lost it."

Simone, whose eyes were bright with anticipation, nodded. "You climbed him like a tree."

"Stoppit." Jazzy buried her face in a fluffy white throw pillow. "But yes. I did. And it was amazing."

"So are you dating? Are you doing it again? What is happening now?"

Jazzy lifted her head. "That's the thing. Nothing. He ran out in the morning apologizing for the weird emotional place he's in, even though he didn't need to apologize because I wanted it too, and— Ugh, god! Then it was so . . . so awkward.

"We had this weird coffee shop moment, the one that got written about, right? We like . . . pretended to not know each other. As if we were starting over. Which seemed like the best idea. And then Keith said we should be seen together sometimes, that ticket sales were through the roof, and that's very cool but . . . he . . . " She bit her lip.

"Oh. He doesn't want that. Mateo, I mean."

Jazzy glanced at the door, surprised to find her eyes filling with tears. "He doesn't. I mean, he had just lost his mom and he needed a . . . a moment. And I loved it. And I wouldn't take it back or anything. But I overheard him telling Jason in no uncertain terms that we are *not* together, so I guess . . . " She shrugged, a sad little gesture. "Besides, I . . . "

"Don't do showmances," they finished in unison. Jazzy managed a tiny smile.

Simone's eyes widened after a moment. "Wait, what about Jason?"

"He told Jason that there was no way we were together and he didn't like me like that. And if that's what he wants, then . . . Wait, also, what's going on with you and Jason?"

Simone waved her hand dismissively. "Oh, we had fun, but I need a little more substance at this stage of my life. But back to Mateo. He absolutely wants you. You've been practically ignoring him all week and he is giving you puppy dog eyes every time you're not looking."

Jazzy rolled her eyes. "Are you okay with the break-up? And no he isn't."

"After the last one? This is cake. And you love him."

Jazzy plucked at a thread on the pillow. "Maybe."

"Jasperanza."

Jazzy chuckled. "Not my real name."

"Jasperanza Persephone Summers, you have to tell him you love him."

"I don't love him." She pulled the pillow to her chest and hugged it, feeling stubborn while her eyes still stung.

"Liar."

She glared at Simone for a moment, but finally she couldn't help herself. Tears began flowing down her cheeks. She'd reached some sort of breaking point. The opening of a show was exhausting. Her unfamiliar feelings for Mateo were exhausting. Confusing. His whole existence in her life felt like an upheaval.

Yet she knew that she would still do anything to make him smile. Even if he didn't feel the same way about her.

Simone pulled Jazzy into her arms and let her cry for a few minutes. "See, we don't just cry for no reason over boys who mean nothing. Tell him your truth. If he's brave, he'll tell you his."

Jazzy nodded, wiping her eyes. She sat up. "You're right."

"Also, you have to fuck him again." Simone was all practicality.

Jazzy chuckled. "Stop saying 'fuck'."

"Stop being a prude and go get your man."

§

The last preview, a matinee, was over and opening night loomed large. The show had been extremely successful. Jazzy was grateful for the next day off so she could rest up for what was sure to be an incredible opening night.

"Hey, Jazz, got a second?"

She looked up from her show bag, disappointed to see Jason standing in her doorway, and not Mateo. "Sure."

He stepped inside and closed the door. "Just wondering about your dinner plans," he said, every bit the charismatic charmer he played onstage.

Jazzy slung her bag over her shoulder and straightened. Jason was standing much too close. "I'm going home. I need to rest tomorrow. Two days until opening, y'know."

He stepped another inch closer. "So you don't want to go out, have a little fun?"

"Jay, you know I always have fun with you. But this?" She indicated how close he was. "Not gonna happen. Besides, weren't you and Simone . . ."

Jason's smile barely faltered as he stepped back.

"Simone and I have an understanding."

"Noted." Jazzy opened the door to the hallway. "But no."

"No harm trying." His grin grew. "I knew Mateo was a liar."

Jazzy stopped short. "What?"

"Man, Jazzy, come on. The whole company knows. You love him, he loves you. We can all see it. Just do the thing already."

She looked up into Jason's face and felt herself blush.

"Ha, see?" He laughed aloud as he followed her into the hallway. "You two kids are made for each other. Go get 'im. I'm gonna go see if Simone is still here."

"Goodnight, Jason." Jazzy stood where she was, letting his words sink in. After a moment, she turned on the spot, determined to be normal and go home to do her normal routine like a normal person who had everything under control.

§

"It's not like I don't want him. You know?" Jazzy shoveled a forkful of quinoa into her mouth. Patti sat on the coffee table, clearly hoping for a bit of the still sizzling broiled salmon. "I do, obviously. Sorry you had to see that, by the way. I hope you averted your eyes."

Patti blinked.

Jazzy sighed. She'd gone through her post-show routine—shower, make dinner, prep her show bag for opening night—but couldn't get Jason or Simone's words out of her head. She chewed violently as she contemplated her situation.

"If we get together, like for real, then that is . . . It's a whole thing, right?" She held out a morsel of fish.

Patti gobbled it down immediately and glanced up expectantly, hopeful for more.

"Like, there will be press. There will be interviews. It will be much too weird. We're co-stars! It's so cliché! And yes, okay, I love him, yes. That's true."

She paused.

"I love him."

Patti blinked.

Jazzy slowly set the nearly empty bowl down on the coffee table. Patti eagerly dove in, licking the sides. Slowly, Jazzy stood.

"I love him. *That's* the point, right?"

Patti just continued her salmon quest.

"You don't care. I do. And if I love him, why . . . Why shouldn't we . . . Why shouldn't I . . . "

Within minutes, she was storming down Amsterdam Avenue, fire within her, desperate to tell him, to feel the starburst again.

It was nearly ten when the elevator doors opened into the penthouse. She saw Mateo across the expanse of the great room, in the kitchen. For a moment she paused between the elevator doors.

She imagined the security guard had told him a wild, blonde woman with fury in her eyes was on her way up. She imagined her skin emitting heat Mateo could already feel. She imagined he could see how fast she was breathing. She wondered if he felt the passion she'd worked up on the walk over.

Mateo tossed the dish towel he was holding onto a chair and started across the room, as if he'd been expecting her.

She met him in the middle.

They stopped just short of touching. Jazzy put her hands on her hips and stepped closer, until their noses were just an inch apart.

Looking directly into his eyes, she demanded, "Say it. Say I'm just a friend. To my face."

She tipped her chin up. "I dare you."

# Twenty-Three ♫

She watched Mateo's expression turn from confusion to understanding to desire, though he still seemed a little hesitant.

Jazzy was *done* being hesitant. She was done wondering and waiting and hoping. She was demanding an end to this hot-and-cold thing they'd been doing. It was now or never.

"The *truth*, Mateo."

His warm brown eyes held everything she needed to know. His gaze seared into her soul. "You were *never* just a friend, Jazzy."

Before she could think, his lips were on hers, soft, demanding, warm. This wasn't the many stage kisses they had shared. It wasn't the fireworks kiss on the boat. It wasn't the desperate kiss of a man who needed to forget.

This was the ending of a movie. And the beginning of the next chapter. She wrapped her arms around his neck and gave in to all of it. Whatever trials—or gossip blogs—might come their way, she knew she could handle it. Because she had this solid, golden man to wrap his arms around her and make her feel like she was home.

"Never," Mateo whispered as he kissed his way along her jawline. "You were never, ever just a friend. I saw you in H&H and I knew I wanted you, before all of this. Before the show, before my mom . . . Hell, maybe since I was fifteen and your light beamed off that stage."

When he pulled away, she could swear the air was sparkling. She cradled his face in her hands. So this is what love felt like. To be unafraid to hold someone, to open up to them. Now she understood. "You looked into my eyes and I thought I was seeing stars."

Mateo smiled softly, brushing his nose on hers. "Star dust."

The charged air around them changed, settled. Mateo, walking backwards, tugged her by the hand into his bedroom where he stopped her right beside the bed. He lifted one of her hands to his heart and took a deep breath. "I can't promise I'm okay right now, that I'm not in a weird place. But I can promise you that I will never hurt you, Jazz. I want this if you want this. I'm so sorry I ran out on you, but I thought maybe . . . I thought maybe you just felt sorry for me."

"No. No." Jazzy felt her whole chest constrict. She'd never done this before. For the first time, she wanted to. No more rationalizing, no more fear. "I denied it for a long time, Mateo. Because I don't do—"

"Showmances, yes." Mateo chuckled.

"But I—" Jazzy took the deepest breath, the one she took when she was going for a high belt. "—that text I sent."

She had never felt more vulnerable. He'd cracked the hard shell she'd put around herself, and she could feel it fall away forever. But saying the actual words . . . that was another story entirely. She toyed with the hem of her sundress.

Gently, Mateo tipped her chin up.

She met his lambent gaze, full of understanding, full of . . . Oh!

"I love you, Jazzy."

Surprising herself, she laughed joyfully and flung her arms around his neck. "I love you, too."

This time when he kissed her, she felt as though she were bursting from the inside out. As though starlight was rocketing through her.

With her in his arms, he fell back onto the bed and she laughed again. His full Mateo smile, that one that made her forget her own name in the coffee shop, spread wide across his face. He cupped her face gently in his hands. For a few long moments, they gazed into each other's eyes, as if saying everything they hadn't yet said, everything that would be said in time. And then they were kissing, kissing for an eternity.

She toyed with the bottom of his shirt until he got the hint. His jeans and boxers were next, and in one swift motion, her sundress joined the pile on the floor. Sitting at the edge of the bed, Mateo beckoned her to straddle his lap.

He curled his hand around the nape of her neck. "I'm yours, Jazz. I think I always have been."

It was familiar now, the perfect way his lips molded onto hers. The way she hungered for him, needed him close. Closer.

He caressed her everywhere as he whispered all the words that she had always longed to hear. He wanted her, he saw her, he loved her. Her skin sang wherever he touched her.

She whispered that she would do her best to take away his pain. He told her that she would never have to be lonely. He pulled away for a moment and beckoned her back once he'd slipped on a condom. Craving him, she straddled him again and slowly guided him inside of her. At last, with New York twinkling at them from the picture windows, they melted together again.

With Mateo's large hands supporting her, she felt safe. Cherished. She explored the curve of his neck, hunting for that scent of citrus. She breathed against his skin, memorizing every curve. She tasted salt on her tongue, desperate to consume him, to know all of him.

"Jazzy." He breathed her name against her neck, trailing his tongue up to her ear. "I never want to be without you again."

She arched back, the angle creating a new and delicious sensation. Gazes linked, they moved together as if choreographed, bodies slick against one another. He ran his free hand down her stomach until his thumb found her center.

Her head fell back and instead of losing herself in him, in his touch, she felt found. No one had ever touched her like this, seen her like this. Made her feel this free. Under Mateo's gaze, she felt like her truest self, able to be exactly who she was. She rocked her hips, her orgasm building, the pleasure rocketing through her as he increased the pressure of his thumb. She lifted her head back up and met his gaze.

Oh, that smile. It pushed her right over the edge. She cried out his name. Thighs quaking, she tightened her hold on him, feeling his skin everywhere against hers. He buried his face in the crook of her neck.

"I love you, Jazzy. God, I'm so in love with you." His hands tangled in her hair and his whole body shuddered on his release. She could feel him breathe against her as slowly, they stilled. She pulled back to look at his beautiful face.

"I love you, too." When she kissed him, she felt as though a question had been answered.

A few minutes later, she lay beside him, fulfilled. She let her fingers wander around his bare chest. "I was so alone, Mateo. And now I have Simone and Blane and Carson and you . . . "

"Especially me." He kissed the top of her head.

"Thank you."

He looked into her eyes. "For what?"

"For making me see that life isn't just about work, and for seeing me as a whole person. You woke something up inside me. A whole universe I didn't know existed. There's no going back now."

He pulled her closer and she could smell her perfume in the crook of his neck. He buried his face in her messy hair. "Good."

§

Jazzy took another bite of the delicious pancakes Mateo had put in front of her. He was across the kitchen, flipping the last few in a frying pan. They didn't say much, just kept catching each other's eyes and grinning. He was in just his boxers. She wore his t-shirt and nothing else. The sun streamed into the penthouse, and Jazzy was all lit up inside. Part of her felt brand new. And the part that was still the old Jazzy—the meticulous, organized, but much too single-minded part—approved.

Mateo flipped his pancakes onto a plate and placed it on the island next to hers. He held her gaze as he spread butter. His smile was her secret now, all hers.

There was so much of him that she wanted to discover, so much she didn't yet know. But that smile.

That smile was only for her. She caught a drip of syrup with her index finger and put it in her mouth.

"Seriously? You just can't do that." Mateo had paused with a forkful of pancakes and was watching Jazzy as she playfully licked her finger.

"Why not?" She darted her tongue out to catch another drip of syrup.

He groaned and stood, shoving his plate aside. Grabbing the hand with her syrupy finger, he pulled her off of her stool and lifted her with ease onto the counter.

He pulled her ass closer to the edge and pressed into her.

Jazzy chuckled, and then gasped. "Ohh, that's why. So sorry about that."

Mateo grinned, but his eyes were lit with passion. "Don't apologize. Just deal with the consequences."

Jazzy did, exuberantly, unsurprised but delighted by how sexy and easy and *everything* he was.

§

"So what are we gonna do?" Jazzy was toweling off her hair as she walked into the living room, now wearing one of Mateo's fluffy bathrobes.

Mateo was lounging on the low sofa, but sat forward when she came in. He too wore only a bathrobe, as the morning had been quite adventurous. He held out his hand.

She took it and slid onto the couch next to him, folding her legs underneath herself.

"Do about what?"

"The cast. Opening. Frickin' Roger at *OMGCeleb*."

Mateo stared up at the ceiling and frowned. "That's a good question." He put one arm on the back of the couch behind her and with his other hand, he cupped her chin. "I'm in this. For real. Possibly for always."

She grinned, even as she said, "Let's not get ahead of ourselves."

"I'm not going to lie to myself about anything I feel." He shrugged. "So you take the lead, Summers. I'm in this, and I would very much like to shout it from the rooftops. But if that's not what you want, if you want to take it slow, that's fine with me. We can keep it quiet for now."

Resting her head on his arm, she reached up to trace the curve of his cheek, the line of his jaw. "I think it's probably best to keep it quiet. At least until we talk to our teams. And maybe have dinner first."

"That's fine." Mateo took both of her hands in his. "But I want you to know: this isn't a PR stunt, this isn't a one-time thing. I am yours, Jazzy. All of me."

Jazzy felt sparkles again, felt such affection for this beautiful man holding her hands, she thought she might burst. "I am absolutely yours. But I'm also—"

"An uptight pragmatist?" Mateo's eyes sparkled with the thought of their first encounters.

She threw her head back and laughed. "No, an unprofessional has-been."

"I'll show you unprofessional." He pressed her into the couch as he kissed her.

Breaking the kiss, she put her hands on the sides of his face and looked into his eyes. "Just for a bit. Until we figure out what to say."

He nodded. "I'm ready when you are."

§

Jazzy texted a thank you to her neighbor for feeding Patti before joining Mateo at the counter the next morning. The last day and a half seemed surreal and she blushed at the thought of all the ways Mateo had explored her.

Time to get back to the world. She could hear his nervous excitement as he chatted with Kara.

Opening night.

Kara slid their drinks to them, eyeing them suspiciously. "One hot, one cold."

"Thank you, Kara." Mateo's hand brushed Jazzy's as they both reached for their coffees.

She thrilled at just that simple touch.

And it was apparently visible.

"Oh my god. It's happening." Kara clasped her hands together over her heart.

Mateo's eyes went wide, clearly confirming what Kara suspected.

"It is, isn't it? I'm right?"

Mateo glanced at Jazzy. She met his eyes and gave a tiny shrug as she pried the lid off of her coffee.

Mateo simply winked at Kara and put a finger to his lips. Then he slipped a twenty into the tip jar.

"Thanks," he whispered.

Kara practically swooned.

§

The cast practiced each choreographed fight so no real injuries were sustained. Simone had the most physical job in the show, and was breathing hard after the fight call before opening night. She collapsed next to Jazzy, who sat on the floor of the stage, stretching. "Happy opening."

After a moment, she spread her legs into a split, as Jazzy was doing. They joined hands and took turns bending forward with their feet touching, pulling each other into the stretch.

Jazzy's legs were aching a bit more than usual, and she warmed when she realized why. Mateo had given her quite the workout. She grinned widely.

"Happy opening. Finally."

"Can you believe?"

"I cannot. I am so excited for you. And Mateo. God, this is a long time coming. Congratulations."

"Thank you. Pretty cool when your dreams come true."

Jazzy smiled at Simone and then caught Mateo's eye over her shoulder. He gave her the secret smile.

Simone's gaze was trained on Jazzy's face and she turned to see what she was looking at. She gasped quietly. "Oh my god, it's happened. You're together, aren't you." She leaned in as Jazzy did, until their faces almost touched. "Tell me, Jazzlinka."

Jazzy bit back a smile. "Not my real name."

"Spill!"

Jazzy couldn't help it. She collapsed into laughter, which Simone joined. "Just keep it quiet," Jazzy whispered. "We have to talk to our teams about press or whatever."

Simone tsked and she swiftly pulled her knees up to her chest in one fluid motion. "No. Just be in love. Be together. *Teams* be damned. Everyone already loves you together and wants you together. So just *be it*."

"Gather round, kids!" Carson called and strode toward the middle of the stage. He gathered the cast into a circle and took Blane's hand. Blane reached for Mateo's. Mateo reached for Simone's, who held onto Jazzy's. Around the circle it went until they were a cohesive unit.

"I love a prayer circle." Carson's voice was low and reverent. "Whether you have a god or you're an atheist, I would like to start our show by putting positive energy into the world. Is that okay with everyone?"

As one, the cast nodded.

"You can say anything here—out loud or just in your heart—but this is a place where you are safe and unjudged. I'll start tonight. I want to thank Blane for being such a wonderful boyfriend. I know a lot of people might think it's too much togetherness to do a show together, but I wouldn't want to share this with anyone else."

Blane smiled and kissed Carson quickly. "I'll go next. I feel the same, Carson. And I want to congratulate Simone on making fucking history tonight. We're so proud of you. May the Tony gods smile upon you."

"They better!" Jason shouted from the other side of the circle. Simone had to briefly let go of Mateo's hand to dab at her eyes.

"I just did my make-up, y'all, come on. Thank you. And I would like to congratulate Mateo. It's your debut, baby! We're so proud."

The cast murmured their assent and Mateo bowed his head.

"I'm so grateful to costuming for those white jeans I wear in the second act. There's already an Instagram devoted to them." Jason made everyone laugh. Parker, Max, and a few others offered up some positivity next.

Jazzy cleared her throat. "Thank you, all of you. I've always felt slightly . . . removed. And you have all embraced me like family. You are my family. I am so excited for the run of this show, and I'm so glad I get to do it with all of you."

"Me, too." Mateo smiled at them all in turn, each of them getting a little bit of his magic. "I know how weird it must be to accept an irrelevant pop star into your cast, and you were all so patient and kind to me through all of it . . . "

Simone cleared her throat.

Mateo laughed. "Okay, through *most* of it. But the way you were all there for me, especially with my mom—" His voice cracked a bit and Simone let go of Mateo's hand and instead gathered him close to her side. Mateo lifted his eyes to the ceiling. "I wish she could be here."

Carson started it. They all moved to Mateo and gathered in a tighter, closer circle, arms now around each other. For a few moments, they bowed their heads in silence.

Mateo broke it. "Thank you. All of you. And Jazzy."

Jazzy looked into his eyes, which held universes.

"Thank you for accepting me for who I am."

The air palpably changed and Jazzy was sure it wasn't just her who could see the sparkles.

"Actors, clear the stage. Actors, clear the stage. Your opening night audience is entering in five."

Carson grinned widely. "Let's do this, queens!"

# Twenty-Four ♫

"Ten minutes to places."

Jazzy looked up at the speaker and grinned, hearing the calls of 'thank you ten' from around the hallway. She caught Mateo's eye in his dressing room mirror.

"You ready?"

He grinned. "I'm ready."

Jazzy stepped farther into the room. "I got you something." She pulled the small package from behind her back with a flourish.

Mateo took it. "That is so thoughtful . . . wait. Should I have gotten you something? Is that a thing?" He looked at her, panicked.

She chuckled. "Not at all. I just noticed you didn't have much personal stuff in here. Open it!"

"Okay. Well, thank you." He tore the gold wrapping off of the picture frame. When he saw what it was, he put a hand over his mouth. His eyes became shiny with tears.

"I hope it's okay. I wanted you to know that she's here with you tonight."

Mateo stared down at the framed photograph of him and his mother. Jazzy knew it had been one of the last times they were photographed together before she got sick and they disappeared. It was on a red carpet for something for MTV, though Jazzy didn't know what.

Marisol was looking up at her tall and handsome son, love glowing in her expression. Mateo gazed down at her, adoring.

Behind them was a curtain full of tiny gold stars.

"How did you find this?"

"I remembered seeing it when I Googled you the first time. So I went back to find it a couple of weeks ago and contacted the photographer. He was thrilled to give it to me. For you."

Mateo seemed a bit overcome as he gathered her close and breathed into her hair. "Thank you."

"I love you," she whispered.

"Me, too," he whispered softly back.

They stood that way for a moment.

"Five minutes to places, five minutes. Happy opening, everyone!"

"Will you two please, I am literally begging you, just get it *together*."

Jazzy pulled away from Mateo and rolled her eyes at Carson. "We're not all you and Blane, you love monster."

"Who's a love monster?"

"Carson," Mateo said as he lovingly placed the framed photo on his dressing table.

Simone appeared behind Carson in the hallway. "We all know that, Blane especially."

"I'm not a monster!" Carson protested as Jazzy and Mateo followed him down the hallway.

"Beg to differ!" Jason called from the stairwell.

Jazzy listened to the cacophony of her cast all teasing one another as places were called.

Another opening, another show.

Now that she and Mateo had confessed their love, their chemistry was off the charts. The kiss at the end of Act One sent the audience into near paroxysms. Jazzy felt the difference, too. Working with Mateo was easier than anything she had ever done. Now that they were completely honest offstage, it translated onstage perfectly. He gave her everything, and she gave him the same. They were open and vulnerable, and it showed. By the time that the town was saved and they were in love at the end of Act Two, the audience was on its feet before the curtain came down.

At the curtain call cue, Jazzy stood at stage right and looked across. Mateo stood at stage left, grinning from ear to ear. They heard the crowd's ovation for Simone and knew that was their cue. They ran to center stage, took each other's hands, and together walked downstage to the lip. Once there, Jazzy stood back and gestured to Mateo, who took a bow to screams and applause. She barely heard the bow music over the roar of the crowd.

Mateo gestured to her and she took her bow, and the screaming intensified. Then he took her hand and they joined a line with the rest of the cast. All of them acknowledged the tech booth and the orchestra, and then took a bow all together. Jazzy waved to her parents, to her vocal coach and agent, in the front rows.

But the audience couldn't seem to stop clapping and cheering. The frenzy continued and the cast stayed onstage, basking in the love. What an incredibly satisfying reaction.

She could feel Mateo begin to laugh. His grip on her hand was strong, then he moved it to the small of her back. She looked up at him and he bent down to speak in her ear.

"Jazzy, marry me." His voice was full of glee and hope and promises, his eyes filled with adoration.

She tipped her head back, laughing aloud. "Let's go to dinner first."

"I can work with that."

As she gazed at him, in her mind she heard Simone say *just be it*. In a flash of memory, she saw Blane and

Carson snuggling together in her living room. She saw Jason giving of himself freely and openly. And for the first time ever, Jazzy Summers thought, *Fuck it.* She caught Mateo's eye and held his gaze. She nodded slowly, and squeezed his hand. She hoped he could hear what she was thinking. *The rest of it be damned. Let's do this.*

Mateo's eyes widened, understanding her completely. "Really?"

"Really." She'd never been so sure.

He took her hand, twirled her into his arms and dipped her, his signature Mateo not-suitable-for-work grin wide and beaming like the sun. When his lips finally melded with hers, the audience went wilder still.

Jazzy knew that sometimes there would be mess and things she couldn't control. That she couldn't always make emotions disappear because she wanted them to. She knew that life could throw devastation or elation at her at any moment. That her routines would be disrupted. And she'd never be alone.

But the familiar starlight was bursting inside of her.

She'd never wanted anything more.

*fin*

# Epilogue ♪
## Eighteen Months Later

OMGCELEB
EXCLUSIVE: INSIDE
JAZZY SUMMERS' AND
MATEO WILLIAMS'
SPRING WEDDING

Kittens, it was the event of the season. You would not believe. In a resort in the Berkshires, Tony nominee Mateo Williams and Tony winner (finally!) Jazzy Summers, who met while starring in *Bridges That Burn* on Broadway, tied the knot in an outdoor ceremony filled with love and tears. Even this blogger got his hankie out! Mateo was gorgeous in a suit the color of Jazzy's eyes, a deep, rich blue. Jazzy wore a gorgeous gown made of shimmery gold silk and a flower crown of dahlias and eucalyptus.

*Click here for the People Exclusive pics!*

The original cast of *Bridges That Burn* sang Jazzy down the aisle: a harmonized a cappella "Tonight" from *West Side Story*. Could she have walked to her new husband to a more romantic song? There were tears shed as the two lovebirds said their vows in a ceremony performed by their best friend, Simone Baxter, fresh off of her first Tony win for Featured Actress in a Musical. No one kept their cool when their friend Kara, who wore a coffee-colored A-line dress, read Shakespeare's Sonnet 116. Mateo promised to bring Jazzy joy for the rest of her days. Jazzy promised he would never have to go through anything difficult alone.

Once those two crazy kids kissed under the biodegradable confetti, it was over to the reception where a forest wonderland awaited us—literal trees! Soft globe lighting! The lushest of blooms! A floral display hung above the dance floor and it felt like that night, we were all fairies. Truly magical.

Once we got a heartfelt welcome from Jazzy's proud papa, we had a delicious dinner, then the two gorgeous kids cut their cake, and we danced the night away.

Though I don't condone handing out sparklers to one hundred people who have been drinking, there was a send-off at midnight. We all shouted our congratulations to Jazzy + Mateo. Then our two lovers ran to their cabin under the vast night sky, which sparkled with starlight.

*fin*

# Hearts of Broadway:

## A Contemporary Romance Series

Stay tuned for the final book in the Hearts of Broadway series. Evie + Ethan, Paige + Alex, Jazzy + Mateo, and Dion + Henry will be back soon!

§

Enter a glittering world where everyone has a song in their heart. Each book in the Hearts of Broadway series follows a Broadway star on the journey of falling in love. And when these artists fall, they fall hard.

A national tour, a brand-new musical, a co-star who makes life miserable, and one too many rejections: navigating a challenging career is already a complicated dance. So when they meet the people who tug on their heartstrings, managing the choreography of their lives gets more difficult . . . and exciting.

Showtune references abound and each book comes with its own playlist, which you can find on your favorite streaming app. Read together or stand-alone, the characters in the Hearts of Broadway series will sweep you off your feet.

# Acknowledgements

Uncial Press and my editor, Judith B. Glad, took a chance on me and have made me a better writer, reader, and thinker. Jude, your unending patience and attention to detail are irreplaceable. Thank you.

Jennifer Ashley Tepper and her books, *The Untold Stories of Broadway,* gave me so much insight into the lives of Broadway performers. Invaluable history.

L. Morgan Lee, congratulations on your nomination for Featured Actress in a Musical. I wrote this book before your nom, and I could not be happier that it is already outdated.

My sensitivity reader, August Forman, was the first to read this book and gave me nothing but insight and kindness while they were in the *middle of tech week.* August, you are a superstar. Thank you.

My street team and all of the wonderful writers, especially Kelly Kay, who I now get to call my friends: you are aggressively positive and uplifting and I love you all.

Erin O'Shea, David Mitchell, Amy Nolan, Tyler Dean Kempf, Brittany Ellis, Ashley Yates, Charlotte Ellison, Christopher Owen, Julie Gimbert, and Lindsay Nevitt: I would, very honestly, be nothing without you.

Miguel Long, you inspired Mateo. Thank you for being the sunshine of my life.

I am unendingly lucky to have such wonderful in-laws. Johnsons and Hankes, thank you for all of the enthusiasm and support.

Lena Ewald, you taught me to work hard and love harder. And to always be up for a bloody Mary. Thank you, Grandma.

Mom, Dad, Lisa, Alesha, and Lilli: none of this would happen without you. I love you to the moon and back.

Mike Johnson, Alfie and Oliver have the best cat dad in the world. I'd marry you again in a second.

# Asopao de Pollo

**Ingredients:** *Serves 4-6*

6 cups water
1 potato cut into 6 pieces
2 pounds skinless chicken thigh
1/4 teaspoon salt
1 teaspoon dried oregano
1 tablespoon olive oil
1/4 cup sofrito
1 8 oz can no salt added tomato sauc
1 packet Sazon seasoning with annatto
1 green bell pepper, diced
1 red bell pepper, diced
1 medium onion, diced
4 cloves garlic, minced
1 cup sliced pimento-stuffed green olives or alcaparrado
(optional)
1 chicken bouillon cube
¼ cup fresh cilantro, chopped
¼ cup fresh culantro, chopped
1 cup medium-grain rice
smoked ham, cut into 1/2-inch cubes

1. Season the chicken thighs with adobo seasoning and dried oregano.

2. Heat oil in a medium pot, add the chicken, cook until golden brown on all sides for about 7 minutes, and set aside.

3. Add to the pot the onions, peppers, ham, garlic, oregano, Sazon, tomato sauce, and cook until fragrant.

4. Stir all of the ingredients right into the sofrito before adding the chicken back.

5. When all of the ingredients are in the pot, pour the 6 cups of water into the caldero (pot), add the salt, bouillon cube, and sliced potatoes.

6. Add the rice. Over the cooking time, you can add more water if needed as the rice cooks and absorbs the liquids.

7. Bring the soup to a boil, then turn down the heat, and allow it to simmer for up to 25 minutes.

8. Stir in the olives, cilantro, and culantro for another 5 minutes, and serve.

9. On the side, we eat it with tostones (fried plantains) or tostones de pana (breadfruit fritters) and/or with a slice of avocado.

# About the Author

With over ten years of wedding planning experience and a lifetime onstage, Avery Easton knows romance. When she was seven years old, in a pink Snoopy notebook, she began writing stories and hasn't stopped since. If she's not reading or writing, you can find her cross stitching or belting out showtunes. She lives in Chicago with her husband and two adorable cats.

If you would like to make a donation to Broadway Cares/Equity Fights AIDS, please visit BroadwayCares.org.

§

If you would like to connect with Avery, find her @averyeastonwrites

on Instagram & TikTok or at her website:

https://msha.ke/averyeaston/

§

*When I Met You* is available as an eBook from Uncial Press. Uncial Press brings you extraordinary fiction, non-fiction and poetry. Put a world of reading in your pocket.
www.uncialpress.com

Made in the USA
Middletown, DE
24 October 2023